DEATH OF A LADY

Jane Austen Investigations
Book One

Laura Martin

SAPERE
BOOKS

DEATH OF A LADY

Published by Sapere Books.

24 Trafalgar Road, Ilkley, LS29 8HH

saperebooks.com

ISBN: 978-1-80055-937-0

CHAPTER ONE

Hampshire, December 1795

"It is like something out of one of those dramatic novels you read," Cassandra Austen said excitedly, pulling on her younger sister's arm as she jostled to get a better view.

Jane tried lifting herself up on her tiptoes, but she was still far too short to see past the heads of the people approaching the grand doorway in front of them.

"*Everyone* in town has been talking about the Westworth's ball, and when our invitation arrived it was just too thrilling."

Letting her excited sister's voice wash over her, Jane smoothed down her dress and tucked a stray strand of hair behind her ear. Her mother had always cautioned her to present the best version of herself in case someone was watching.

"Come girls, don't dawdle," their mother said now, ushering them forward as their turn arrived to greet their hosts.

"Mr and Mrs Austen, how delightful to see you again. Thank you for coming tonight."

"Thank you for the invitation, Lord Westworth, Lady Westworth, it was an honour to receive it," Mrs Austen said, dipping her head before stepping to the side. "I don't think you have met my daughters, Miss Cassandra Austen and Miss Jane Austen?"

"No," Lady Westworth said slowly, casting an appraising eye over the sisters, "we haven't met, but I hope you enjoy the festivities tonight and will take part in the dancing."

Before either of the sisters could answer, Lord and Lady Westworth's attention had moved on to the next set of guests and the Austens were swept inside.

"I have never seen anything so spectacular," Jane murmured as they stepped into a grand ballroom. Above their heads a chandelier glittered, lit by the light of a hundred candles, and all around the room were candles in sconces and candelabras strategically placed to show the room at its best. Already the ballroom was a crush of people, and despite the icy temperatures outside it was sweltering within.

"I wonder where Edward Stanmore is?" Jane recognised most of the people in attendance from their dances in the Assembly Rooms and various balls and dinners over the last couple of years. There were a few faces she couldn't place, perhaps friends from London or more distant relatives of the Westworths, but no one who stood out as the long-lost brother of their host, and in whose honour tonight's ball was being held. "Tell me the story again, Cassandra."

Cassandra linked her arm through Jane's and pulled her away from their parents, indicating she and her sister would take a walk around the ballroom.

"According to Mrs Dunmore, who heard it from Mrs Lamb who works in the kitchen here at Stanmore Hall, Lord Westworth wasn't originally meant to inherit the title and the estate. He had an older brother, but that brother went to India many years ago and was reported to have died there. From what I understand, Lord Westworth took his case to the House of Lords when he came of age in order to confirm he was eligible to the title, as his brother hadn't died in this country and there was some uncertainty around his death."

"Just a little," Jane murmured.

"Then years later, out of nowhere, the brother reappears and Lord Westworth travels to India to bring him home."

"Extraordinary. It *is* like something out of a novel," Jane said.

Cassandra nodded. "I'm curious as to what happens to the title now that he's back."

Jane was about to open her mouth to answer when she was stopped short by a young man with tousled hair stepping in front of them. It was clear he hadn't seen them; his gaze was directed back over his shoulder at the small group he had left. He turned just in time to avoid colliding with Jane, although he did have to stop abruptly and seemed to teeter before catching his balance. A dazzling smile bloomed on his lips and Jane felt the full force of his charm as he looked her directly in the eye.

"My apologies," he said, his voice low and clear. "I wasn't looking where I was going and almost flattened you."

"There was no harm done," Jane said quickly, wondering if the man would introduce himself or simply carry on his way.

"I know you," he said, leaning his head to one side. "Miss Cassandra Austen and Miss Jane Austen."

Jane blinked. She prided herself on being a keen observer of people and she was certain she would remember a man with a smile like this, whenever they had met him before. "You have us at a disadvantage, Mr…"

"Mr Lefroy, Tom Lefroy. It is a pleasure to meet you." The young man bowed courteously.

"Are you sure we have met before, Mr Lefroy?"

"No, we have not. But I have heard much about you. I am fortunate enough to be staying with my aunt, Mrs Anne Lefroy, for a few weeks and she has described you so vividly it is like we have been introduced already."

"I cannot think what she could have said to make us so easily recognisable."

Mr Lefroy leaned in a little closer and smiled. "She speaks very highly of you, Miss Austen."

Although the words were completely innocent, Jane felt the heat rise in her cheeks. Mr Lefroy was looking at her intently, his eyes only occasionally flicking to Cassandra. Jane knew she was passable in appearance, but her sister was normally the one to capture the attention if they were stood side by side. Now she felt a frisson of excitement that Mr Lefroy was looking at *her* with his dark eyes.

"Perhaps you would save me a dance this evening, Miss Austen?" he said, still looking at Jane. "If you have any space on your dance card."

"I do." Jane swallowed and then smiled, feeling her tongue stick to the roof of her mouth and wishing she had a refreshing glass of lemonade in her hand. "And I would be honoured to accept your offer to dance."

"Wonderful. Shall we meet for the third?"

Jane nodded and watched as Mr Lefroy took his leave and disappeared into the crowds.

"Jane," Cassandra said as they stood side by side at the edge of the ballroom, "I do believe you are blushing."

"Nonsense," Jane said, shaking her head just a little too vehemently. "I do not blush."

At that moment the musicians struck up the first chords, inviting the dancers to the dancefloor. Neither Jane nor Cassandra had partners for the first dance, but as they gathered near the edge of the dancefloor a young gentleman approached and asked Cassandra to dance, leaving Jane on her own looking on.

She didn't mind, she quite enjoyed watching the dancers, catching glimpses of Cassandra twirling round and round, parading up and down arm in arm with her partner. Cassandra looked happy, smiling at the man she was dancing with and saying a few inaudible words when they came together before the steps meant they were pulled apart again for the next part of the dance.

"I'm sorry," a breathless voice said as a small body barrelled into her. Jane instinctively reached out to steady the young woman. It was Emma Roscoe, a friend she had known much of her life. "Jane, I'm so glad it's you."

"Whatever is the matter, Emma?"

Emma Roscoe's cheeks were flushed and her normally immaculate appearance wasn't quite as put together as usual. There were a few stray strands of hair that had come loose from their pins and one puff sleeve had slipped from her shoulder, revealing a little more skin than she customarily would. She glanced over her shoulder, as if checking for who might be following her.

"Emma?" Jane said again.

"I can't say anything here, but I would appreciate your counsel, Jane."

"What has happened?"

"I heard something I shouldn't…" Emma pressed her lips together and shook her head. "I must not speak of it here, not until I have things straight in my head. Perhaps I have things wrong."

"Do you want to go somewhere more private to talk?"

"Yes, but not now. Can you meet me at ten o'clock? I promised I would dance the second with Mr Newbury and my mother will not let me hear the end of it if I let him down."

Jane nodded. She had heard a clock chiming nine times about fifteen minutes ago, so she would have time to dance the third with Mr Lefroy. "Where shall we meet?"

"In the library, it is quiet in there. The card tables are set up in the drawing room so I think we should be able to talk in private."

Jane nodded, feeling a surge of anticipation. Something out of the ordinary had happened tonight, something that had caused a normally sensible young woman to feel more than a little unsettled. "Are you sure there is nothing I can do now for you?"

"No. I must find Mr Newbury." Emma reached out and squeezed Jane's hand. "Thank you, Jane, I'm sure you will know what to do." With one final glance back over her shoulder she slipped away, leaving Jane feeling uneasy as well as concerned for her friend.

"One more dance, you cannot deny me that."

"We have danced two together, anymore and the gossips will be circling." Jane felt uncharacteristically giddy as Mr Lefroy took hold of her hand and looked into her eyes.

"Let them gossip. I find tonight I cannot make myself care what they say."

"You will regret it tomorrow when our names are linked and you have to explain our recklessness to your aunt."

"I do not think I could regret anything when it came to you, Miss Austen."

Against her better judgement Jane allowed Mr Lefroy to lead her back to the dancefloor. There was a lull in the music and she heard the chimes of a grandfather clock in the distance, probably the grand clock in the hall they had passed on the way in. She counted ten chimes, suddenly remembering her meeting with Emma Roscoe, but already it was too late to bow out of the dance. She was trapped by a press of bodies and before she could even utter a word of protest she was swept away into the procession.

Once the dance was finished, she hurriedly took her leave of Mr Lefroy, laughing as he pressed her to take a stroll around the ballroom later in the evening, happy that he would only let her leave once she had agreed. There was no time to find Cassandra to tell her where she was going, already it must be ten or fifteen minutes past the hour and Emma would be waiting for her.

Jane bent her head, keen not to catch anyone's eye and invite conversation that might delay her further. It seemed to take forever to weave her way through the ballroom and she was relieved when she stepped out into the airy hall. There were a few groups of people out here, gathered away from the noise in the ballroom but still close enough to enjoy the music and festivities. The door opposite the ballroom was thrown open and Jane could see there were three tables set up for cards, all three full with others standing round looking on, waiting for their chance to step in and claim their place in a game.

Turning her attention to the rest of the house, Jane made her way through the grand hallway. It was darker down here, with just one or two candles flickering at increasing intervals. The Westworths were generous hosts, but it seemed they hadn't wanted to open up their whole downstairs to the guests as this part of the house was quiet and uninviting.

"Where could the library be?" Jane murmured to herself, trying a couple of doors to find them locked. Her third guess was the right one and she let out a sigh of relief as she opened the door to reveal the grand bookshelves of the Westworth's considerable library inside.

The room was in darkness and Jane hesitated at the doorway. If Emma was inside, then surely she would have brought a candle with her? It would be strange to be sitting here in the gloom. Perhaps Jane had left it too long to escape from the ballroom and Emma had become frustrated with the wait. With a ball of guilt building in her stomach Jane turned to leave, but something stopped her.

There was a sense of the room not being quite empty. She couldn't explain it, but she felt as though there was a presence there. "Emma?" she called softly.

There was no answer. Taking one step into the library she paused, reluctant to go in any further without a light.

Jane could feel her pulse quickening as she realised there was an unfamiliar scent in the air. A mixture of rose water and something more metallic, more earthy.

"Emma, are you here?"

Making up her mind, Jane returned to the hallway and took a candlestick from an alcove before re-entering the room. For a moment she couldn't make sense of what she saw. Sticking out from behind the huge mahogany desk was a delicate foot clad in a satin shoe. The shoe had a little pearl flower on the top and for a few seconds Jane couldn't bring herself to look anywhere else but the flower.

She didn't want to take another step, didn't want to see the rest of what was behind the desk, but she knew she had to.

With her heartbeat pounding in her ears Jane took a couple of quick steps forwards and looked down, feeling all the air being sucked from her lungs.

Lying on the ground was the body of Emma Roscoe. Her eyes were open and unblinking, her lips parted ever so slightly, but there was no breath passing them. Jane swallowed as she saw the bloom of blood on Emma's dress and in the centre of her chest the handle of a knife sticking out.

CHAPTER TWO

Eventually, Jane managed to get enough air into her lungs to call out. She wasn't sure what she shouted but it was enough to summon someone who had been further down the hall.

The next few minutes seemed to pass in a blur as more and more people poured into the library until eventually Lord Westworth arrived and took charge. Jane was escorted, still shaking, to a quiet room and as she left the library, she overheard Lord Westworth instructing his butler to clear all the guests back into the ballroom and then send for the magistrate.

"What happened?" Lord Westworth asked as he followed Jane into a tidy room set out with comfortable armchairs. Lady Westworth was with him and fussed around Jane, making sure she was seated before she attempted to answer.

"Miss Roscoe…" Jane began, trailing off. Desperately, she tried to compose herself. It was vital she didn't fail her friend now, and the quicker she could impart her information the more useful it would be. "Miss Roscoe asked me to meet her in the library," Jane said, her voice steadier this time. "I was a little late and at first I thought no one was there." She took a deep breath, trying to push the picture of Emma's body from her mind. "I took a candle from the hallway and when I re-entered the room, I saw her body." Jane felt the tears running down her cheeks and raised a hand to brush them away.

"Why did you…?" Lady Westworth began but was silenced by her husband.

"Perhaps we had better leave the questioning to the magistrate, my dear. He will know what questions to ask."

"Of course," Lady Westworth said, patting Jane on the hand in a motherly fashion. "I will send someone to find your parents and your sister."

The Westworths looked completely shocked by the events of the evening and Jane could see the tremor in Lady Westworth's hand as she smoothed down her skirts.

A middle-aged man entered the room dressed in a butler's livery and leaned in to murmur in Lord Westworth's ear, though the words were still audible to Jane.

"The guests are all gathered in the ballroom, my lord, and I've put the footman Jones outside the library door to ensure no one enters until the magistrate arrives. I've sent one of the grooms to Petersfield House to inform Lord Hinchbrooke."

"Good. What is the talk amongst the guests?"

"I think everyone knows what has happened now. Miss Roscoe came with her aunt and uncle; I have taken them aside and put them in the yellow room, but they are understandably distraught."

"Understandably," Lord Westworth murmured. He turned to Jane. "Please excuse me, Miss Austen, I should talk to Mr and Mrs Roscoe."

Jane nodded absently. She knew a shock like this could affect one's body in strange and inexplicable ways, but she felt as though she were floating outside of herself. Everyone's words were coming to her as if they were drifting through a cloud and she felt separated, cut off from the rest of the room.

"Jane," Cassandra cried as she burst into the room, followed closely by her parents.

Jane let her body relax into Cassandra's familiar arms.

Jane had always thought of herself as good in a crisis. If the chickens got loose from the coop or the dogs took off chasing a rabbit, she would always be the calm one, the voice of reason. When her mother was worrying about finances or her father was fretting about how best to look after her brother, she would guide them through the difficult decisions with her calm and concise reasoning.

Finding a dead body was another thing entirely, though. For half an hour she doubted she would have been able to put together more than half a dozen words into a coherent sentence. Her hands trembled every time she tried to raise the glass of water she had been passed to her lips and if she closed her eyes to steady herself, she saw the image of Emma Roscoe's body in her mind.

It was a relief in many ways when she heard a commotion outside the room she was seated in, clutching at Cassandra's hand, and a couple of seconds later Lord Hinchbrooke walked in.

Her father rose and the two men exchanged greetings in low voices.

"Miss Austen, thank you for waiting for me."

Jane looked up and gave the magistrate a weak smile, more of a twitch of the lips than anything else.

"I am sorry we do not meet again in more pleasant circumstances."

Jane had met Lord Hinchbrooke on a number of occasions and always found him to be friendly and jovial despite their difference in social rank. He was a viscount, and she had it on good authority he took his role as member of the House of Lords very seriously. She expected he had the same attitude towards his position as magistrate, which pleased her, for many saw the role as a nuisance and nothing more.

"I am sure you are eager to get home, but I think we share the desire to understand what happened to Miss Roscoe tonight."

Jane nodded, mentally trying to compose herself. She owed it to Emma to do everything in her power to help find who had taken her life. "I will do anything I can to help."

"I'm really not sure…" Mrs Austen began to say, but Jane's father shot her a warning look.

"I think Jane can decide what she is capable of, my dear."

"Perhaps we can begin with your account of events leading up to you finding Miss Roscoe," Lord Hinchbrooke said softly.

"I really think this might be best done tomorrow," Mrs Austen said, fussing around in a distracting manner.

"Please, Mother," Jane said, a little sharper than she meant to. "I wish to talk to Lord Hinchbrooke. I want to tell him what happened. Anything that might help."

Lord Hinchbrooke smiled at her encouragingly. He had a pleasant, round face with bushy eyebrows and greying hair. His demeanour was friendly and Jane could see he had a talent at getting people to relax around him. It was a good skill for a magistrate to possess.

"Earlier this evening I bumped into Miss Roscoe at the edge of the dancefloor. It was whilst Cassandra was dancing and I was left on my own for a few minutes." Jane took a shaky breath and felt an unbidden tear slip from her eye and onto her cheek.

"This is too much," Mrs Austen said, standing up and pulling Jane by the hand. "I must insist we do this another time."

"Mother," Jane said, wrenching her hand away. "Please."

"Might I suggest I talk to Miss Austen in private?" Lord Hinchbrooke said, bestowing his amiable smile on Mrs Austen.

"We can get through these couple of questions quickly and then you good people can get home."

"Jane will need a chaperon."

"I am happy to sit with her, Mama," Cassandra said. "If that is acceptable to Lord Hinchbrooke?"

"That sounds like a perfect solution." He watched as Mr Austen led his wife from the room and then turned his attention back to Jane. "Are you happy to continue?"

She gave a nod.

"Do you mind if I take notes?"

"No, I don't mind."

"You were saying you saw Miss Roscoe earlier in the evening?"

"Yes." Jane fiddled with the material of her dress, pinching the fabric and then smoothing it down. "Miss Roscoe was shaken, she said she had heard something she shouldn't have and she asked me if I would meet her later to discuss it."

"Were you a particular confidante of Miss Roscoe?"

"No," Jane shook her head. "We are old friends, but we are…" she took a shuddering breath before correcting herself, "…*were* not that close."

"Do you have any idea why she might have asked for you to be the one to meet her?"

Jane considered for a moment, tilting her head to one side and thinking back to the moment in the ballroom when Emma had brushed past her, harried and shocked in her demeanour.

"I am known to have a clear head and to be practical rather than overcome by emotion," Jane said slowly, "but if I am truthful, I wonder if I was just in the right place at the right time. I was the one she ran into, and she reached out to me because I was there."

Jane watched as Lord Hinchbrooke jotted something down in a small, leather-bound book, muttering under his breath and looking at the writing as if it were foreign and not produced by his own hand. As he tried again Jane noticed the tremor that built in intensity whenever he tried to touch the pen nib to paper.

"What happened next, Miss Austen?"

"Miss Roscoe asked me to meet her at ten o'clock in the library to discuss it, away from the curious ears in the ballroom. I agreed, but I was distracted as Mr Lefroy asked me to dance." Jane took a deep steadying breath. "It was almost a quarter past ten when I left the ballroom. I can't help but wonder if I had been on time whether Miss Roscoe would still be alive."

"Don't think like that, Jane," Cassandra murmured, reaching out and taking her hand.

"Miss Austen, there is only one person to blame for the death of Miss Roscoe, and that is the one who killed her. Now, I am fairly certain that was not you, so I beg you please do not blame yourself."

"I didn't know which room was the library, I have never been inside Stanmore Hall before, so I tried a few doors until I found one that was unlocked." Jane closed her eyes for a moment, knowing it was important to get the sequence of events right. Every detail might be significant and she owed it to Emma to not make a mistake. "I opened the door and stepped into the library, but at first, I thought the room was empty because it was completely dark. I could see the bookshelves, so I knew it was the right room, but I assumed Miss Roscoe had left because I was too late."

"What made you stay?"

"It sounds strange, but I felt as though the room was occupied. I smelled something that was out of place — a faint hint of rose and a metallic smell."

"That would have been the blood." Lord Hinchbrooke went to note something down again and this time cursed under his breath as he seemed to struggle to grasp the pen tight enough for him to make a mark and the tremor started again.

"I stepped out of the room into the hallway and picked up a candlestick and then went back into the library." Jane swallowed and let the memory of finding Emma wash over her. "I saw her foot first, sticking out from behind the desk and I can remember thinking what a pretty satin shoe she had on."

After letting out a short, sharp laugh, Jane felt her hands fly to her mouth as if trying to claw it back in. It all seemed so ridiculous, so absurd, and even though she had seen Emma lying there dead with her own eyes she still couldn't quite believe it. It felt as though any moment her friend would appear in the doorway and explain away the misunderstanding with a laugh or roll of her eyes.

Lord Hinchbrooke was regarding her intently but there was only kindness in his dark brown eyes. "What did you do?"

"I went round the edge of the desk and saw the … knife … and the blood all around it. I think I crouched down to see if she was still alive, but her eyes were unmoving and her chest was not rising and falling."

"You did very well to check."

"Then I stumbled back a bit and called out for help."

"Did you touch anything? Move anything?"

Jane took a moment to think, to go over those last few moments in the library in her mind before shaking her head.

"Lots of people arrived and then Lord Westworth ushered me in here."

"Thank you, Miss Austen, that is a very thorough account." Lord Hinchbrooke gave her a gentle smile and Jane felt herself relax a little, thinking this part of the ordeal was likely nearly over. "I do have a couple more questions for you, if you are able? Have you any idea what it was that Miss Roscoe might have overheard?"

Jane shook her head. She had been thinking hard about this but there was no way of knowing what had happened in the minutes leading up to their encounter in the ballroom where Emma had seemed so flustered.

"And can you think of any reason why anyone would have wanted to cause Miss Roscoe harm?"

Jane's eyes widened as the reality of the situation hit her. Someone had wanted to cause her friend so much harm that she was now lying dead in the next room. She closed her eyes and tried to take a few deep breaths, the way her father told her mother to when something threatened to overwhelm her. It felt as though her throat was closing up and there was no space in her chest for the air. Beside her Cassandra rubbed her back and murmured soothing sounds but it all felt so distant.

There was a darkness that clawed at her and Jane could feel it closing in from all sides. She tried to think of more positive things, anything really other than the image of Emma Roscoe lying unmoving on the library floor, but it was impossible to put it from her mind.

Slowly, with great effort, Jane pushed back at the darkness, feeling it recede little by little as she breathed deeply and focussed on Cassandra's fingers on her back.

"I'm sorry," Lord Hinchbrooke said, "I have been inconsiderate." He ran a hand through his greying hair and gave Jane a smile that didn't quite reach his eyes. He looked tired and Jane wondered what he had been doing when he was called to attend Stanmore Hall. It was strange that he hadn't been at the ball tonight as he was one of the Westworth's neighbours, but Jane didn't pretend to understand the complex links between the titled gentlemen.

"I think it might be time for me to take my sister home," Cassandra said gently. It was said in such an unassuming way that only Jane heard the hint of grit in her voice. "I am sure Jane will be happy to return tomorrow if you need to ask her anything else."

"Yes, you must go home. You have been very helpful, Miss Austen, thank you for taking the time to tell me what happened tonight. If you do think of anything else then please do send me a note."

Feeling a little wobbly as she stood, Jane leaned on her sister's arm and headed for the door, pausing with her hand on the handle. "Lord Hinchbrooke, you will find out what happened?"

"I will endeavour to discover the truth, Miss Austen."

"Thank you."

As she stepped out into the hall Jane looked back over her shoulder and saw Lord Hinchbrooke try once again to write something in the notebook he had resting in his lap but once again his hand shook and this time, thinking he had no audience, he cursed and threw his pen down in disgust.

"Come, Jane, let's get you home," Cassandra said as they walked through the hall.

People were gathered in little clusters. A group of servants were looking worried huddled in the shadows away from the guests and some young men were talking in low voices outside the door to the ballroom.

Jane peered into the ballroom, but apart from a couple of stragglers it was now empty. Lord Hinchbrooke must have released all the guests to return home before he came to talk to her earlier. Unbidden, Jane's gaze flicked to the room further down the corridor, her eyes fixing on the firmly closed door to the library. She wondered if Emma was still lying there on the floor, her foot sticking out from behind the mahogany desk, her eyes glazed and unseeing.

"Don't think about it," Cassandra said quietly, as though reading her thoughts. "Not now. There will be plenty of time to remember Emma once you have had a rest."

"Oh, my darling Jane, what an ordeal," Mrs Austen said as she rushed out from the drawing room where earlier the card games had been set up and pulled Jane into a tight embrace. She regarded her daughter's pale, drawn face and turned to her husband. "Mr Austen, we must leave at once. Jane is exhausted and needs her bed."

Jane's father approached a footman who slipped away to arrange for their borrowed carriage to be brought round.

For the first part of the journey home the Austen family sat in silence, all too overwhelmed by the events of the evening to say anything. Jane's mind was flitting all over the place, wondering if there was a detail she could remember, anything that might help the investigation.

"Lord Hinchbrooke seemed competent," Cassandra said quietly after a few minutes, her hand searching for Jane's in the dark.

Jane nodded, grateful for her sister's observation.

"I have heard good things about him as a magistrate," Mr Austen said. "So many are not interested in the intricacies of the position, especially when they have other responsibilities."

He shook his head, his grey hair bobbing up and down with the movement. "I remember our last magistrate, Mr Utteral, he could not bring a thief to justice if he saw them steal something with his own eyes. He just wasn't interested."

"Lord Hinchbrooke doesn't seem like that," Cassandra said.

"No, I do believe he will do a good job," Mr Austen said, giving Jane a reassuring smile, "and not simply pin the crime on the shiftiest servant or a local vagrant."

"What are you saying, Mr Austen?" Mrs Austen interrupted, her voice a little shrill. "You aren't suggesting it might have been one of the *guests*?"

"I don't see why it couldn't be," Mr Austen said matter-of-factly.

"These are our friends, our neighbours."

"Not all of them."

"I think Papa is right," Jane said. "Emma wanted to talk to me about something she'd witnessed. Surely the affairs of Lord Westworth's servants wouldn't have caused her so much consternation."

"Hmmm," Mrs Austen said, pressing her lips together.

"Perhaps it is something to do with this confusion with Lord Westworth and his brother?" Cassandra mused.

"No," Mrs Austen said, raising a hand to stop this line of speculation. "I will not hear about it. Lord Westworth is highly respected and his wife is involved in numerous charitable organisations."

"What about the long-lost brother though? Did anyone even see him tonight?"

They all fell silent.

"It is a strange situation, but I do feel we should not speculate on things we know nothing about," Mrs Austen said, fixing each of her daughters with a hard stare.

Jane and Cassandra both acquiesced and remained silent.

The road outside the gates to Stanmore Hall was bumpy and even worse in the dark. The carriage had been borrowed for the evening from a friend of Mr Austen and the driver must have been eager to get home for he barely slowed for the uneven patches, making the carriage rock from side to side.

Jane closed her eyes, wishing she was already in bed where the horror of the night's events could be lost in the oblivion of sleep and the comfort of Cassandra's warmth beside her.

CHAPTER THREE

It was a relief when the first rays of sun began to peek through the curtains. Jane had tossed and turned the whole night. Every time she closed her eyes she was unable to see anything but Emma Roscoe's blank stare and the bloom of blood on her dress.

Jane quietly rose from bed, careful not to wake Cassandra who seemed to be sleeping peacefully. Often Jane envied her sister's ability to slumber as if she had not a care in the world. Cassandra always fell asleep quickly at night and rarely anything disturbed her for a good eight hours. Jane, on the other hand, struggled to keep the thoughts from swirling around in her head, her mind beset by ideas that wouldn't leave her alone until she had risen and found a pen to write them down.

It was her writing desk she now turned to, pulling back the curtain enough to let some of the dawn light into the room, but not so much as to disturb Cassandra. She picked up the piece of paper at the top of the neat stack and read what she had last written. The writing was small and spidery, all the better to fit more on the page. Her father never begrudged her paper or ink given how invested he was in all his children's education, but she was well aware they were expensive commodities and tried not to waste any.

Most mornings she cherished this time before the rest of the household was up and awake. It was her private time, the time she liked to use to write, but today she found she couldn't concentrate. Every sentence she had to re-read three times and she knew anything she wrote this morning she would not be happy with and would end up scratching out and writing again.

Instead, she pulled open one of the drawers and took out a small notebook. It was delicately bound with an embroidered flower on the front, a recent birthday present from Cassandra. It was one of her most treasured possessions and Jane was in the habit of carrying it round with her most places. It was surprising how often an idea struck her when she was out walking across the fields or performing some mundane chore like shopping for cloth in town. She would quickly whip out her notebook and jot down a few words to remind her of what she had seen or heard or what thought had occurred to her, ready for her to mull it over and come back to it later. It was also in this notebook that she would write her night-time ideas, those thoughts that kept her awake at night if she did not put them down on paper.

Jane paused for a moment, gathering her thoughts, then started to write.

Emma Roscoe.
Found in library, stabbed in chest, shortly after ten o'clock.
Knife — from where?
Last seen by me in the ballroom at a quarter past nine.
What did Emma observe that she shouldn't have?
Who could have stabbed her? Guests, servants? Someone from outside the house?

Jane read through what she had written and let out a low moan of frustration. She barely knew anything. It was a list of questions with no answers, and thus far all her assumptions had been based around the idea that Emma had borne witness to something she shouldn't have.

Dropping her pen in disgust Jane stood and crossed to the small wardrobe in the corner of the room. She opened it carefully, placing her hand over the hinges to shield Cassandra's ears from the high-pitched squeak emitted when the door was halfway open. From inside she took her coat and slipped it on, feeling on the shelf above the rail for her gloves, then closing the door with equal care before leaving the room.

The whole upstairs was quiet, but downstairs Jane could hear the humming of Mrs White, their cook. Jane crept past the door to the kitchen and then quietly turned the key in the back door and slipped on her boots before stealing out into the garden.

The air was icy and there was a thick frost on the grass, but Jane didn't mind the cold temperatures when everything looked this beautiful. Winter was secretly her favourite time of year. She loved it when the ponds froze over and when the snow fell thickly from the sky. They were lucky enough never to be short of firewood and Jane enjoyed sitting next to a warm fire, curled up in her favourite armchair, happy with a book whilst the wind or rain raged outside.

Treading carefully, Jane wandered through the garden, trying to clear her head of the events of the night before.

"Good morning, Jane." Her father's voice surprised her out of her reverie. He had his thick winter coat on as well as his boots, but underneath she could see he was still in his nightwear. "Don't catch cold or your mother will never let you hear the end of it."

Jane smiled and walked over to join her father, linking her arm through his.

"Good morning, Papa. Did you sleep?"

"Barely. I was worrying about my girls." He bestowed a loving smile on her and Jane stepped in even closer to share some of his wonderful warmth. "I am going to guess that you did not sleep a single wink."

"No."

"Understandable after everything you went through last night."

"I just keep thinking there must be something more I can do, some way I can help poor Emma."

Her father patted her on the hand, his bare on top of her gloves. "You told Lord Hinchbrooke everything you remembered, didn't you?"

"Yes, I think so."

"Then best to leave it to those who know what they are doing."

"Do you think Lord Hinchbrooke has had to deal with something like this before?"

Mr Austen contemplated the question for a moment and then shook his head slowly. "I doubt it. Mostly the magistrates sit in judgement of the local disputes and petty crimes, but I know Lord Hinchbrooke is keen to be more than your average magistrate."

Jane was inclined to agree. The magistrate had seemed genuinely interested in what had happened to Emma and she had believed him when he said he would endeavour to discover the truth.

"Do you know him, Papa?"

"Only by reputation. He inherited his title when he was young and has spent the last twenty years working to improve the conditions for those that live and work on his land. He is known to be a fair and good master and I am told he is formidable in parliament."

Jane nodded in approval. He sounded exactly the sort of man she wanted looking into Emma's death.

"I am impressed he came out so late for the matter, it shows his commitment to his neighbours and his role as magistrate. It really is going beyond what is expected in his situation."

"Papa," Jane said quietly, wondering how best to phrase what she wanted to say. "I think I have told Lord Hinchbrooke everything I know, but I hate the feeling of waiting around hoping for news."

"Sometimes I wonder if patience is one of the hardest virtues to master."

"For me I think it is."

"I understand your desire to be involved, Jane dearest, and I know what a sharp mind you have, but some things are out of our reach however much we want it."

"It is because I am a woman, is it not?"

"I know your talents, my dear, but even I would have qualms about letting you get involved in a matter like this."

"I do not plan to involve myself exactly, I do not think that possible, but I wondered if you would object to me walking over to Stanmore Hall this morning and enquiring if there were any more questions Lord Hinchbrooke would like to ask of me, just to be sure?"

Her father looked at her with a sad understanding in his eyes, appraising her for a moment. "I will not stop you, although it may be wise to leave before your mother rises. I doubt she will want to let you out of her sight today if you are still here when she gets up."

"Will you explain to her where I have gone?"

"Of course."

"Thank you, Papa."

Jane didn't wait around for him to change his mind, instead hurrying indoors to dress quickly. In a way she was pleased he hadn't told her to take Cassandra with her. She loved her sister dearly and relied on her more than anyone else in the world, but today she craved solitude. She wanted to walk in silence so she could gather her thoughts before she reached Stanmore Hall, and Lord Hinchbrooke.

Upstairs in their shared bedroom Jane was careful to dress silently, wishing the fire had been laid in the grate but stripping down to her chemise and petticoats anyway and pulling on a dress that would be suitable for the long walk over the muddy fields. When she crept past her parents' room she could hear the easy, throaty breathing that signalled her mother was still asleep and it meant Jane was confident enough in her timings to slip into the kitchen and beg for a piece of bread from Mrs White before she set off.

It wasn't snowing when she left, but the sky was dark and the clouds looked heavy with precipitation. Jane pulled her collar up around her neck and bent her head against the wind, knowing she would be frozen through by the time she reached Stanmore Hall. Normally she was a keen walker, venturing out in almost any weather, never minding if the rain was beating down on her or the heat of the summer making her perspire, but today it was a little too cold even for her. Before she had reached the end of the lane near the rectory her fingers felt stiff and cold and the tip of her nose was numb.

"Keep going, Jane," she muttered to herself, pushing through the discomfort and increasing her pace to try and infuse some warmth through her body.

The gates to Stanmore Hall looked even more imposing in the daylight and Jane paused for a second before she continued up the sweeping drive. At the top of the wrought iron were the figures of four lions, mouths open and complete with sharp teeth bared. It sent a shiver down Jane' spine and made her want to look away.

The long drive curved round so you couldn't actually see Stanmore Hall until you were over halfway up it. The bottom portion was lined with trees — big, well-established oaks on either side whose branches met over the middle of the drive and made a canopy high above.

Jane often wondered what life must be like for the lucky few with titles and land and wealth to be able to do whatever they wanted. She was aware she was in a relatively privileged position in the world, but her life was nothing like that of the gentry. She had a comfortable home and had been fortunate enough to be allowed a formal education for a few years until the money had become too tight. She enjoyed warmth and the knowledge that her belly would be full at the end of each day. Every year she would get a new dress and there were enough funds for their home to be well furnished. It was much more than many people had, but it would be an unrecognisable existence for the likes of Lord and Lady Westworth.

She was about halfway up the drive when she heard a clattering of hooves in the distance and a minute later a rider dressed all in black thundered past, not slowing to avoid her. Jane had to step back onto the grass to ensure she was safe from the horse and rider, and she only caught a glimpse of his face as he whipped past.

The man had dark hair and dark eyes and the shadow of a beard, as if he hadn't shaved for a day or two. He was tall and thin and wore a frown on his face, and seemed so preoccupied that Jane thought it likely he hadn't even seen her.

As she approached the front door she slowed, suddenly uncertain of herself. Lord and Lady Westworth had been inviting the night before, but then they had voluntarily opened their house up for the ball. Today, whilst they were coming to terms with the tragedy that had occurred here they might not want to receive visitors, especially one who had come with the firm purpose of inserting herself into the proceedings.

Knowing she had come too far to turn back now Jane rapped on the door, surprised to find it opened almost immediately by Waters, the butler.

"Good morning," she said with her friendliest smile. "I am Miss Jane Austen, and I was here last night when…" she faltered and then pressed on. "I have come to see Lord Hinchbrooke if he is still here."

"Please come in, Miss Austen. I will let Lady Westworth know you are here."

Jane stepped into the entrance hall, her eyes immediately seeking out the door to the library. She wondered if Emma's body had been removed and if so where it had been taken. It wasn't something she had ever needed to think about before — what happened to a body when the manner of death was under investigation?

"Miss Austen, how are you this morning?" Lady Westworth said as she sailed out of the dining room. On the surface she looked composed and every inch the calm and collected viscountess, but Jane could see some subtle signs she wasn't as put together as she might usually be. There were a few loose strands of hair at the nape of her neck as if she had hurried her maid along, and she was worrying a piece of skin by the side of her thumbnail with her index finger as she spoke.

"Please excuse the intrusion, Lady Westworth, I know you must be eager to return to some semblance of normality, but I hoped I might have a few moments of Lord Hinchbrooke's time. I assume he is still with you?"

"Yes, he is. He agreed to stay last night so he could conclude things as quickly as possible today."

Jane felt her eyes widen, wondering if her trip here had been in vain. Although she would be very glad to hear Lord Hinchbrooke had made significant progress with finding out what had happened to Emma.

"Have you remembered something else, Miss Austen, something from last night?" Lady Westworth took a step closer and Jane could see there was a flash of concern in her eyes. "Lord Hinchbrooke said anything we remember out of the ordinary may help."

"I'm not sure. Is he busy?"

"Waters, see if Lord Hinchbrooke is happy for Miss Austen to go in and see him."

The butler who had first greeted Jane marched briskly to one of the many doors off the main hallway and knocked loudly. After a moment he entered and Jane could hear the low hum of voices being exchanged. She felt a bubble of anticipation. If he refused to see her she knew there was nothing she could do about it. She would have to begin the long walk home with the feeling of failure in her heart.

"Lord Hinchbrooke is happy to see Miss Austen," Waters announced as he reappeared through the doorway.

"Please, go in. Would you care for any refreshment?" Lady Westworth smiled magnanimously and Jane felt a rush of gratitude towards her hostess. It was a difficult time for the Westworths, but they had been nothing but accommodating.

"A cup of tea would be much appreciated."

"Of course. Waters, will you see to it?"

Jane approached the door the butler had come out of a few moments ago and knocked softly, hearing the shuffling of feet before Lord Hinchbrooke opened the door in person and greeted her with a warm smile.

"Come in, Miss Austen, it is a pleasure to see you again."

Stepping into the room Jane felt the warmth of the fire draw her closer. Lord Hinchbrooke closed the door behind her and invited her to sit and his relaxed manner made her immediately feel more at ease. She could imagine him upholding the law, smoothing over arguments between disputing parties and generally making the local area a better place.

"How are you this morning, Miss Austen?"

"I am sorry to intrude," Jane said, wishing she had rehearsed what she was going to say on the way over. "I have had an unsettled night and I knew I needed to speak to you again."

Lord Hinchbrooke didn't look annoyed or immediately dismiss her, which was reassuring, so Jane took a deep breath and continued.

"I thought I might be of some help to you."

"Oh?"

"I know it is not considered the done thing to sing one's own praises, but I hope you will forgive my immodesty. I am a quick thinker and logical. I have a great desire to see whoever murdered my friend brought to justice and I am willing to do whatever small or menial job you need from me to help the process along."

"You're proposing you act as my assistant, Miss Austen?" To his credit Lord Hinchbrooke did not laugh but Jane could see he was far from convinced.

Jane started to say no and then paused. "Yes," she said finally. "I know it is not how you would normally operate, but this is an extraordinary event and I hoped you would consider the merit of the idea."

Lord Hinchbrooke looked thoughtful and Jane's hopes climbed that he might be inclined to at least consider her proposition.

"I appreciate your desire to help, Miss Austen, but I can see no role for you," Lord Hinchbrooke said gently.

In any other circumstance she would have appreciated him letting her down so kindly, but Jane felt a stab of irritation deep in her gut. If she were a man this conversation might have gone a different way.

He reached out for his cup of tea, set on a small table to one side, and took a long sip. As he set it back down she noticed how it clattered in the saucer and an idea started to form.

"I understand your reticence, Lord Hinchbrooke. It is a strange request I make of you, but I truly think I can be of some assistance to you. If I could beg your leave to be personal for a moment?" She waited until he inclined his head, the twitch of a smile on his lips. "I have noticed you struggle with a tremor in your hand, worse when you try to do something. It kept you from writing your notes yesterday."

"You are very observant, Miss Austen."

"I spend much of my time writing. One day I hope..." She trailed off, not knowing if revealing her dream to become a published author one day would enhance her chance of him accepting her help or hinder it. "It does not matter. I write notes and prose and letters. I have a neat hand and I write quickly; I can keep up with whatever you are saying and transcribe it into notes."

"A useful skill, Miss Austen."

"Useful to you, Lord Hinchbrooke. I can be quiet and unassuming, blending into the background whilst I take your notes and whoever you are talking to will barely know I am there."

"What do your parents think of your plan?"

"My father is an enlightened man. He ensured both my sister and I received a formal education and is happy for me to make decisions for myself."

"Very enlightened," Lord Hinchbrooke murmured. "I don't know…"

"At least give me a chance. One hour and if I have not made myself indispensable then you can send me home."

Lord Hinchbrooke regarded her for a long moment and then to Jane's surprise nodded his head. "I suppose one hour cannot hurt. I will have to ask you to promise whatever we do discuss you will keep strictly to yourself."

"Of course."

"Good."

Jane felt a little of the despair that had threatened to engulf her over the last twelve hours begin to lift. It wasn't much, but it was a start to atoning for letting Emma down the night before. If she could help Lord Hinchbrooke find out who had killed her friend, then it would appease some of her guilt.

There was a soft knock on the door and after a moment Jones, a smartly dressed footmen, entered the room.

"Lord Westworth asked me to inform you that the undertakers are here my lord, ready to take Miss Roscoe's body back home."

"Thank you. Please ask them not to touch anything yet."

Jane swallowed. That meant Emma's body was still in the room next door, still lying on the floor but now cold and missing that vital spark of life.

"I must examine the body before it is taken away, Miss Austen. I will not put you through the ordeal of seeing your friend again."

Jane took a deep breath and shook her head. "I have offered to help you, Lord Hinchbrooke, and I will not shy away from the job."

"Miss Austen, I do not think it is wise."

"Please, Lord Hinchbrooke. I will stand well back and if needed can step outside."

He relented with a heavy sigh and passed her his notebook and pen. Clutching it to her chest as though it were a warrior's shield ready to protect her, Jane followed Lord Hinchbrooke out of the drawing room and into the library, trying not to regret her offer to help before she had even begun.

CHAPTER FOUR

The curtains were drawn in the library and it took a few moments for Jane's eyes to adjust to the gloom. At first, she focussed on her breathing, trying to look anywhere but the big mahogany desk and the body she knew lay behind it.

"Miss Austen?" Lord Hinchbrooke enquired gently. "There is no harm in you stepping outside."

Jane shook her head, waiting for her heart to settle before she met his eye. "I am quite composed," she said softly, brandishing the notebook and pen in her hand. "Please begin whenever you are ready."

Lord Hinchbrooke crossed to the heavy curtains and with a gentle tug pulled one aside. It let a beam of light into the room disturbing the darkness and illuminating the dust that floated in the air.

Knowing it was time to be brave, Jane took a step forward and then another. The shoe that had been visible turned into a leg and then the crinkled-up skirts of Emma Roscoe's ballgown. It had been a pretty gown, stripes of dark and pale pink with a lace trim around the neckline. The sort of dress her mother would try to encourage her to consider for a ball or a dinner party, but which Jane would dismiss as being just a touch too cheerful.

With her whole body shaking, Jane took one final step and the rest of Emma Roscoe's lifeless body came into view. Her skin had a horrible waxy sheen and was completely devoid of colour now. Even her lips looked a muted purple rather than the rosy pink they once had been. Someone had closed her eyelids and for that Jane was grateful, but the knife was still sticking out of the young woman's chest although the blood around it had dried to a darker red.

"Will you take notes?" Lord Hinchbrooke asked, waiting for her to nod before continuing.

Jane fumbled open the notebook and rested it on her left hand, waiting for the magistrate's words.

"The body of Miss Emma Roscoe lies supine on the floor of the library. She is positioned behind the desk with her head pointing in the direction of the windows." He paused, crouching down to get closer to the body. "There is a knife still in situ, the handle is approximately seven inches long. The blade is embedded up to where it joins the handle and as such was likely wielded with some force." He glanced over at Jane to check she was keeping up.

"I thought there would be more blood," Jane said, taking another step closer.

Lord Hinchbrooke carefully placed his hand on Emma Roscoe's dress, a few inches below the knife wound.

"There isn't much, although it does depend a little on the angle of the knife." He peered at the point where the knife entered Emma's body. "I wonder if the knife pierced the heart itself, causing blood to flood into the pericardium. Even a small amount of blood is enough to put pressure on the heart and stop it from beating. Death is not so much from exsanguination as it is from the heart being unable to beat."

Jane hovered the pen over the paper, wondering if Lord Hinchbrooke wanted her to include his theories or only the facts. "That sounds an awful way to die."

"It would have happened quickly. You can see by the way she has fallen she did not suffer; she did not stumble around the room grasping at furniture. She was stabbed here and fell here."

It was something to be grateful for, although Jane could not begin to imagine what must have gone through Emma's mind in the seconds between the knife entering her chest and her last breath leaving her body.

With great care, Lord Hinchbrooke inspected each of the young woman's hands in turn, peering at the fingernails and taking a moment to unclench the fingers where they had curled.

"I have learned to always check under the fingernails. Sometimes a wisp of fabric or other such clue can be caught when the victim reaches out to grasp at their assailant."

"Is there anything of the sort here?"

"No, her fingernails are clean with nothing caught in them."

Lord Hinchbrooke paused for a moment, sitting back on his haunches and regarding the body in front of him. "Such a waste of young life, and what for? Without a doubt the reason for her death will be something petty or selfish. In all my years as the local magistrate I have never come across a motive that I could truly understand. What sort of person thinks their money or their sordid secrets are worth more than a young woman's life?"

"Have you dealt with many murders, Lord Hinchbrooke?"

"Unfortunately, more than I ever imagined I would. Most have been drunken fights that have gone too far or men who have hit their wives hard one time too many but murder all the same. There have been a few puzzling cases like this, but I am pleased to say there has only been one case in my time as magistrate I have not got to the bottom of."

"Then I am glad you are investigating Miss Roscoe's death."

Lord Hinchbrooke gave her a sad smile and nodded in acknowledgement.

"I am going to search Miss Roscoe now, Miss Austen. I will be respectful, but I understand this could be distressing."

Jane swallowed and took a step closer, watching as Lord Hinchbrooke carefully patted the fabric of Emma's dress to ensure nothing was concealed in it. After a minute he gave a grunt of satisfaction.

"Please make a note that no other injuries were found on external examination and nothing concealed about her clothes." He paused, groaning as he got to his feet, his movements slow and stiff. "We have a number of questions to answer. One, where is the knife from? Did the assailant bring it with them or was it more opportunistic than that? Two, why did Miss Roscoe not cry out or try to fight off her attacker, did it mean they were well known to her? Three, was there any blood transferred from Miss Roscoe to her attacker, and if so why did no one notice anything?"

Dutifully, Jane noted these questions in the notebook, waiting for a moment for the ink to dry before closing it as Lord Hinchbrooke made his way out of the room. She paused by the door, glancing back into the room, feeling a pang of sadness and guilt as she saw the solitary foot poking out from behind the desk.

"Have you finished?" Lord Westworth was pacing up and down the grand hallway, a pocket watch in one hand and a frown on his face. "The undertakers are keen to remove the body and her presence is unsettling the servants and my wife."

"I have finished."

"Miss Austen, you are still here. Is something amiss?" asked Lady Westworth.

Jane shook her head, wondering how best to explain her presence. She was saved from Lady Westworth's curious stare by the magistrate.

"Miss Austen has kindly offered to assist me with my enquiries." He offered no further justification for Jane's presence but the quiet authority he delivered the statement with was enough to signify the matter wasn't up for discussion. "I will also need to question the members of your household, Lord Westworth. Is there a room I can use that is private?"

"Certainly. The blue drawing room is comfortable and private."

"Do you really need to question all of the servants?" Lady Westworth looked shocked by the idea of the disruption this would bring to her household.

"Each and every one unfortunately, Lady Westworth. At present it is impossible to know who might hold that vital piece of information. I wonder if I can ask you to set an example of cooperation, Lord Westworth, and be the first to talk to me. I am sure your servants are more likely to step into the interview with ease if they are following your lead."

Lord Westworth glanced uncomfortably at his wife but nodded all the same. "Anything we can do to help."

"Good. Shall we begin now?"

Jane tried to make herself as unobtrusive as possible as they stepped into the blue drawing room. It was an airy room on the southwest side of the house with large windows on two aspects giving the room an open and bright feeling. The furniture, like that in the rest of the house, was beautifully upholstered and on the walls there were a selection of oil paintings depicting Italian cities and classical scenes.

In one corner of the room was a small writing desk and chair perfect for her to perch on out of the line of sight of whoever Lord Hinchbrooke was interviewing. It would allow her to observe the proceedings and make notes without becoming too much of a distraction.

"Should Miss Austen be here?" Lord Westworth said, glancing in her direction.

"Yes." Once again Lord Hinchbrooke didn't offer any explanation in his including Jane in his investigation, instead settling back in the chair and moving on to his questions before Lord Westworth could protest further. "Can you tell me how you knew Miss Roscoe?"

"I didn't."

"Not at all?"

"I have perhaps seen her in the village before, but I doubt I have ever spoken to her."

"Yet here she is at your ball."

Lord Westworth gave a dismissive swipe of his hand. "My wife dealt with the guest list. We attend a few of the local events when we're not in London, but I really don't pay much attention to the minor gentry."

"Did you speak to Miss Roscoe at the ball?"

"Lady Westworth and I greeted all of our guests at the door so I assume I said good evening to her, but I confess I cannot recall her arriving."

"And not at any other time?"

"No, I didn't speak to her any other time."

"Did you go into the library at any point during the evening?"

"No, not once the ball had started. I moved between the ballroom and the drawing room where the card tables had been set up but didn't venture anywhere else."

Jane jotted down a few words to detail Lord Westworth's answers.

"Did you see anything suspicious?"

"No."

"Nothing that could help with the investigation into Miss Roscoe's death?"

"Unfortunately not." Lord Westworth spread his hands as if laying himself open to Lord Hinchbrooke's scrutiny, leaning back in his chair.

"Thank you for your help, Lord Westworth," Lord Hinchbrooke said, smiling genially. Only when the viscount made a move to stand did he speak again, his tone light as if the question were an afterthought. "This strange business with your brother, can you tell me about it?"

Jane leaned forward, eager to see Lord Westworth's reaction. She made a little note to herself to ask Lord Hinchbrooke if this was a recognised questioning technique. It appeared he had asked the simple, straightforward questions first, putting the viscount at ease, waiting until the other man thought the interview was almost over before swooping in with the queries he really wanted the answer to.

"There's not much to tell that isn't already public knowledge," Lord Westworth said slowly. Jane was impressed by his composure; she only noted the slightest flicker of panic in his expression.

"Indulge me. I don't socialise much, so I have not heard what the gossips are saying."

Lord Westworth sighed and leaned back in his chair. "There is a large age gap between my brother and me. I was only a child when he travelled to India. My grandfather purchased some land between Surat and Bombay many years ago, but it sat vacant and unused ever since. The idea was that my brother would assess the potential for making money from it and if it was unlikely to turn a profit he would organise the sale."

Relaxing as he got further into the story the viscount shifted in his seat to make himself comfortable. "By all accounts it was not a vital trip, my brother was young and foolhardy and not ready to settle down and learn the skills needed to run the estate and look after the interests of the title he would inherit. My father agreed to the trip to allow him to get some of the youthful exuberance out of his system."

It was the privileged few who would be able to fund a trip purely to rid a son of his *youthful exuberance*. Jane wondered how much it would cost for a passage to India in a comfortable cabin and a few months' stay in a reputable establishment in Bombay.

"Before my brother left my father had an accident. He was thrown from a horse and hit his head and he lay unconscious for many weeks. The expectation was my brother would cancel his trip but…" Lord Westworth shrugged. "Sometimes we do not make the right decisions in life."

"Your brother went anyway?"

"Yes. He assumed my father would regain consciousness and resume his position as head of the family, but he didn't. Three months after Edward left England our father died. Mother wrote, of course, but we do not know if the letters ever reached him."

It was a fascinating story and Jane had to try her hardest not to interject with the many questions she had flooding her brain. She knew Lord Westworth was telling just the bare bones of the tale and likely many details at this point even he did not know, but she had the urge to press him for more.

"We received a couple of letters, one when he first disembarked his ship and the second a few days later, then nothing. We waited and waited and after eight months my mother sent a man to investigate."

"What did he find?"

"At first, nothing. Not even a trace of my brother. It was a terrible time, those years of not knowing, and then he wrote saying he had come across the story of an Englishman killed in Madras."

"Madras is a long way from Bombay."

"Yes, it is. At the time I think my mother was desperate to put the whole ordeal to rest. My brother was gone and she couldn't bear spending any more of her life wondering if he would ever return. She set about having him legally declared dead."

"I cannot imagine that was straightforward."

"No," Lord Westworth said quietly. "It took seven years to settle the legal side of things, after that I could inherit the house and the money. The title was more of a complex issue. Eventually the matter had to go to the House of Lords."

"I do remember something of it a few years back."

"After the evidence was presented, it was agreed I should inherit the title. This was eleven years ago, nine years after Edward disappeared. We hadn't heard anything from my brother in almost twenty years."

"Yet here he is in your house, after all this time," Lord Hinchbrooke murmured. "How did that come about?"

Jane had been jotting down notes, names of places and dates so later they could piece together a timeline if it were needed, but now she let her pen rest in the fold of the notebook and focussed on listening, engrossed in the story.

"I received a letter from a man named Hooper who claimed to have travelled on the same ship with my brother to India. He had heard about Edward's disappearance and wrote saying he was convinced he had seen my brother alive and well in Bombay only a few weeks earlier."

"You believed him?"

"There was no reason for him to lie, no personal gain from sending the letter."

"What did you do?"

"I booked a passage on a ship and travelled to India to search for him. The letter detailed when and where Mr Hooper had seen Edward and it was surprisingly easy to track him down."

"You recognised him?"

"Yes."

"There was no doubt in your mind he was your brother?"

"He looked different, but twenty years will do that to a man." Lord Westworth paused, and Jane saw he waited for Lord Hinchbrooke to look up and meet his eye before continuing. "There is no doubt in my mind that the man I brought home with me is my brother. He has the same mannerisms, the same laugh, the same look in his eye when he is sad."

"Does he remember you?"

"He recognised me, but his memories are a little patchy. There are snippets, certain things he does remember from our childhood, but not everything."

"What happened to him?"

"He fell ill soon after disembarking and lay delirious with fever for months. When he woke up he had no memory of his previous life and no contacts in India to tell him who he was or where he was from. His luggage and belongings had long since been plundered so he had no way of working out what his life had been before."

Lord Hinchbrooke nodded, and Jane wondered if such a thing were possible. Harry Williamson, a young man in her father's congregation, had been kicked in the head by a horse five years ago and he had laid unconscious for over a month. When he had woken up everyone had rejoiced but he was not the same man as before the accident. Even now he struggled with finding the right words to express himself and was prone to bursts of anger that were triggered by inconsequential events. Perhaps Edward Stanmore *could* have lost his memory for twenty years.

"Forgive me for all the intrusive questions," Lord Hinchbrooke said with a soft smile, "I know it cannot be easy dredging up all these memories. What will happen to the title now?"

Lord Westworth shrugged, looking much more relaxed than Jane thought he should. By law the title, the estates, all the money from the inheritance should have gone to the eldest brother, Edward Stanmore. It had been his birthright, even though he had been absent all these years. She doubted the matter would be resolved quickly and would probably involve many years of legal wrangles.

"Who knows. For now, my brother is happy to be home with his family and does not wish to think of anything else. One day I am sure we will need to involve the lawyers, but that is not one of Edward's priorities right now." Lord Westworth grasped the arms of the chair and leaned forward, signalling the interview was over.

"Thank you for your candour; it is much appreciated at this early stage of our investigation."

Lord Westworth nodded, levering himself to his feet. "Who would you like to speak to next?"

"Either your brother or Lady Westworth, please."

"Lady Westworth will be in shortly. My brother..." he trailed off, spreading his hands out in front of him. "He went out for a ride earlier this morning and I do not think he has returned as yet."

They watched as the viscount left the room. Lord Hinchbrooke got up and closed the door after him. "What do you think?"

Jane blinked in surprise. The magistrate had been generous in letting her stay, in giving her a job to do, but she had expected he would be resistant to her forming opinions on what they heard, let alone putting them up for discussion. She took a moment to think, to gather her thoughts before speaking. "It is a fascinating story," she said slowly. "But that is exactly what it feels like: a story."

Lord Hinchbrooke motioned for her to go on and Jane was pleased to see her idea hadn't been dismissed immediately. *She* knew it had merit, but often it was hard to get oneself heard as a woman. "It felt rehearsed, as if Lord Westworth had thought about what he wanted to say and stuck to it, almost word for word."

"It did feel as though he were telling a tale," Lord Hinchbrooke agreed, "although that doesn't necessarily mean it was made up."

"True, it is rather a fantastical set of events, and the homecoming of his brother is going to be the one thing he is asked about again and again. I suppose he could want to know what he was going to say each time some friend or neighbour enquired." She thought for a moment and then shook her head. "Even so, everything felt too slick, too smooth."

"Did you think he was lying?"

"No, not about everything. I think he wanted to dazzle us with the spectacle of the tale, to distract us with the absurdity of it. I don't think he minds us questioning the events of his brother's homecoming, but I wonder what he was trying to hide in the middle of what he *did* tell us."

"It is an absurd story, isn't it? I wonder if this long-lost brother has anything to do with Miss Roscoe's death, or if it is merely a distraction, a curiosity."

Jane stood and stretched, placing her hands in the small of her back and leaning back a little. It was a trick she used when she was writing for a long time to stop her back from complaining later in the evening. "Miss Roscoe saw something," Jane said as she ignored Lord Hinchbrooke's curious glance, "but there is no way of knowing whether it had anything to do with Lord Westworth and Edward Stanmore, or something else entirely." She shook her head in frustration. "How do you do this? We're not getting anywhere."

"Patience, Miss Austen. Patience and perseverance. You will never find the snippet of information you are looking for in the first interview, but the tenth, or even the hundredth, that is where it will be hiding. Each person you speak to builds the picture a little more, and it is only when the picture is complete that you can see the piece that doesn't fit."

Jane contemplated the advice but was stopped from answering by a knock on the door followed immediately by it swinging open to reveal Lady Westworth looking agitated.

"Lady Westworth, is something amiss?"

The viscountess managed to stumble into the room, her face pale with just two lone spots of colour on both cheeks.

Jane moved quickly, rushing forward and guiding the older woman to a chair, making sure she was settled before stepping away. "Shall I call for a glass of water, Lady Westworth?"

"No," Lady Westworth almost shouted the word, stopping Jane just before she pulled on the bell cord to summon a maid.

Jane shot a glance at Lord Hinchbrooke and the magistrate shook his head, taking his seat across from where Lady Westworth was sitting.

As they both watched Lady Westworth took a deep, shuddering breath and closed her eyes. "I know who did it. I know who the murderer is."

CHAPTER FIVE

"You know who murdered Miss Roscoe?" Jane sank down in front of Lady Westworth, desperate to prise the name out of the viscountess.

Lady Westworth flicked her a glance and then dismissively turned her attention back to the magistrate. "A kitchen maid is missing. The servants have had strict instructions they are to go about their jobs as normal, there is to be no break in the routine. So, you see there is no reason for us not to be able to find the maid in question. She must be guilty."

"Is there anything else that makes you think this woman guilty? Anything she has said or done?" Lord Hinchbrooke enquired calmly.

"Is this not enough? Why else would the silly girl flee?"

Jane felt the swell of anticipation deflate a little. The disappearance of the maid was hardly compelling evidence.

"Did the maid know Miss Roscoe?"

"Does it matter?" Lady Westworth threw her hands up in exasperation.

"It is certainly suspicious," Jane said, realising the best way to get more information out of the viscountess was to agree with her. "What is her name? Has she worked for you for long?"

Lady Westworth sniffed and for a moment Jane thought she might refuse to answer unless Lord Hinchbrooke repeated the questions, but after a long few seconds she began to speak.

"Dorothy Macgill, she is a kitchen maid and has been with us for two years."

"She must have friends amongst the other servants if she has been here for two years," Jane said.

"I do not take an interest in the private lives of my servants, Miss Austen. I dare say she does have friends below stairs, but I am not privy to those relationships."

"Who would be?" Lord Hinchbrooke asked much more directly than Jane would have been able to.

"Mrs Lamb, the cook, I suppose. She is in charge of all servants who work in the kitchens." Lady Westworth looked from Jane to Lord Hinchbrooke in disbelief. "I cannot believe you have not raised the hue and cry. Dorothy Macgill has fled the house when given explicit instructions not to, in the wake of a murder. I may not have experience of the law but even I can see that is highly suspicious."

"As you say," Lord Hinchbrooke murmured, "highly suspicious. It is merely a case of gathering the information before charging off on horseback, scouring the countryside."

"Perhaps we could ask Mrs Lamb to join us?" Jane said.

"Very well." Lady Westworth stalked over to the corner of the room and pulled on the bell cord, summoning a footman within seconds. "Please ask Mrs Lamb to come upstairs for a few moments."

Lady Westworth paced backwards and forwards across the large room as they waited for the cook. With one eye on the clock and the other on the viscountess, Jane counted six minutes between the footman hurrying away and the hesitant knock on the door signalling the cook's arrival. Stanmore Hall was large, but it wasn't palatial and there was no way it would have taken the footman six minutes to fetch the cook. Although there could be a reason Mrs Lamb hadn't been able to leave the kitchen immediately, Jane wondered whether it signified a reluctance to be interviewed.

"Come in, Mrs Lamb, thank you for taking some time to talk to us." Lord Hinchbrooke stood and motioned for the cook to approach and take a seat.

Mrs Lamb's eyes flickered to her mistress who nodded abruptly, hovering in the corner as if not sure whether to stay or leave.

"Lady Westworth tells us one of the kitchen maids is missing this morning, Mrs Lamb," Lord Hinchbrooke said softly, motioning for the cook to sit down. She looked uncomfortable on the delicate upholstery and kept shooting glances at Lady Westworth as if the mistress of the house might soon tell her to stop taking liberties and get back to the kitchen.

"Yes, my lord. Dorothy Macgill."

"When did you last see her?"

"Last night, whilst all the commotion was going on. With the ball I had the maids up early working and I sent Dorothy and another girl to bed about nine so they would be up this morning to prepare breakfast." Mrs Lamb paused, clearing her throat nervously. "Dorothy came downstairs when she heard the fuss to see what was happening last night."

"How was she then?"

Mrs Lamb looked confused. "She seemed well, my lord."

"Was she flustered or in a state of agitation? Was she dressed for bed?"

"You can't think Dorothy…" Mrs Lamb began.

"Just answer the question, Mrs Lamb," Lady Westworth said sharply. "If the girl was acting strangely tell Lord Hinchbrooke."

"No, my lady, she was shaken, like the rest of us when she heard what had happened, but she wasn't acting strangely. Once I knew she wouldn't be needed I sent her straight back to bed and that was the last I saw of her."

"She was in her nightclothes?"

"Yes, with a dressing gown over the top."

"Does she share a room?" Lord Hinchbrooke asked quietly.

"No, she has a small room to herself upstairs."

"Would you be able to show us, Mrs Lamb?" He glanced over at Lady Westworth and gave her a reassuring smile. "Please do not exert yourself, Lady Westworth, I will check the room and let you know what we find."

He rose, his eye catching Jane's and indicating with a miniscule movement of his head that she should follow him.

It was fascinating to see the inner workings of such a grand house. Jane had been invited as a guest to a few large estates over the years, but often you only got to see the drawing room and dining room. Here they were being led through the family areas into the realm of the servants. Mrs Lamb took them first down a couple of steps into the kitchen area that sat partially underground with some natural light filtering in from windows set at the level of Jane's head. Down here it was a bustle of commotion with chatter and the noise of people going about their work, clinking cutlery and dishes as they prepared for the day ahead.

The servants' stairs were situated at the end of the corridor that ran alongside the big kitchen. They were uncarpeted and narrow with an unpolished wooden handrail. Mrs Lamb led the way up, passing the ground floor again and then continuing up three more flights until she paused, out of breath, at the top.

"It's just along here, my lord."

The corridor was narrow here at the top of the house with doors leading off to each side at regular intervals. Jane assumed they must all be bedrooms for the servants and wondered at the size of the rooms to fit so many in.

Mrs Lamb paused in front of a door and pushed it open, revealing a small, neat room inside. It had a bed and a chair alongside a little table and a chest of drawers pushed up under the window. On the bed was a patchwork quilt, something that looked lovingly made and had been smoothed neatly down at some point. The only other personal item in the room was a small vase that held a single sprig of holly, the berries still red and bright against the dark green of the leaves.

"Thank you, Mrs Lamb," Lord Hinchbrooke said. "I will take a look around. Please do go back to your work and I will call for you if there are any further questions."

Mrs Lamb bobbed into a curtsey and stepped out of the room and Lord Hinchbrooke dropped his voice. "Go with her, find out about this maid's personal life, family, courtships, that sort of thing. She will likely be more at ease with you than if I question her formally."

Jane nodded, slipping out of the room and walking fast to catch up with the cook. "Mrs Lamb," she called, waiting for the cook to turn around, surprised to see her face streaked with tears.

"I can't believe it of Dorothy," Mrs Lamb said, her voice cracking. "Everyone is saying she must have had a hand in this because she's run away but I won't believe it. She's a good girl."

Jane reached out and rubbed the cook gently on the back. "You know her the best, you're with her all the time."

"I am. And I know she's a good girl," Mrs Lamb repeated.

"Perhaps we could go downstairs and have a nice cup of tea and you can tell me about Dorothy?" Jane said, wondering if it was going to be as easy as that to gain the cook's confidence. "I have Lord Hinchbrooke's ear and I am sure I can put in a good word for her."

Mrs Lamb sniffed and nodded, leading the way down the winding staircase to the basement kitchen and motioning for Jane to step into the private room off the main corridor. It was much bigger than the servants' rooms upstairs, with a bed tucked in one corner and enough space for a table and chairs in the middle of the room as well as a comfortable armchair by the fire.

"You sit down," Jane said, taking charge, "and I will ask one of the girls to bring some tea." She slipped out of the cook's room and into the kitchen proper, finding it unsettling when all the chatter stopped as she appeared. At home they only had Mrs White and Lizzie the maid and both were treated as an extension of the family. Jane and Cassandra were expected to help out with the day-to-day chores and running of the house at home, whether that be by peeling potatoes for dinner or washing sheets on laundry day. Here there was much more of a divide and Jane knew Lady Westworth would only come down to the kitchens to give orders or discuss the menus for the day, but still it was strange when all the servants stopped and stared at her.

"Mrs Lamb has asked for some tea," she said, not knowing who to direct her request to.

A young kitchen maid bobbed her head in acknowledgement and brushed her hands on her apron before reaching for the brass kettle.

Retreating, Jane made her way back to the cook's room, finding the interlude had given Mrs Lamb a chance to compose herself a little.

"Tell me about Dorothy," Jane said as she turned one of the chairs from the table round to face Mrs Lamb, who had taken a seat in the comfortable armchair by the fire. "Has she been working here long?"

"About two years. She came from the Willoughby's house in the village. They hired her when she was just a girl and trained her up, then two years ago the Willoughby's decided to move to London. Dorothy is a local girl, so she wanted to stay in the village. We had a position come up at the right time."

"Is she a good worker?"

"The best. She grew up on a farm so doesn't struggle with the early mornings like some of my girls and I've never had cause for complaint about her work." Mrs Lamb paused, and Jane got the impression she was mulling something over as if deciding whether to say it.

"Until recently?" Jane ventured.

Mrs Lamb looked up sharply. "Yes," she said eventually. "Nothing all that noticeable."

"But you run a tight kitchen," Jane said with a smile.

"I spot the little things, the details. It is what enabled me to rise from fourth kitchen maid to cook in less than a decade."

"That's quite an achievement." Jane paused as one of the young maids knocked on the door and brought in a tray of tea, setting it on the table before flashing Mrs Lamb a worried look.

"Thank you, Polly, get back to work now, dear. Not long until lunch time."

Jane waited for the young woman to leave and for Mrs Lamb to pour out the tea.

"You were saying about the little details?" Jane prompted as she took a sip from her cup.

"Dorothy has always been one of my best workers, but these last few weeks she's not been as sharp as normal, like letting the toast burn on the fire or not adding eggs to the cake mix until she was reminded."

"It sounds like she has been distracted."

"Yes, that's exactly it."

"Do you know what by? Has she had any bad news or unexpected visits."

"No. Her family are in the village and she goes to see them every Sunday after church and on her afternoon off each Wednesday. Apart from that she spends all her time here."

Jane nodded, taking another sip of tea, trying to decide whether to risk the next question she wanted to ask. So far, she hadn't got anything more helpful than the maid had seemed distracted, so she reasoned she had nothing to lose. "Lady Westworth seems to think Dorothy is connected to Miss Roscoe's death, given the timing of her disappearance. Do you think that is possible?"

"Certainly not. I do not wish to speak ill of my employer, but Lady Westworth does not know Dorothy at all. *I* know her. I know her character and I am certain she has nothing to do with the unfortunate events of last night."

"Can you explain her disappearance?"

Mrs Lamb shook her head and shrugged at the same time. "Perhaps she got spooked. A dead body in the house would be enough to scare a delicate young woman."

Jane nodded, sitting back in her chair and finishing off her cup of tea. "Would you be able to give me the address of her family? I am sure Lord Hinchbrooke will want to enquire whether they have seen her."

Mrs Lamb stood and rummaged in a drawer, pulling out a small piece of paper and then carefully poring over a book of addresses until she found the right one, copying it onto the paper in a looping hand.

"Thank you, Mrs Lamb, I appreciate all your help and I will tell Lord Hinchbrooke what a good worker Dorothy is and how you consider her above suspicion."

The cook nodded, still staring into her cup of tea as Jane slipped from the room.

CHAPTER SIX

"I've asked for the horses to be saddled," Lord Westworth said as Jane walked up the stairs from the kitchen and into the grand entrance hall. Lord Hinchbrooke had donned his coat and hat and looked poised to launch himself out the door. "I have two groomsmen and two stable boys I can send out to help with the search and three footmen and my valet who are able to ride from the house." Lord Westworth was animated in his expressions and there was an excitement in his eyes Jane hadn't seen before.

"Send them out on the major routes. Miss Macgill will be on foot so I daresay it should be easy to catch up with her if she is heading for one of the nearby towns."

Jane coughed quietly, brandishing the piece of paper in her hand. "I have the address of her family in the village. I thought I might see if anyone there had seen her."

"Good," Lord Hinchbrooke said with a hint of a smile on his lips. "I will join you in the village." He turned back to Lord Westworth. "Instruct your men to be discreet and gentle. The girl has not been proven guilty of anything but leaving without permission and there could be a hundred good reasons for it. I need to speak to her, but I do not wish her to be carted back here in ropes, embarrassed in front of everyone she has ever known."

Lord Westworth gave a short, sharp nod and then marched out of the house, no doubt to give instructions to the men he had gathered outside.

The magistrate turned back to Jane and lowered his voice. "Tell me you can ride, Miss Austen."

"I can ride."

"Good. Let's go find this poor girl shall we, before Lord Westworth releases his hounds on her."

They walked in silence out of the house, around the path to the courtyard and over to the stables on the other side. Jane was not dressed for riding, but she had sturdy boots on and a coat that had kept her warm in all weathers so she knew she wouldn't freeze. It was a little awkward getting herself settled in the side saddle, but once she was up she felt herself forgetting the discomfort as the thrill of the chase began to take over.

"Did you find anything in Dorothy's room?"

They set off at a trot down the long drive, the dust already settling from where the rest of the mounted household had ridden before them.

"I found two things of note, alongside the sprig of holly."

"The sprig of holly?"

"Interesting, wasn't it?" Lord Hinchbrooke said, looking over to her with a smile. "There's a holly bush in the garden you can see out of her window, tucked to the left side of the house."

Unsure of the relevance, Jane asked, "What else did you find?"

"The first was a burnt scrap of paper in the grate. It was too charred to be able to make out what it had once said, but its presence is important all the same. The second was a chamber pot scrubbed clean and hidden under the bed."

Jane wrinkled her nose, wondering if Lord Hinchbrooke was a genius or just a little eccentric. "I understand your excitement about the scrap of paper," she said slowly, "but a chamber pot? Surely under the bed is the most likely place to store it and the cleanliness is something merely to be thankful for?"

"Do you know how many servants there are employed in a household such as this, Miss Austen?"

Jane tried to quickly calculate but had to shake her head.

"Certainly twenty as a minimum, perhaps more when you take into account gardeners and stable boys. That is a lot of chamber pots if they are all to have their own. Especially when you consider the three privies outside and the communal female servants' bathroom upstairs." He smiled at her and leaned in a little whilst maintaining a steady pace on his horse. "I also asked Lady Westworth and although she was aghast at my question she confirmed the maids were expected to use the outside privy during the day and the communal chamber pot in the bathroom at night if needed."

"So why did she have one?"

"That is the question."

"Do you know the answer?"

Lord Hinchbrooke shrugged. "I have an idea, but we will soon see."

"Do you think we will find Dorothy Macgill at home?"

"She is a young woman, certainly no more than nineteen and I doubt she has ever left Hampshire. However, if she is involved in the events of last night I expect she will not want to stray too far from the people and the places she knows."

As they rode through the fancy wrought-iron gates Jane felt the wind whip around her neck and send shivers down her spine. Even though it must be approaching midday the sky was grey and grim and made the hour appear much later. The road was quiet and on the five-minute ride into the village they did not see anyone else. Even the main street was quiet, with only a few shoppers braving the icy temperatures and bowing their heads against the wind.

"Do you know this address?" Lord Hinchbrooke asked her, motioning to the piece of paper Mrs Lamb had written the street name down on.

"Yes. It isn't far." Jane led the way on a narrow road that branched out from the high street to a neat row of little farm cottages on the outskirts of the village. They were tiny in size and can have contained only one room on each level, but the one they stopped in front of was well kept and had a neatly dug flower bed on either side of the door.

Lord Hinchbrooke dismounted, cursing quietly as his leg seemed to buckle underneath him for a moment. He was stiff and Jane could see the effort it took him to pause a moment, then when he was balanced he tried again. This time the movement was smoother and if you weren't watching carefully, you wouldn't even notice the tremor as his hands fell to his side. It was gone completely by the time he had moved to assist Jane from her horse and loop the reins over a nearby fence post.

The door to the little cottage was freshly painted and it swung open before they even had time to pass through the gate outside.

"Good afternoon, my lord," a woman with a lined face and streaks of grey in her hair said as her eyes widened when she realised who had come to pay her a visit. She would be one of Lord Westworth's tenants, but everyone knew the magistrate by sight and reputation.

"Good afternoon. Is it Mrs Macgill?"

"Yes, my lord." She looked as though she were a startled animal with eyebrows raised high up on her forehead and mouth open in an expression of shock.

"I am Lord Hinchbrooke, and this is Miss Austen. I am here in relation to a tragic event at Stanmore Hall last night."

"Would you like to come in, my lord? Our home is humble, but you are welcome to sit by the fire."

Inside was as neat as outside, with a pristinely swept floor and no hint of dirt or mud anywhere. The fire was crackling in the grate and even though the area was cramped the older woman had done her best to make it homely with patchwork covers over the chairs and a picture above the fireplace on the wall. There was a rocking chair by the fire and a scratched wooden table that looked as though it must double as the area where the woman prepared the meals. Two girls played quietly by the fire, their thin faces clean and hair neatly brushed and pulled into long plaits down their backs.

"We are looking for Dorothy, Mrs Macgill," Lord Hinchbrooke said quietly, pulling off his gloves and warming his hands by the fire.

"I haven't seen her," Mrs Macgill said quickly. "Is something wrong?"

"We just need to talk to her, to see if she knows anything about the events of last night."

"You can't suspect my Dorothy. She's a good girl."

Jane glanced at Lord Hinchbrooke and stepped forwards, motioning for Mrs Macgill to take the rocking chair whilst she perched on the seat facing it.

"Dorothy left the house at some point before the household got up this morning," Jane said quietly, "and we need to know why. I can assure you Lord Hinchbrooke only wishes to talk to her, there is no assumption of guilt."

"My Dorothy is a good girl; she wouldn't have anything to do with the affairs of the guests."

"It does seem unlikely," Lord Hinchbrooke said, "which is why I am keen to speak to her, to find out what she knows." He paused and then crouched down in front of the older woman. "I think I have a fair reputation as a magistrate, do I not?"

Mrs Macgill nodded.

"I give you my word I will treat Dorothy with respect and an open mind. I merely wish to speak to her, and to do so before any other interested party catches up with her."

For a fraction of a second Mrs Macgill's eyes flickered up to the ceiling and then she shook her head. "I would help you if I could, Lord Hinchbrooke, but I have not seen my daughter since last Sunday."

"She did not visit on Wednesday?"

"No. And she is not here now." Mrs Macgill stood, crossing her arms over her chest. "Now I don't expect you to believe me so please check upstairs and anywhere else you wish. You can even check in the pot on the stove for all I care." The words flowed from her and only when there was silence did she seem to remember who she was talking to. "My lord," she added hastily.

Jane had to smother a smile and was pleased to see Lord Hinchbrooke wasn't about to take offence.

"I would be remiss in my job if I did not take you up on your offer to check," he said slowly. "Perhaps, Miss Austen, you wouldn't mind accompanying Mrs Macgill upstairs?"

Mrs Macgill stalked up the stairs with as much dignity as a queen, head held high and nostrils flaring with defiance.

There was only one room at the top with a double bed pushed up against one wall and a single bed in the opposite corner. On the floor was a trunk and a small wardrobe took up most of the rest of the room.

"She's not even hiding in here," Mrs Macgill said, flinging open the door to the wardrobe.

Jane peered under the bed and into the darkness of the wardrobe then nodded in satisfaction.

Back downstairs they found Lord Hinchbrooke in the small back yard watching the chickens as they pecked at the scattered seed on the ground.

"You have no idea where Dorothy might have gone, Mrs Macgill?"

"No."

"Does she have any family elsewhere? Or perhaps a young man she is stepping out with?"

"No, we don't have much family."

"And a young man?"

"No."

"Thank you for your time," Lord Hinchbrooke said as he guided Jane towards the door. Mrs Macgill restrained herself from slamming the door after them, but the sentiment was obvious by the speed at which it shut behind them. "She knows where Dorothy is," Lord Hinchbrooke murmured as they made their way to where the horses were tied.

"What makes you say that?"

"If your sister disappeared what would be your first reaction?"

"To ask if she was harmed or unwell in any way."

"Exactly. Mrs Macgill was most concerned that we knew Dorothy was a good girl, but not overly worried as to whether her daughter was lying in a ditch or kidnapped by highwaymen."

Jane considered this for a moment, turning back to look at the cottage. "If she isn't here then where is she?"

Lord Hinchbrooke shrugged. "She's local. She will have friends, people she grew up with. People willing to risk a little trouble to help a girl they've known for most of their lives."

A flicker of movement caught Jane's eye in the upstairs window of the cottage next door to the Macgill's. It was a flash of colour, there one second, gone the next.

"Next door," she said, feeling certain of her sudden realisation. "She's in the cottage next door."

Lord Hinchbrooke frowned and followed her gaze to the window.

"Neighbours are close," he said. "And it would explain why Mrs Macgill was so keen for us to search her house and be on our way." Without taking his eyes off the upstairs window he tied his horse back up and motioned for Jane to stay behind him.

Quickly they moved to the front door and Lord Hinchbrooke rapped on the wood. Jane had to resist the urge to lean forwards and press her ear against the door to try and hear what was going on inside.

One minute passed and then another. Lord Hinchbrooke knocked again, this time louder and more insistent.

"I definitely saw movement," Jane said quietly.

He knocked for a third time, hammering on the door until he eventually heard footsteps inside.

A young woman opened the door a crack, peering out from the gloom inside. She was neatly presented but her clothes were patched and discoloured. There was a child on her hip, a little boy about two years old.

"Can I help you?" she said, her voice low and shaky.

"My name is Lord Hinchbrooke, I am here for Dorothy Macgill."

"I don't…"

Lord Hinchbrooke interrupted her, and Jane was surprised at the change in his demeanour and how serious his voice sounded. "We know she is upstairs. I merely need to speak to her but if you impede my investigation any further, I will ensure you and all your family spend a few nights in the local jail to remind you of the consequences of lying in a situation as grave as this."

The young woman glanced down at her baby and hesitated.

"I don't have all day, Miss…?"

"Macgill. Rose Macgill."

"Dorothy is your sister?"

The young woman nodded.

"I mean her no harm."

"Let him in, Rose," a voice said from the darkness.

Slowly, Rose took a step back and opened the door fully, revealing a house nearly identical to the one next door and a young woman standing halfway down the stairs.

"I'm Dorothy. It's me you're looking for."

"You'd better come in," Rose said, "unless you're going to take her straight away."

They entered the cottage and Rose bade them sit, motioning for them to take the chairs by the fire. Dorothy hovered nearby, moving nervously from foot to foot and seeming unable to keep still.

"Miss Macgill, Dorothy," Lord Hinchbrooke said, his voice reverted back to normal, "Lady Westworth tells me you fled Stanmore Hall when all the servants had been given orders to stay put."

Dorothy pulled a face and then nodded.

"Can you tell me why?"

"Sit down, Dorothy," Jane said, feeling agitated just looking at the nervous young woman. "This may take a while and there is no need to stand on ceremony."

Dorothy nodded and Jane carefully took out the notebook and pen she had been using to jot down all the information they had gathered so far.

"I didn't have anything to do with the murder," Dorothy said quickly.

"You can see how suspicion might fall on you, given that you ran away the day after."

"But I didn't do it," Dorothy said, an edge of panic in her voice.

"Why don't you tell us what did happen?" Lord Hinchbrooke said kindly. Jane realised this was one of the reasons he was so good at his role as magistrate. He had a way with people, a gentleness that made people want to trust him alongside an air of competence. She saw Dorothy consider the man in front of her and after a moment decide to trust him.

"Last night, after Mrs Lamb relieved me of my duties I didn't go straight to bed," Dorothy said, biting her lip and throwing a nervous look at her sister. "I went out into the garden…" She trailed off.

"To meet someone?" Lord Hinchbrooke prompted.

"Yes. I've been walking out with William Wilson, one of the gardener's assistants for a couple of months. No one from the house knows about it because Lady Westworth has a rule about maids and courting so we kept it quiet."

Jane sat forwards, wondering if Dorothy had seen something unusual on her way out of the house, something that might be relevant to Emma Roscoe's death.

"I needed to speak to him about something important," Dorothy said, her hands now clutching at the skirts of her dress. "We had arranged earlier in the day to meet once Mrs Lamb let me go. He was there waiting for me."

"What happened, Dorothy?" Lord Hinchbrooke pressed her.

"We talked and then I heard someone moving about in the shadows. Our conversation was private and I got worried someone had overheard. I rushed back inside and went straight up to bed, but I couldn't sleep." She took a deep breath and continued. "Then I heard the commotion when that poor young lady was found and came down to see what was happening."

Lord Hinchbrooke was nodding thoughtfully, as though trying to piece all the information together.

"This morning when I went down to the kitchen everyone was saying that Miss Roscoe overheard something she shouldn't and that was why she had been killed."

"You thought it might have been her in the shadows whilst you were meeting William Wilson?"

Dorothy nodded. "I panicked. I didn't see how it could have been true, but I know how easy blame is laid on."

Jane leaned forwards, her eyes flitting over the young woman in front of her. She looked distressed, unsure of herself, certainly not like a murderer.

"Someone overheard us talking, and then Miss Roscoe dies with a secret she is going to reveal," Dorothy said, tears flooding to her eyes.

"What is your secret, Dorothy?"

Dorothy shook her head and looked down at her hands.

"Does your sister know?" Lord Hinchbrooke asked.

Dorothy's head jerked up, an expression of shock on her face. She studied Lord Hinchbrooke and then slowly nodded.

"You're with child?" he confirmed.

"Yes. About four months gone."

"Congratulations, Dorothy. Is William going to stand by you?"

She nodded, the tears falling onto her cheeks now. "We're going to get married just as soon as we have enough money to pay for a house of our own."

Jane sat back in her chair, looking at the young woman. She was an unlikely killer, but her fiancé was a possible suspect, especially if he thought Miss Roscoe might reveal something to Lady Westworth that could jeopardise their future together.

"Can I trust you, Dorothy?" Lord Hinchbrooke said, sincerity in his voice.

"Yes."

"Stay here. Don't do anything foolish, don't try to run. Lord Westworth has people out looking for you. I will tell him to call them off, but you need to stay inside until I can get the message to them."

"I will."

He stood and Jane followed, leaving the cottage and making their way to the horses. They both remained silent whilst he helped her up into the saddle and mounted his own horse, aware of the Macgills' faces at the windows.

"What did you think?" Lord Hinchbrooke said as they rode out of the village into the narrow lane.

Taking a moment to organise her thoughts. "I can certainly see how a vulnerable kitchen maid who is scared she is going to lose her job or, worse, be accused of stabbing someone, would work herself up into believing her secret condition could somehow be a motive for murder." She paused, shaking her head. "But I wonder if it is merely the overactive imagination of a scared young woman."

"If Miss Roscoe had overheard Dorothy and her gardener discussing the pregnancy and the future of their unborn child, would she have been so agitated when she saw you in the ballroom? Would she have wanted to take your advice on it?"

Jane looked down at her gloves for a moment and then closed her eyes, remembering the uncertainty in Emma's eyes. "No," she said, completely certain. "Emma was a kind young woman, someone who did charitable acts not only because she knew she should, but because she wanted to. She might have wanted to help the young couple, but it wouldn't have caused her to be that concerned."

"I didn't think so. The affairs of servants do not register in the same way," he slowed his pace, pulling on the reins so his horse was walking leisurely, giving them time to talk before they re-entered the Westworth estate. "We should question the gardener's assistant of course, Dorothy's young man, but I wonder if we have dashed off down the wrong path here." He gave a deep sigh and then seemed to rally. "Indulge me, Miss Austen, what do we know?"

Jane felt a wave of gratitude to Lord Hinchbrooke. It felt good to be doing something. Already she felt a little of her guilt lifting even though they had not yet worked out what had happened last night. Jane couldn't go back and change the fact she was late for her meeting with Emma, that was something she would regret for a very long time, but she could do her best to find out who had killed her friend and see they were brought to justice.

"Miss Roscoe was stabbed in the library last night at some time before twenty past ten. Earlier in the night she had witnessed something she wanted to talk to me about, but we don't know what. Dorothy Macgill disappeared from Stanmore Hall early this morning, but it would seem there is an innocent explanation." She paused, shaking her head.

"Do you know what we're missing?"

"Everything. A motive, a murderer, an idea of how it happened."

"Do not be morose, Miss Austen. We are making good progress." Lord Hinchbrooke smiled encouragingly at her.

"In all this, the person that stands out is Mr Edward Stanmore. It is as if he is a ghost. He wasn't seen at his own party yesterday; he hasn't been available for us to question today," Jane said. "It is he we need to speak to. I'm sure if you insisted he make himself available he would have to."

"True. Let us question the gardener's assistant and then see what we make of the mysterious Edward Stanmore."

CHAPTER SEVEN

William Wilson was digging over a bed of soil in the walled garden. As Lord Hinchbrooke and Jane entered through the heavy gate, he paused what he was doing and leaned on his fork, regarding them for a moment. He pulled off his cap as they approached and gave them a nod of greeting.

He was young, only a year or two older than Dorothy. He was tall and muscular with a square jaw and full lips but his eyes were set a little too close together for him to be called handsome.

"Are you William Wilson?"

"Yes, my lord."

"We have just been speaking to Miss Dorothy Macgill."

There was a flicker of unease in the young man's eyes as he tried to work out how much Dorothy might have told them. "You saw Dorothy?"

"Yes, we did. She is well, just a little shaken by the recent events at Stanmore Hall."

Slowly the young man nodded and Jane saw how he shifted from foot to foot as if preparing to run.

"You look scared, Mr Wilson," Jane said softly.

The young man's eyes flicked to her as if trying to work out her role.

"There's been a murder and the magistrate is coming to talk to me. Course I'm scared."

"Let me ask you a question, Mr Wilson," Lord Hinchbrooke said. "Did you kill Miss Emma Roscoe?"

"No. I never even saw her. I never even went into the house last night."

"Good," Lord Hinchbrooke said, and Jane saw the confusion in the gardener's eyes.

"That's it. You're just going to believe me?"

"I'm just going to believe you. I do have a few more questions, but they're not trying to trap you."

The gardener seemed to consider this for a moment and then gave a nod. "What do you want to know?"

"Simply tell me exactly what happened yesterday evening and what you saw."

"We work in the gardens until sundown, but in winter of course that is quite early. I had agreed to help in the stables with the horses with all the guests arriving, and that is what I did until about eight o'clock." He shifted and focussed over Jane's shoulder for a moment, his eyes following something in the garden. "Damn crows," he muttered. "Excuse me, Miss."

Jane watched the crow hop about on the hard soil for a few seconds, head turning this way and that, before it spread its wings and flew away.

"Mrs Lamb always lets some of the girls go up to bed early when there is a big party, so at least a couple are fresh for anyone who wants an early breakfast the next day. It is never a set time so I told Dorothy I would wait for her from eight o'clock onwards out in the garden."

"Where is it you met, Mr Wilson?"

"In the main garden, just out of sight from the main house behind the big holly bush."

"You must have waited a long time."

"Perhaps an hour. Dorothy was in a fluster; she was petrified someone would find out about the ba..." he trailed off realising he had almost let slip too much.

"We know about the child," Jane said quietly. "Dorothy told us."

William took a moment to digest this, looking none too pleased someone knew their secret. "Well, she's terrified Lady Westworth will find out and send her packing. We know once we're married Mrs Lamb will have to let her go, but it is a scary prospect raising a family on just an assistant gardener's wage."

"What did you talk about last night?" Jane was beginning to warm to the young man and with every sincere word she became more and more convinced that he did not have anything to do with the Emma's death.

"The baby mostly. We agreed we would wait another three weeks and then get the banns read in church. We can't hold on much longer than that. It has been hard enough keeping the pregnancy hidden for as long as we have."

Jane suddenly saw the relevance of the cleaned chamber pot stashed under the bed. Morning sickness was a cruel phenomenon to saddle women with when they were emotional and exhausted in pregnancy. She wondered how many times Dorothy had needed to dash from the kitchens to vomit, her stomach turned by the cooking of eggs or kippers. She thought of Mrs Lamb's observant, kind eyes and wondered if the cook was really in the dark as to the condition one of her kitchen maids found herself in.

"We had just agreed on the banns when there was a rustling in the bushes between us and the house. Dorothy was convinced there was someone there, someone listening. She started crying, thinking someone had overheard what we had been talking about and would go immediately to Lady Westworth and get her dismissed."

"What did you do?"

"I checked the bushes but couldn't see anyone, so I sent Dorothy in, to go up to bed. I told her not to worry."

"You didn't see anyone?"

"No, only the rustle in the bushes and it could have been the wind."

"Thank you, Mr Wilson, we will let you get back to your work," Lord Hinchbrooke said, offering Jane his arm. "I wish you well in your marriage." He paused, seeming to consider something for a moment. "If you do find yourselves struggling then please come and see me. I have a large garden and there is always work, and we have workers cottages on the estate."

"Thank you, my lord."

They walked briskly out of the walled garden, closing the heavy gate behind them.

"That was a kind thing to do."

"Our modern society is rather set up against the young people, do you not think?"

Jane considered for a moment. "How do you mean?"

"They are encouraged to marry, to settle down and have children, yet as soon as the woman marries they go from two incomes to one, and in a couple of months with three mouths to feed."

"A woman can hardly continue with her job as a live-in maid when she has a baby of her own."

"Very true. But in the way we have things set up at the moment, surely it is the responsibility of those of us who have the means to do so to make the social changes that make life easier for everyone, not just ourselves."

"What would you propose?"

"Well, ensuring that young families like Dorothy and William are adequately housed as part of their job, and then as any children get older offering a couple of hours a week of paid work for the woman in the laundry or wherever, somewhere extra hands are always needed."

"It is a nice idea," Jane said, regarding her companion out of the corner of her eye. Although she knew the society version of his background, she realised Lord Hinchbrooke was a complex man that a few sentences couldn't sum up. She wondered what had made him into the man he was today, what had given him such progressive ideas about society, and what allowed him to quietly and confidently accept her into his investigation when most men would have turned her away with a patronising pat on the hand. "I can see the merit in it, but I think the difficulty would be in making these sorts of changes widespread. Whilst it is noble to help three or four families in this way, to make a real difference you would need to encourage others to follow your lead."

"I do not dispute that, but perhaps it is enough to start with three or four families. We can only do what we can do in this life, Miss Austen. Not everyone was put on this earth to change the world." He smiled at her and Jane realised they were almost back at the house.

"Wait," she said. "Before we ask to speak to Edward Stanmore shall we have a look at this infamous holly bush, see if we can see signs of anyone sneaking around in that area?"

"That is not a bad idea."

They strolled round into the garden and Jane glanced over to the house. She yearned to be back inside, ideally near a roaring fire. Somewhere she could warm her frozen fingers and slip out of the thick coat. She felt suddenly wearied, having had very little sleep the night before, even though she knew no matter how tired she became she would be determined to press on.

"Here it is," Lord Hinchbrooke said, looking back at the house as he indicated the holly bush.

"William and Dorothy must have been standing around this side," Jane said as she walked around the large bush, indicating the side furthest from the house. They would have been completely hidden here from anyone looking out of any of the windows as well as from most of the rest of the garden due to how the area had been planted.

Only the patch of grass behind them was clear of any foliage.

Jane circled around the bush, wondering if she would know what she was looking for if she saw it. Lord Hinchbrooke did the same and with a wave of his hand called her over.

"Look," he said, indicating an area in a flowerbed that had been flattened more than elsewhere. There was no distinct boot print, but a compacting of earth in a way that might happen if someone had lingered for a moment or two behind the bush. "Nothing conclusive, but I would suggest William and Dorothy did hear someone moving through the bushes whilst they were having their talk."

Jane nodded, frowning. "It wouldn't have been Miss Roscoe. She was sensible enough to know never to stroll through a darkened garden unchaperoned. The risk of scandal is almost unparalleled."

Glancing over at her companion Jane wondered if he had noticed that they too were unchaperoned. Her father might be progressive in his ideas, but he would never have agreed to her coming to Stanmore Hall if he had known she would be charging round the countryside with just Lord Hinchbrooke for company. Reputations had been ruined over far less. No doubt her father had assumed she was sitting in the drawing room with Lady Westworth, sipping tea whilst awaiting an update from the magistrate.

Lord Hinchbrooke seemed oblivious to the potential scandal and just nodded in agreement.

"Unless she was out here to meet someone illicitly."

Slowly, Jane shook her head. "Miss Roscoe was not engaged, but there was an informal arrangement between her family and the Petersworth family in Winchester that she would marry their eldest son when it was felt they were both of an appropriate age."

"That doesn't preclude an illicit liaison."

"That is true, but I think unlikely."

"I defer to your judgement on this matter, you knew the young lady."

Lord Hinchbrooke straightened up and took a moment to stretch out his back before offering Jane his arm. She wondered about her assertation that Emma was too sensible to be sneaking about in the gardens. How well had she really known her friend? Emma Roscoe had always seemed shrewd and certainly wise enough to follow the rules of society, aware as they all were of the perils of stepping outside the boundaries. It was possible she had merely appeared to do so, and in the darkness had allowed herself to follow her heart.

As they walked across the crisp, frosty grass Jane's thoughts flicked for a moment to Mr Tom Lefroy, the young gentleman she had met and danced with the night before. How long ago those carefree dances seemed, when anything in the world had been possible. Jane knew it was no time to think of courtship, or to remember the sparkle in Mr Lefroy's eyes as he'd smiled at her. When she had done right by Emma and her killer had been brought to justice, perhaps then her thoughts could turn to Mr Lefroy.

"I could murder a warm cup of tea," Lord Hinchbrooke murmured as they re-entered Stanmore Hall. "Poor choice of words, but you understand the sentiment."

"Let me see what can be organised whilst you arrange to call off the hunt for Dorothy."

CHAPTER EIGHT

"You're still here, Miss Austen," Lady Westworth's cultured voice rang out as Jane ascended from the kitchen below. She had asked for tea from one of the maids downstairs, knowing it was a little presumptuous, but she had seen how cold and drawn Lord Hinchbrooke looked once they'd stepped in from the icy wind.

"Yes, Lord Hinchbrooke has requested my assistance for a little longer."

"Remind me how exactly you are assisting him?"

"I am acting as his scribe, for his notes on the case."

"Ah. Of course." Lady Westworth smiled at Jane then, her demeanour relaxing. "Did you find the girl, Dorothy?"

"Yes," Jane said, pressing her lips together to remind herself not to let anything slip about the young woman's pregnancy. "Lord Hinchbrooke is arranging to discuss the matter of the search with your husband." She shifted, not wanting to say too much but knowing Lady Westworth was both her social superior and her hostess. "I hope it is not too much of an imposition, but I asked for one of your kitchen maids to bring up tea for Lord Hinchbrooke. He is a little cold after spending so long outside."

"It is no trouble at all. Whatever he needs to aid him in getting to the bottom of this matter."

For a long moment they both stood facing one another, Jane unsure whether it would be impolite to leave but not wanting to be caught up in any questions about Dorothy. She was thankful when Lord Hinchbrooke emerged from one of the doors nearby and beckoned her inside.

"Lord Westworth has agreed to find his brother so we can talk to him," Lord Hinchbrooke said as he settled back in the armchair he had been occupying earlier in the day. "This should be interesting."

Jane took her seat in the corner with the little desk and opened the notebook in anticipation. So far today she had filled five pages with notes on the interviews they had conducted. Whilst they were waiting for Edward Stanmore, she took up her pen and filled in everything they had learned from Dorothy and William and their trip to study the holly bush.

"Lord Hinchbrooke, I presume?" Edward Stanmore's voice was deep and throaty as if had smoked one too many cigars.

Lord Hinchbrooke stood and inclined his head then reached out to shake the other man's proffered hand. "This is Miss Austen; she is assisting me by taking some notes."

"Good afternoon, Miss Austen," Mr Stanmore said and for a moment Jane felt the weight of his scrutiny.

She recognised him as the man who had ridden past her furiously earlier that morning on the drive. He was tall and thin with dark hair and hollow cheeks. His eyes were also dark, so dark they almost looked black, and he had a haunted look about him as if he had seen too much of this world.

"Thank you for coming to speak with us," Lord Hinchbrooke said and indicated Mr Stanmore should take a seat.

"Terrible business," Mr Stanmore muttered.

"It is."

"Do you know who killed her yet? My brother was all excited at the prospect of one of the maids disappearing."

"That was proved to be an innocent misunderstanding."

"I suppose it was always unlikely, a maid stabbing a guest in a murderous rage." He paused and motioned for Lord

Hinchbrooke to start his questions. "Please ask whatever you need."

"The ball last night was thrown in your honour?"

"Yes," Mr Stanmore grimaced. "It was something my brother and I argued about. He thought it was right to celebrate my homecoming, to show there was no animosity between us. I…" Mr Stanmore trailed off.

"Go on."

"I am just grateful to be restored to my family. I didn't see the need for the whole county to be invited."

"Did you attend the ball?"

"I had a headache in the afternoon. I get them every few weeks ever since I was ill in India. Completely debilitating things; I can't get out of bed, have to lie in the dark and hope the flashing lights and pounding pain subsides."

"You had one of these headaches yesterday?"

"Yes. My brother was considering cancelling the party, but he thought it would send the wrong message. We agreed I would rest for the first part of the evening and make an appearance once the ball was properly underway." He paused and glanced over at Jane, smiling as he caught her eye. There was something hypnotic about the way he spoke and for a moment she had been so caught up in his story she had forgotten to note anything down. Quickly she bent her head and started to scribble furiously.

"Is that what happened?"

"I rose from bed about half past nine and took a while to dress. I was heading downstairs when I heard the commotion and my brother informed me about the tragedy that had occurred."

"So, you did not attend the ball at all?"

"No."

"You did not see Miss Roscoe?"

"No."

"Have you ever met Miss Roscoe before?"

"No, never. I have been back in England for a few months and in that time I have largely kept to the estate. Sometimes I will venture into the village or the surrounding countryside, but I rarely talk to anyone."

"How are you finding being home?" Jane asked.

Mr Stanmore paused and turned towards her before answering. "Very strange, Miss Austen. For all those years I was in India I felt as though a large part of me was missing but I had no idea what. I did not have any clue as to who I was or where I had come from. When my brother found me, it felt as though so many things clicked into place, but still, I do not really feel like I belong."

"I would love to hear your story," Jane said, giving him her warmest smile. Mr Stanmore had an easy charm about him, a confidence seen in some born into wealth and status, which was surprising given how long he must have lived without knowing who he was. "If it is not too painful to tell it."

"It is a curious tale. If I can trust your discretion, Miss Austen, then I will be happy to tell it."

"My lips are sealed, Mr Stanmore."

"Perhaps I could suggest we stretch our legs. I hate being cooped up inside. That is, if you have no further questions for me, Lord Hinchbrooke?"

"You didn't see anything unusual? Anything suspicious, last night?"

"No, nothing at all."

"Then I have no further questions."

Mr Stanmore stood and brushed out a minute crease in his trousers. "I will ask the footman to fetch our coats. I am wary of safeguarding your reputation, Miss Austen, so I propose we stay in full view of the house at all times. Perhaps you would be so kind as to inform Lady Westworth where we are, Lord Hinchbrooke."

The magistrate inclined his head, catching Jane's arm as she went to follow Mr Stanmore from the room.

"Be careful, Miss Austen," he whispered, looking genuinely concerned. "Stay in view of the house at all times."

"I will."

Jane hurried from the house to find Mr Stanmore waiting outside with her coat and gloves. She wasn't fully warm from her last expedition outside but the thrill of anticipation of what might come next in their investigation propelled her forwards.

"May I suggest we do a few loops of the formal gardens," Mr Stanmore said, heading in that direction. "They are nothing much to look at this time of year, but the paths are dry and even and we are in good view of the drawing room."

"It is lovely to get some fresh air," Jane said, wishing her fingers were not so icy. "This must be quite a change from India."

"For all the years I was in India I had vague memories of winter. I could remember playing in the snow and ice skating on the frozen lake. The images were blurry, devoid of the details, but they were there all the same. When I returned to England it was as if all those gaps and blanks were filled in."

"What happened to you all those years ago?"

Despite her motivation for being here, her need to get to the bottom of what had happened to Emma Roscoe, she was also genuinely interested in Edward Stanmore's story. Over the years she had heard of men who had disappeared on their travels, fallen victim to shipwrecks or accidents whilst in more perilous lands, but never had she come across anyone who had been missing for so long and successfully made it back.

"I am sure the start of the story is common knowledge. I was sent to India to appraise some land for my father to see whether it was worth developing it or selling it. Before I left my father had an accident, but he was expected to recover so I set off as planned."

Jane nodded, this matched what Lord Westworth had told them earlier on.

"The sailing was smooth and I arrived in Surat as expected. I stayed in a hotel for a few days to acclimatise before setting off to inspect the land. It was positioned halfway between Surat and Bombay, a very rural area. I had a local guide who spoke good English and together we travelled on horseback for twelve days. We were about four days ride from our destination when I started to feel unwell." Mr Stanmore grimaced, and Jane realised it must be difficult for him to relive the moment his life had gone so wrong. "It was the start of monsoon season, and the rains came earlier than expected. My guide, who had been so helpful until that point, took us on the wrong path and we travelled about fifty miles too far east of our destination. By the time he realised his mistake, I was feverish and unwell."

Stanmore was building a picture of a string of calamities that on their own may not have meant twenty years' exile from his family, but together had whipped up to form the perfect storm.

"The rains were torrential and there were frequent mudslides on the road; one such disaster meant we could not go back the way we had come." He shook his head and Jane glanced up at him, seeing his gaze was fixed on a point far in the distance. "By then I was almost delirious, and my guide left me in a small village under the care of the locals. He planned to rush back to Surat and bring a doctor and supplies."

"Do you remember all of this happening?"

"Again, parts of it. Over the years little fragments would come back to me. It was only when my brother arrived that together we retraced my steps and could build the whole story."

Jane nodded, wondering what it must be like to have snippets of memory you couldn't place, floating in a sea of darkness.

"I understand I was unconscious for a long time. Some sort of infection of the brain. The villagers cared for me as much as they could and a few months later I recovered enough to spend more of my time awake."

"What happened?"

"I didn't know who I was or how I had got there. It was like I had awoken in a nightmare. The villagers were unbelievably kind and patient, helping me walk, teaching me a little of their language."

"What about the guide?"

"Of course, I couldn't know at the time, but when my brother and I enquired twenty years later it turned out a man had been killed in a mudslide on the road to Surat. We have no proof, but I suspect that was my guide."

"And the only person who had known what had happened to you." Jane could see how Edward Stanmore could have remained missing for so long.

"I stayed in the village for three months after I had recovered consciousness, slowly building my strength. In that time, I reasoned I must have travelled from Bombay as it was the closest city, three days ride away, and where many English start their journeys in India."

"Oh dear — Bombay was the opposite direction to which you'd come."

"I set out for there, hoping something would trigger a memory or someone would recognise me and tell me who I was."

"Meanwhile when your family sent investigators to look for you, they traced the wrong route, as your guide had taken you off course?"

"So I am told." He shook his head sadly. "All the time I missed out on, that is what grieves me the most."

"What have you been doing for the last twenty years?"

"When I reached Bombay, I was penniless and disheartened. I could not sail for England and seek answers there as I had no money, but that was my aim in those first few months. I fell in with a Dutch businessman. He gave me a job and slowly I worked my way up in his company. By the time I had enough money saved for a passage I had started to build a life for myself in Bombay."

"You gave up on coming home."

"I didn't know if there was a home to come back to. I could have been an orphan or disowned by my kin. As far as I knew, no one had come looking for me."

"Did you ever remember more?"

"Yes. As the years went on, I would get flashes of memory, like a painting or picture in my mind. They would be momentary, but I saw faces, hints of a family."

"So how did your brother come to find you?"

Jane was finding the whole story fascinating. If it had been written in a book she would have thrown down the story in frustration at how far-fetched it all was, such a series of coincidences, but sometimes real life was stranger than fiction.

"I travelled to Surat to conduct some business and whilst there a man named Hooper approached me, adamant he knew me, that we had sailed together for India twenty years earlier. I was wary of being conned and think I might have scared him away, but I understand he wrote to my brother all the same. A few months later Arthur came to find me and this time was determined not to give up until he had."

"Did you recognise him?"

"Not really. There was a vague hint of familiarity about him, but it had been a long time. What I did recognise were his descriptions of home."

Mr Stanmore fell silent and gazed up at the house beyond the formal gardens. It was an impressive building, built of red brick and grey stone with wide pillars framing the doorways. Large rectangular windows gave it a symmetrical appearance and it was beautifully maintained. It was clear the owners had substantial wealth and the staff to upkeep it so well.

"It must have been strange coming home."

"It was. In a way it felt like I was stepping into someone else's life."

"Do you ever regret it? Do you wish you were back in India?"

"There are things I miss, of course. The smell of the earth after the first of the monsoon rains, the lush green of the jungle and the faint roar of the tiger roaming in the distance, and that brilliant blue of the sea, shimmering in the sunshine like nowhere I have ever seen before." He tore his gaze from the house and turned back to Jane. "But I always felt a big part of me was missing. I couldn't marry because I didn't know if I already had a wife somewhere, I couldn't settle never knowing if one day someone from my past would come looking for me."

They walked in silence for a minute and Jane could see Mr Stanmore was deep in thought.

"I have struggled to adjust a little to life in England, but it does feel like this is the right place for me."

"It must be unsettling to see your brother after so many years, grown and with a life of his own."

A smile flitted across Mr Stanmore's lips. "Arthur is a force of nature, a man I am proud to call my brother. *He* has made this whole homecoming bearable."

Jane paused, knowing she had to ask the next question but aware it was a little indelicate. "What will happen to the title now? Will your brother continue as Lord Westworth, or will it pass to you?"

Mr Stanmore snorted and shook his head. "Who knows. The lawyers are currently debating what is the legal standing and then I assume it will go back to the House of Lords. They are the ones who passed the title on to Arthur in the first place." He ran his hand through his hair. "The thing they don't seem to understand is I don't want any of it. For years I didn't even know who I was. I have no need for a title, a grand estate."

"Surely if you do not wish to contest it then it should be straightforward?"

"I do not pretend to know how these things work. I hope between us my brother and I can resolve it."

"You really would let him have the life that could have once been yours?"

"It wasn't ever mine and I do not think it is mine to take now. For the next few months all I want to do is explore my memories and then I will make the decision as to whether to return to India or stay here."

"And if you stay here?"

"I am sure there is a modest house somewhere the family owns that I can settle in. I do not need anything ostentatious."

She glanced up at the man walking beside her and wondered if he was sincere in his declaration that he would not take the title or the estate from his brother. If he had not fallen unwell in India, he would be a viscount, and a wealthy one at that. He would own Stanmore Hall and the surrounding estate and farmland. She was certain there was property in Kent and Sussex as well that belonged to the Stanmore family, in addition to the land in India. The Stanmores had been wealthy and influential for generations, she wasn't sure if she completely believed Edward Stanmore was willing to give that all away to his brother.

"Do you have any other questions for me, Miss Austen?" Mr Stanmore pulled her attention back to him.

"I'm sorry, I have spent the last ten minutes peppering you with questions. You must think me unforgivably rude."

"Not at all, Miss Austen. I understand the bizarre nature of my story and how people find it fascinating. If it did not involve me personally, I would feel the same."

"Thank you for being so generous with your time."

Mr Stanmore bowed and they turned back to the house.

Jane wondered whether anything she had just heard had any bearing on the murder. It *was* a bizarre story, one that affected a number of people who had been at the ball the night before, but she couldn't see an immediate connection to her friend. Emma did not know Lord and Lady Westworth well and Jane wasn't certain, but she suspected she had never even met Edward Stanmore. It was hard to make a connection between Emma's death and what Edward Stanmore had told her.

"Miss Austen," Lord Hinchbrooke said as she returned to the drawing room. "You must tell me all about the mysterious

Mr Edward Stanmore. Let us see if we can make sense of this puzzle."

Jane related what she and Mr Stanmore had discussed, trying to remember the exact wording the man had used, knowing it was important to be precise. As she spoke, she noted the pertinent facts down in the notebook Lord Hinchbrooke had given her, so it was documented for him to look over later.

"What do you make of it all?" the magistrate asked.

"As he was talking, I thought to myself what a preposterous story," she said slowly. "There were an awful lot of coincidences, a whole series of events that had to occur to stop Mr Stanmore from finding out who he really was or to stop his family from finding him."

"Indeed."

"All of the elements are possible — the infection that spread to his brain and led to him lying unconscious for weeks on end, I have read of such things happening in foreign countries."

Lord Hinchbrooke nodded thoughtfully.

"And the guide being killed in the monsoon, the weather meaning they walked a long way from their original route, meaning no trace of Mr Stanmore was ever found. Individually you can see how all these things *could* have happened."

"Yet you struggle to believe it."

Jane sighed and closed her eyes, flopping back in the armchair even though she knew her mother would be mortified to see her in such an unladylike position.

"I struggle to believe it," she said slowly. "Yet I cannot see what any of it has to do with Miss Roscoe."

"No, unless it pertains to what she overheard." Lord Hinchbrooke stretched and stood.

There was a brisk knock on the door and without waiting for a reply it flew open, revealing Lady Westworth.

"Your sister is here, Miss Austen. I assume to escort you home. Unless *her* scribing skills are needed as well."

Lady Westworth stepped aside to reveal Cassandra, who had a worried look on her face.

"Jane," she said rushing past Lady Westworth. "You've been gone hours. Even Papa is getting worried."

Glancing at the clock on the mantelpiece Jane saw it was quarter past four, much later than she had expected.

Jane stood as did Lord Hinchbrooke and Cassandra's eyes flicked to him momentarily.

"I am sorry for detaining Miss Austen for so long," he said with a warm smile. "She has been helping me with a few notes, but we are finished now. Thank you for all your assistance today, Miss Austen."

Feeling suddenly bereft, Jane realised she didn't want to leave like this. Although the day had been full and eventful, she felt they were no closer to finding out what had happened to Emma. She didn't want to leave now and risk missing out on the vital piece of information that allowed the pieces of the puzzle to fit together.

"If you need any further help, Lord Hinchbrooke, I would be happy to assist."

"I will keep you abreast of any developments, Miss Austen. I know how deeply you have been affected by Miss Roscoe's death."

"Thank you."

"Come, Jane, we need to get home."

"One of the footmen is seeing our carriage is prepared for you," Lady Westworth said as Jane reluctantly stepped from the warm drawing room, pulling on her coat and her gloves.

"The horses were already harnessed so it should be round momentarily."

"That is too kind, Lady Westworth, we would not like to impose on your hospitality any more than we have already," said Cassandra.

"It is getting dark," Lady Westworth said, the hint of an indulgent smile pulling at the corner of her lips. "What sort of hostess would I be if I allowed two of my guests to go traipsing through the countryside after sundown?"

"Thank you," Cassandra said, pressing her fingers into Jane's arm, indicating they should accept the kindness.

The carriage rattled to a stop outside and within a minute they were settled on the plush seats with Stanmore Hall retreating behind them.

"Jane Austen, what on earth has come over you?" Cassandra exclaimed as they started down the drive.

For a moment she thought about feigning ignorance to Cassandra's meaning but knew her sister would not let her get away with such behaviour.

"I feel so guilty, Cass," she said quietly.

"You did not murder poor Miss Roscoe; you have nothing to feel guilty about." Cassandra was never so direct in her speech with anyone but Jane.

"If I had not dallied on the dance floor…"

"You cannot know things would have been different, Jane." Cassandra shook her head. "Anyway, it does not mean you can go running around forgetting about your reputation and your good sense."

"I did not forget."

"Then you chose to show it blatant disregard."

Jane fell silent.

"When I arrived, you were sitting unchaperoned with a gentleman, the door closed and not even a maid in sight to safeguard your reputation."

"Lord Hinchbrooke is the magistrate…"

"He is a man. In the eyes of many a very eligible, unmarried man."

"I was assisting him. That is all."

"*I* know that."

They fell silent and Jane sighed. Cassandra was of course right. All day she had been reckless with her reputation. She knew the consequences of even a little gossip, the stigma a young lady never quite recovered from. Every year there was someone of their acquaintance that fell victim to the strict standards of society. The lucky ones were hurried into a rushed marriage and told to be grateful. The unlucky ones, refused by the men who had compromised them, were shunned by those they thought friends and lost any hope of an advantageous match.

"Don't say anything to Mother," Jane said quietly. "I think Lord and Lady Westworth were too distracted by the events of last night to realise I was left unchaperoned and Lord Hinchbrooke is unlikely to say anything."

"Your secret is safe," Cassandra said more gently as Jane rested her head on her sister's shoulder. Suddenly she felt very weary, as if every muscle and bone in her body had tripled in weight and it was a great effort to move them. It wasn't far home in the carriage, but perhaps just long enough to rest her eyes for a few minutes.

CHAPTER NINE

Flexing her fingers, Jane's eyes flitted over the page she had been writing, satisfied with her progress. She had slept well, exhausted by the events of the last couple of days, but had woken up restless and feeling unable to settle. Knowing she could not expect her parents to be indulgent enough to allow her to traipse up to Stanmore Hall again, and aware the hospitality of the Westworths may be finite, she had drifted around the house all morning, unable to concentrate on any task but not content with sitting quietly with only her thoughts for company.

After lunching, her father had regarded her with concern in his expression and sent her upstairs to rest, but every time she closed her eyes all she could see was Emma's satin shoe poking out from behind the desk in the library.

Instead, she had taken out the story she was working on and delved back into the world of *Elinor and Marianne*. She loved her brothers, but it was her sister Cassandra who was her closest companion. It was Cassandra who she confided in, Cassandra who could rile her to anger in just a few words, Cassandra who could soothe her if disaster struck. In Jane's mind there was nothing like the relationship between sisters and in writing *Elinor and Marianne* she got to explore all of the messy web of family relationships.

This afternoon she had written in a frenzy, scribbling down the words and not caring for neatness. At first, she had worried that her haste would make for poor writing, but she was pleased with what she had produced and for a few hours at least it had taken her mind off Emma and the events at Stanmore Hall.

"You have a visitor," Cassandra said, bursting into the room in a flurry of excitement.

"Lord Hinchbrooke?"

"No, Jane, why would you think that?"

"He promised he would keep me informed of any developments in his investigation."

"It is Mr Lefroy, he's downstairs with a beautifully wrapped gift and asking for you. Mother is all in a flap and fussing around him like he is a long-lost child."

Jane stood too quickly, almost knocking over her ink bottle, managing to save it with only a few splashes escaping on to the blotter on the desk. Quickly, she rushed to the mirror, trying to ignore the little smile on Cassandra's lips as she patted down her hair.

"Stop it," she ordered her sister.

"I'm not doing anything."

"You're smiling."

"I am allowed to smile."

Jane clamped her mouth shut and regarded herself critically in the glass. She looked a little pale and drawn after the last few days, but that was to be expected. Her dress was light blue with a pretty white trim. It was old but well looked after and sat well on her body.

"Come, Jane, you look lovely," Cassandra said. "Do not keep Mr Lefroy waiting."

As Jane descended the stairs her stomach roiled and she felt a stab of nerves. It was ridiculous, he was merely a man she had danced with at one ball, but all the same she found herself pausing outside the drawing room door.

As gracefully as she could Jane glided into the drawing room, her eyes immediately latching on to Mr Lefroy. Before she had entered he was sitting with her mother, engaged in quiet conversation, but as she opened the door Mr Lefroy sprung to his feet and greeted her with a warm smile.

"Miss Austen," he said, reaching out as she approached and bowing over her hand. "Forgive me for calling unannounced but after the events at the Westworths' ball I needed to see you for myself."

"A terrible tragedy," Mrs Austen said, shaking her head. "Jane knew Miss Roscoe, didn't you, Jane?"

"Yes, we were of an age and I have known her most of my life." She felt the familiar lump form in her throat as she thought about all the things Emma would miss now her life had been tragically cut short.

"How are you coping, Miss Austen?"

"I feel such sadness and I grieve for Miss Roscoe, but also for her family and their loss," she said quietly. "I cannot even begin to imagine how awful it must be to lose someone in such a way." She paused, aware of her mother's eyes boring into her. Sitting in the drawing room was an attractive young gentleman who had come to call on Jane. Her mother would be willing Jane to steer him away from thoughts of tragedy and onto more cheerful topics.

"I find I am unimaginably warm, Mr Lefroy," Jane said, fanning herself with an outstretched hand to add to the effect. "Perhaps you could accompany me on a stroll around the garden?"

"Of course."

A few minutes later, dressed in thick layers and with a hat firmly upon her head Jane stepped out of the back door. The garden was not large and her mother would be watching from the drawing room so it meant they could talk and walk freely without anyone needing to chaperon them.

"I apologise for my mother," Jane said as they stepped away from the house.

"There is nothing to apologise for, Miss Austen."

"You are kind to say it, but I have been of marriageable age for more than two years now. I am aware of the hungry look she gets in her eyes when a gentleman comes to call."

"You have a lot of gentlemen call on you, then, Miss Austen?"

"No, I think maybe that is the problem. She thinks I will scare away all the suitors and live my life as a miserable spinster."

"You haven't scared me away."

Jane looked at him, her spirits lifting a little for the first time in days. "I haven't scared you away *yet*," she corrected him.

"It would be hard to do, Miss Austen."

"Now I am intrigued, Mr Lefroy. What exactly would it take to send you running back to your aunt's house?"

He gave her a mischievous grin and Jane felt a rush of gratitude towards the young man. It was the first time she had properly smiled, the first time she had really felt anything other than the awful mixture of sorrow and guilt and fear since the night of the ball.

"If you released a horde of hungry crocodiles and directed them my way, I think I would struggle to stand my ground."

"You are safe on that front, Mr Lefroy; I fed our crocodiles earlier this morning. One of my father's parishioners was growing tiresome. Is it only murderous beasts you would run from?"

"Murderous beasts and some of my tutors, but certainly not well-meaning mothers." As he spoke, he raised a hand and waved in the direction of the house. Mrs Austen returned the gesture, a smile spreading across her face. "Alas, I fear it is your mother who would chase me away if she knew of my situation."

Jane knew little about Mr Lefroy, only the snippets of information gleaned on visits to Mrs Anne Lefroy with her mother and hearing the letters he had written to his aunt. She knew he was studying law and that his family were proud of him for doing so and she knew his eyesight suffered from the long nights reading by candlelight.

"Your situation?" As soon as she had uttered the question Jane wished she hadn't. She didn't wish to know about the woman he was betrothed to or the debt the Lefroy family were in that required him to find a wealthy wife. Whatever the reason behind his last comment she would rather be kept in ignorance. Shaking her head quickly, she said, "Don't tell me. Instead let us talk of other things, more interesting things."

"I came to call on you yesterday, Miss Austen, but your mother informed me you were up at Stanmore Hall."

"I was."

"Did Lord Hinchbrooke summon you?"

"In a way," she said and then wondered why she was lying to the man beside her. "No," she corrected herself. "He didn't summon me, but I felt an awful restlessness, a need to see if there was anything further I could do to help."

"I am sure Lord Hinchbrooke was grateful for that."

Jane thought of his kindly smile and gentle guidance as she had burst into the middle of his investigation.

"Do you know him?" Jane asked, looking up at Mr Lefroy.

"Only by reputation. Keeps himself to himself I believe. No one has a bad word to say about him, though, and he is known as a fair magistrate."

"That's what I keep hearing."

"What impression did you get of the man?"

"He is kind and thorough. Meticulous and methodical. I think he is driven by this need for the truth, and I wonder if that is why he is such an excellent magistrate. Whereas others see the position as a burden or a stepping stone to something else, he truly wants to ensure the right people are punished for their crimes and the innocent go free."

"It sounds like you have a lot of respect for the man."

"I do."

"Then I am sure he will soon get to the bottom of this awful business. I can't imagine how the young woman's family must be feeling."

With a stab of guilt, Jane realised she hadn't even contemplated visiting the Roscoes to express her condolences. All her thoughts had been about finding out what had happened to Emma and she felt awful that she hadn't considered the wider consequences of what had occurred. Her family would be distraught.

"Nor can I," Jane murmured, wondering if it would be better to visit them or send a letter of condolence.

"I must return to my aunt soon, Miss Austen, but I am told we will be attending the Templeton's Christmas ball next week. I wonder if you have plans to go?"

Her mother had been talking of nothing else but the succession of festive balls and dances they had been invited to for the past three weeks. It was a busy time of year in Steventon and until the events of the last few days Jane had been excited by the prospect of the festivities. It was the chance to see friends and meet new people whilst observing the fascinating interactions between people you saw in the ballrooms and drawing rooms.

"Yes, I do believe we have been invited, although…" she trailed off, unsure what the etiquette was when a friend had died. Jane wouldn't be expected to enter a mourning period, but it felt wrong to think about dancing and frivolity when Emma never would be doing those things again.

"You must think me terribly unkind, talking about balls at a time like this. I confess it is a desire to see you again that drives me to be less sensitive than is proper. I did enjoy our dances at the Westworth ball, Miss Austen, I have not laughed like that in a long time."

Jane looked up sharply and saw the hint of sadness in his eyes. She wondered if it were just his strained eyesight that had driven him to the countryside from his studies in London or if there was something else.

"I did too, Mr Lefroy."

"I will take my leave now, Miss Austen," he said and then hesitated. "I brought you a gift. It is in the drawing room. Why don't you open it and let me know at the Templeton's ball whether you like it or not?"

"Thank you. You are too kind."

"You do not know what the gift is yet. You may find it too presumptuous."

Jane smiled, her curiosity piqued.

"Goodbye," Mr Lefroy said and turned to leave, making his way back to the drawing room. Jane remained where she was, savouring the fresh December air for a few more minutes.

With a silent curse she realised she had been too swept up in the thrill of seeing Tom Lefroy again that she had not asked him if he had noticed anything of importance that night at the ball. "You would make a poor magistrate," she muttered to herself. It would be another reason to attend the Templeton ball in a few days.

As the ends of her fingers began to tingle despite her gloves Jane slowly returned to the house, eyeing her mother and sister as she entered the drawing room and closed the door.

"Mr Lefroy seems a very pleasant young man," Mrs Austen spoke first, her demeanour bubbling with excitement.

"He is."

"Remind me, he is the nephew of Mrs Anne Lefroy?"

"Yes."

"He is young," her mother mused, as if considering whether this was enough of a black mark against Mr Lefroy to dismiss him as a potential suitor. "Although I understand he is a very clever young man and is studying at Lincoln's Inn Fields."

"Indeed."

"Open the present he bought you, Jane," Cassandra said, passing the package over to her. It was heavy, the base rectangular and solid and rising up to a rough pyramid in the middle. On top was a small square piece of card filled with looping writing.

Dear Miss Austen,

This may be a strange present from someone you have only just met, but I believe the best gifts are the ones that encourage us to follow our passions.

Yours, Tom Lefroy

Carefully, Jane untied the ribbon holding it all together and then peeled back the paper. Inside was a heavy notebook, thick and filled with quality paper and piled on top were two inkwells and a beautiful maroon pen.

"Oh Jane," Cassandra said, a giggle bursting out from her lips, "only you could inspire a gentleman to bring you gifts so practical."

Jane carefully took the notebook and opened the front cover. Inside Mr Lefroy had written, in small, neat handwriting. *To Miss Austen, remember to always follow your dreams.*

"What a thoughtful present," Jane murmured, trying to suppress the surge of excitement that was rippling through her. She had only spoken to the man twice and there was no indication anything more than a friendship was being offered her, but she felt her hopes soaring, nonetheless.

"Very thoughtful," Mrs Austen said, peering over at the gift in the wrapping. "It seems he has grasped what you are passionate about in one short meeting, Jane. I shall discuss this with Mr Austen."

"There is no need to discuss anything with Papa," Jane said quickly. "Mr Lefroy has not declared any intention."

"Nevertheless, I will discuss his position with your father," Mrs Austen said, "in case an offer is made."

Standing abruptly, Jane gathered the items of the gift to her chest and excused herself from the drawing room. As she started to ascend the stairs, she heard Cassandra behind her.

"I didn't mean to upset you, Jane," Cassandra said, reaching out for her sister's arm.

"You didn't. I just do not want to build this into something that it isn't. Not yet."

"I understand. Affairs of the heart are rarely straightforward."

Knowing Cassandra was speaking from experience of her own engagement, Jane took pity on her sister.

"Come, it will be only a few days before Mr Fowle's next letter, and perhaps then he will have some news on when he will return and then you can set a date," Jane said. "Until then I need your wise guidance and assistance."

"What do you have planned?"

"I need to visit Emma's family," Jane said with a heavy heart. "I haven't yet offered my condolences and I wish to tell them what a wonderful person she was."

"Let us change," Cassandra said, looking down at their pastel-coloured dresses, "and then I shall accompany you."

"Thank you, Cassandra. What would I do without you?"

CHAPTER TEN

The Roscoes lived a little way out of Steventon, on the road to Oakley. It was a walk that could be done in forty minutes if cutting across the fields, but after the mud she had experienced the day before, Jane suggested they stick to the roads. It would add on about twenty minutes to their journey, but it meant they would arrive looking presentable to the house of mourning.

The house itself was large and a little dilapidated, suffering from a lack of funds needed to upkeep a building that was approaching three hundred years old. Jane had visited only once before, two summers ago when Emma had been struck down with measles. At the time Jane had brought some supplies to her friend, leaving them on the doorstep as she had strict instructions not to step into the house lest she become infected.

"I am not sure I would want to live so far away from any other house," Cassandra said, looking around at the rolling hills that surrounded the dwelling on every side.

"Yes, and Steventon is such a grand metropolis," Jane said, dodging the hand Cassandra went to tap her with for the comment.

"There are at least other houses, other people. I don't think we've passed another dwelling for twenty minutes."

"I like it," Jane said, tipping her head back and looking at the sky. "It's peaceful."

"You would be bored within an hour, without people to watch as they go about their daily business."

They paused for a moment outside the front door, both nervous now they had arrived. Jane felt a wave of nausea overtake her as she looked up at the first-floor windows, wondering which room had been Emma's, which bed would now never be slept in again. She raised her hand and knocked on the door. It was opened almost immediately by a maid who looked exhausted and as if she had spent half the night crying.

"Miss Jane Austen and Miss Cassandra Austen. We are here to offer our condolences to Mr and Mrs Roscoe."

"Will you wait a moment, and I will enquire if they are receiving guests?" the maid said, ushering them into a dark hall. It was neat and tidy but devoid of much furniture and there were spaces on the walls, outlines on the wallpaper where it looked as though pictures had once sat.

They waited in silence, Jane straining to overhear the murmur of voices in the room the maid has disappeared into.

"My dear Miss Austen and Miss Jane, how kind of you to visit," Mrs Roscoe said as she emerged out into the hall. "Do come through; we are in the drawing room."

They followed Mrs Roscoe into the drawing room just in time to see the retreating form of Mr Roscoe disappearing out through the doors that joined the room to the next.

"Please excuse my husband, this is a trying time for us."

"I am so sorry for your loss, Mrs Roscoe," Jane said, tears springing to her eyes. "Emma was such a kind and gentle soul; she will be missed every single day."

"Yes, she will be," Mrs Roscoe said, her voice thick with emotion. "I know she has gone to a better place, but I do wish she could have had a few more years with us on this earth." She shook her head and tried to hold in the sobs but after a moment it all became too much and she rose, pressing a handkerchief to her cheeks.

With a glance at her sister who provided an encouraging nod, Jane stood and moved over to the older woman, reaching out for her hand. The grief in her eyes was stark and overwhelming and Jane realised how lucky she was not to have been blighted by such profound loss in her life. Of course, friends of her parents and distant relatives had passed away, as was the natural order of the world, but she had seven siblings and all of them had made it through childhood without succumbing to any of the deadly illnesses. George had his troubles, but despite the frequent seizures he had survived longer than any doctor had predicted. Never had she felt the all-encompassing grief that Mrs Roscoe was suffering now.

Death was never easy, but to have your only child struck down in their prime must be a blow you never recovered from.

"I keep thinking she is going to come back through the door," Mrs Roscoe said, looking wistfully out the window. "I keep thinking someone will tell me there has been a mistake and it wasn't Emma who was killed."

"I can understand that," Jane murmured.

"My husband went to Stanmore Hall, in the middle of the night after it had happened," Mrs Roscoe said. "He tells me he saw her, that it was definitely her, but I still find myself unable to believe."

Jane closed her eyes for a moment, picturing the pretty shoe sticking out from behind the desk and then the rest of Emma's body cold and stiff, the bloom of blood unnaturally dark on her pale dress.

Mrs Roscoe spun to look at her, a wild look in her eyes. "The undertakers offered to bring her home here, but I don't think I could bear it."

Not knowing what to say, Jane reached out and took the older woman's hand, squeezing it tight. There were no words that could take away the pain, nothing anyone could say or do to make it even a little better.

They stayed like that for a long time, Jane allowing her own tears to spill onto her cheeks as Mrs Roscoe sobbed openly. From outside there was the sound of hooves, but although Jane's curiosity was piqued she did not move from her position. It was only when the deep rumble of a voice in the hallway grew louder that she shifted in surprise.

"Mrs Roscoe," Lord Hinchbrooke said as he entered the room, followed by Mr Roscoe. "May I offer my sincerest condolences?" He blinked in surprise to see Jane and Cassandra, nodding a greeting to them too.

"Thank you, Lord Hinchbrooke," Mrs Roscoe said quietly, still clutching Jane's hand.

"Do you have news, my lord?" Mr Roscoe said, his voice thick with grief and his cheeks flushed as if he had only just managed to stem his own tears.

"Nothing definite yet, but we make progress."

"Lord Hinchbrooke has given me his word he will do everything to find out what happened to Emma," Mr Roscoe said.

Jane knew she and Cassandra should excuse themselves and leave the Roscoes to answer any questions Lord Hinchbrooke might have in private, but she didn't want to miss anything that might be helpful. Even though she didn't want to admit it to herself and it felt terribly vain, she had this notion that she might be the one who was able to untangle the mystery of who had killed Emma. It was a ridiculous idea, she had no experience and no authority to question people like Lord Hinchbrooke did, but still it clung on, burrowing deeper. She knew it was her mind's way of trying to assuage some of the guilt she felt at being late to their meeting in the library.

"Thank you," Mrs Roscoe said quietly, her voice barely audible.

"I came to clarify a few points, to help build a picture," Lord Hinchbrooke said, indicating Mrs Roscoe should take a seat. Jane moved silently beside the older woman, still holding her hand.

"We can go if you would prefer privacy," Cassandra said, shooting a pointed look at Jane.

"Of course," Jane murmured, hoping the Roscoes would not see the harm in them staying.

"No, you girls have walked such a long way," Mrs Roscoe said.

Mr Roscoe looked at them as if he could barely remember who they were, then turned his attention back to the magistrate.

"Emma attended the ball with her aunt and uncle that night, was there a reason for this?"

"I had one of my headaches," Mrs Roscoe said, choking back a sob.

Jane squeezed her hand and murmured soothing noises.

"I keep thinking if only I had been there…"

"You can't think like that, my dear," Mr Roscoe said, his voice gruff.

"My sister-in-law offered to take Emma so she wouldn't miss out on the ball. She was so looking forward to it."

"Did Miss Roscoe have a particular friend; someone she would meet up with when she attended these events?"

"Not so much in Steventon. We are positioned in such a rural location that our social life is split between the families of Steventon and the larger community in Oakley. There were two young ladies of an age in Oakley who were her particular friends. Miss Mary Firth and Miss Elizabeth Lord." She paused, glancing at Jane and Cassandra. "Of course, Miss Austen and Miss Jane were friendly with her in Steventon and then there was Miss Harriet Henby and Miss Lilibeth Burton."

Lord Hinchbrooke glanced at Jane, raising an eyebrow in enquiry.

"Miss Henby has gone to spend Christmas with relatives in Devon and Miss Burton contracted a fever three weeks ago and has been on strict bed rest since."

"So, there were no other young ladies at the ball with whom Miss Roscoe was particularly friendly?"

"No, although Emma would have known some of the young ladies from the wider community, it is just they were not particular friends of hers."

Lord Hinchbrooke cleared his throat and Jane saw he was uncomfortable with the next question he was about to ask. She shifted in her seat, ensuring Mrs Roscoe could feel the pressure of her hand and know Jane was there for reassurance.

"I know this is an indelicate question," Lord Hinchbrooke said, "and it is not my intention to malign the memory of your daughter in any way, but I must ask even the difficult questions, so I get the full picture." He paused, looking from Mr Roscoe to his wife and back again. "Was there a gentleman, perhaps, that Miss Roscoe was courting, or someone who she had hopes for?"

"Certainly not," Mr Roscoe said quickly. "She was promised to the eldest Petersworth son. Their family lives in Winchester and his father and I have been friends for years. Emma knew of the arrangement and was happy with it. There was no one else."

Jane felt the miniscule shift in position from Mrs Roscoe and looked up to study the older woman's face. There was something there, a mere flash of unease that Jane wasn't sure if she had imagined it. She caught Lord Hinchbrooke looking at Mrs Roscoe too and wondered if he had seen it.

"I understand the betrothal arrangements," Lord Hinchbrooke said slowly, "but sometimes young ladies do form an attachment, a liking, for a young gentleman, even when these arrangements are in place."

"Not Emma," Mr Roscoe said firmly. "She knew her duty."

Jane knew vaguely of the Petersworths; they were a wealthy family with the father running a successful shipping and transport business. No doubt the younger Mr Petersworth was learning the family business before taking a wife. Her eyes travelled around the room which was sparsely furnished and she remembered the gaps in the hall where paintings had once hung and wondered if the Roscoes were struggling financially. If so, a match between their only daughter and the Petersworths would have done a lot to alleviate any money troubles.

Lord Hinchbrooke nodded, but Jane could tell that like her, he wasn't quite satisfied with the answer.

"Had Miss Roscoe ever attended a ball at Stanmore Hall before?"

"No, I don't think so," Mrs Roscoe said, shaking her head.

"Did she know Lord and Lady Westworth at all?"

"No. Lady Westworth, I know well enough to greet in the street and exchange a few pleasantries, but she and Emma could not have spoken more than half a dozen times, and only then to say good morning."

"And Lord Westworth?"

"No, not at all."

"How about the brother, Mr Edward Stanmore?"

"Curious business," Mr Roscoe murmured.

"No, I do not think Emma had ever met him. I understand he has barely left the estate."

"Thank you," Lord Hinchbrooke said, catching Jane's eye and trying to communicate something with his expression.

Then realisation dawned as the magistrate asked Mr Roscoe if he would be kind enough to show him Emma's room.

The two men left and Jane patted Mrs Roscoe on the hand, aware she needed to tread carefully but conscious Lord Hinchbrooke would not be able to keep Mr Roscoe occupied elsewhere in the house forever.

"It is a relief to know a man such as Lord Hinchbrooke is determined to get to the truth of what happened to Emma," Jane said, ignoring the incredulous look she was receiving from Cassandra. Sometimes in life you had to be bold.

"Indeed. He is a good man."

"I suppose much of the information he gathers is not relevant," Jane said carefully, "but he must have it all the same to build a full picture and then he can disregard what is not useful."

"Yes, I suppose," Mrs Roscoe said. She was biting the skin around her thumb on her free hand, seemingly oblivious to the fact she was doing so.

"Emma was such a lively young woman. So full of laughter and happiness. I wonder that there was no gentleman who had taken an interest in her, other than the Petersworth son."

Mrs Roscoe shifted, her eyes coming up to meet Jane's.

"It is important Lord Hinchbrooke knows everything," Jane said quietly, "and I can assure you he is most discreet."

For a long moment Mrs Roscoe was silent. In the background Jane could hear the clock in the hall ticking away the seconds, counting down the time until Lord Hinchbrooke and Mr Roscoe were back in the room. She wanted to shake the woman in front of her, to tell her not to be foolish, to not put her daughter's reputation above finding out who had killed her, but Jane knew she had to step more carefully than that.

"Emma was insistent she attend this ball," Mrs Roscoe said, dropping her voice low. "When I told her I had a headache she was distraught, much more so than she normally would be for having to miss a social occasion." The older woman glanced at the door to ensure her husband was not coming back. "I sent a note to my sister-in-law, asking if she would chaperon Emma, but I decided to not tell my daughter until I had the reply. I did not wish to get her hopes up only to dash them again."

Jane nodded, realising she was holding her breath as she waited for the revelation.

"I walked in to find her writing a note of her own. She covered it when she noticed I was in the room and later, once it had been confirmed my sister-in-law could take her, I found it screwed up in the bin." She stood, moving over to a small writing desk in the corner of the drawing room. With a key she unlocked one of the drawers set on top and pulled out a folded piece of paper.

Jane felt her heart pounding in her chest as she took the paper from Mrs Roscoe and unfolded it, looking at the looping writing that covered the sheet.

My dearest S, I fear I may not be able to meet you tonight at the ball, my mother has a headache and we will not be attending. My heart aches for you and I long for the moment we can be reunited. I hold the memory of our last meeting close until we meet again. E

Jane turned the piece of paper over, trying to hide her frustration at the lack of address or even name. *S* could refer to so many people.

"The Petersworth son, the one she was betrothed to, this couldn't be him?"

"No. His name is John, and he was not invited to the ball."

"Do you know who this is?"

Mrs Roscoe shook her head.

"May I keep it, to show to Lord Hinchbrooke? I will ensure it comes back to you."

"Yes, but please do not let my husband see it. I do not want anything to tarnish his memory of Emma."

"Of course."

Jane tucked the note into her reticule and was just snapping it closed when Lord Hinchbrooke and Mr Roscoe came back into the room.

"It is getting late," Lord Hinchbrooke said. "Thank you for your time, Mr and Mrs Roscoe, and for being so patient, answering my questions." He turned to Jane and Cassandra. "You must have a long walk home and it is already growing dark. Perhaps you would allow me to escort you to Steventon?"

"That is most kind, Lord Hinchbrooke," Jane said, standing.

"Thank you for coming," Mrs Roscoe said. "The funeral is in two days. I hope we will see you there."

"Of course, Mrs Roscoe. If there is anything you need, please let us know."

With Cassandra leading the way they left the Roscoe house, waiting a few minutes as Lord Hinchbrooke fetched his horse from the fence he had tied it's reins to. He didn't mount, instead walking next to Jane and leading the horse alongside him. They walked in silence for a few minutes even though

Jane was eager to tell the magistrate about the note and discuss the significance with him.

It was Cassandra who broke the silence first. "Jane Austen, I cannot believe you did that," she exploded when they were out of earshot of the house. "That woman was grieving and you manipulated her."

Jane blinked, surprised at the anger in her sister's voice.

"Was that why you wanted to come here? To gather evidence?"

"Of course not," Jane said, hurt her sister would even think such a thought of her. "Emma was a friend and I wanted to tell her mother how sorry I was for their loss. I can't believe that you think so poorly of me."

"As soon as Lord Hinchbrooke and Mr Roscoe stepped from the room you pounced on that poor woman."

"That may have been my fault," Lord Hinchbrooke said quietly. "I indicated to Jane to find out what she could."

"You never spoke, my lord."

"We both noticed Mrs Roscoe's reaction when I asked if there was perhaps another gentleman Miss Roscoe was interested in. Your sister was quick enough to catch the question in my expression." He paused for a moment and then smiled kindly at Cassandra. "It is supremely difficult when there has been an unlawful killing, especially when it involves someone young, vibrant, in the prime of their lives. I feel deeply for the family, for those left behind, especially for the parents who should never have to suffer the torture of outliving their children."

Glancing sideways Jane saw her sister was mesmerised by Lord Hinchbrooke's soft voice, unable to look away.

"My job, however, is not to commiserate and sympathise. There will be dozens of families close to the Roscoes who will do that. What they cannot do, what they do not have the authority or expertise to do, is to bring the killer to justice." Jane saw the passion in his eyes and realised how devastated he must be if he didn't catch the person responsible. "I admit it does sometimes feel like a burden, but I have vowed to do whatever it takes to discharge my duty and that sometimes means choosing progress over sensitivity."

"I understand your sense of duty, Lord Hinchbrooke," Cassandra said, and Jane was surprised to see her sister press on in argument with the viscount. Normally Cassandra was outspoken at home, but much better at holding her tongue in social situations than Jane, knowing when to stop, when to keep her more controversial opinions to herself. "And I agree as magistrate you have to put your mission to find the killer above all else, but my sister is neither a magistrate nor trained in such matters. She is a young lady of a certain social status who is expected to behave in an appropriate manner at all times."

"There is a fine line to tread," Lord Hinchbrooke said, "between gentle questioning and interrogation. Miss Austen has natural talent at keeping on the right side of the line. Mrs Roscoe is going to feel relieved she has unburdened herself and less traumatised than if a man she did not know insisted she hand over the information."

Jane was surprised Lord Hinchbrooke was arguing for her involvement in the matter. The last couple of days he had been solicitous and kind, encouraging her where he could, but she had thought it likely the magistrate was happy to return to working alone.

"Tell me, Miss Austen, what did you find out?"

Carefully, ensuring not to rip the delicate little piece of paper, Jane dug out the note from her bag and handed it over to Lord Hinchbrooke.

"Mrs Roscoe does not have any idea as to who this might be," Jane said once he had read it, his brow furrowing as he contemplated the implications.

"This changes things quite considerably," Lord Hinchbrooke murmured. "It may be that what Miss Roscoe overheard was not in fact the reason she was killed, perhaps it has something instead to do with this gentleman she was writing to."

"It is quite intense," Jane said, stepping closer and peering at the wording again. It was far from a casual note letting an acquaintance know she would not be in attendance.

"Do you have any idea who this could be?"

Jane closed her eyes, trying to picture the faces at the ball. Apart from Mr Newbury, she hadn't seen Emma dance with anyone, nor stop and talk to anyone in particular. "No," she said slowly. "I recognised most of the gentleman at the ball but would not know many of their first names. There wasn't anyone Miss Roscoe paid particular attention to. Did you notice anything, Cassandra?"

"No," Cassandra said, shaking her head. "In fact, I barely remember seeing her at all."

"She may have avoided this person on purpose, kept her distance so she was not linked with him in any way," Lord Hinchbrooke said. "I have a list of all the guests at home; I am sure I will be able to narrow things down to a few names."

He fell silent for a few minutes, deep in thought. They were walking slowly, minds engrossed in the discussion than thinking about the impending darkness. The sun was setting in the distance and it wouldn't be long before the dusk turned to the dark of evening.

"Will you question them? These gentlemen?" Jane looked up at Lord Hinchbrooke, trying not to sound too eager to be involved.

"I thought I might observe them first, at the funeral. Then I can put my questions to them after."

"Do you think the gentleman in question will come?"

"Yes. If it is someone she knows relatively well, someone local who would be expected to attend, then it would look strange if he didn't turn up."

"We should look out for someone trying to hide their emotions."

"Yes." He glanced at her and grimaced. "Promise me you will not approach anyone without me. Remember, this may be our murderer and I do not want them to feel cornered and as though there is no way out other than more violence."

Next to her, Jane felt Cassandra stiffen.

"Surely it would be better to leave this to Lord Hinchbrooke," Cassandra said quietly.

Jane knew there would be more to come when they were alone. "I am merely going to observe. We are attending the funeral anyway; it is not much to cast an eye over the faces of the other mourners." She turned to Lord Hinchbrooke. "Will you be at the funeral?"

"Yes."

"Then perhaps we can meet afterwards to discuss what we have seen?"

He inclined his head and Jane felt a thrill of anticipation. She wondered if this could have been a simple lover's quarrel. Perhaps Emma's lover had followed her to the library, jealous to think she was meeting someone else illicitly. They had argued and in a fit of anger he had stabbed her.

Jane shook her head slowly, for some reason it felt colder than that, less frenzied. "Did you find out where the knife came from?"

"The kitchen. The cook found they were missing a knife when she did the count at the end of the night."

It meant a crime committed in a moment of heightened emotion, in the middle of an argument, was much less likely.

"So, someone planned to kill her," Jane murmured, almost overwhelmed by a sudden nausea.

"It would seem so. It certainly suggests some element of intent, to sneak down to the kitchen and steal a knife."

"Surely it can't have been one of the guests, it must have been a servant or one of the family," Cassandra said, intrigued despite herself.

"I thought so too," Lord Hinchbrooke replied, "but when I asked Mrs Lamb, she said the kitchen was such a hive of activity that someone could have sneaked in and taken a knife whilst the maids were preoccupied elsewhere, although it would have been a big risk to take."

"It was a very big risk," Jane agreed.

"As is killing someone in the middle of a ball, albeit in a quieter part of the house. We are not looking for someone who lacks courage here."

"I feel we are no closer," Jane said with a sigh. "We have been told so much and yet none of it has been helpful."

Lord Hinchbrooke smiled at her indulgently. "That is your fatigue talking. I feel it too, that terrible sense of failure that I have not yet apprehended the killer, but I assure you we are making good progress." He glanced up at the darkening sky. "I suggest a day of rest tomorrow. I need to go over all the information you captured in my notebook and then I will be fresh for the funeral and the trials of the days that follow."

"You should rest tomorrow too," Cassandra said quickly, linking her arm through Jane's. "You have not slept enough these last few days and the emotional toll is huge."

"I can sleep when this is all over."

"Take heed of your sister, Miss Austen. Sometimes these matters can take weeks to conclude. There is no benefit of you working yourself into a nervous exhaustion in the meantime. Besides, a little distance is sometimes a good thing."

"What do you mean?"

"You write, do you not, Miss Austen?"

"Yes."

"Tell me, when you have been working at your writing for hours on end, days on end, does it all seem a blur when you read back through? You cannot view what you have written with a critical eye, but if you leave it a few days, come back to the manuscript with fresh eyes and a fresh mind, you can see the errors, the little phrases that do not sit right, the things that are out of place." He waited until she nodded before continuing. "A magistrate's job is very similar. You are told all of this information and at the time it is impossible to sort through it. It is only when you take a step back, to let your subconscious put in the work behind the scenes, that you start to see the connections that were invisible before."

"Then tomorrow I shall rest," Jane said, knowing it would be next to impossible. She found it hard to relax at the best of times. Whereas her brothers when home would often sit on the bench in the sunshine, contemplating the beauty of the garden or recline by the crackling fire, she found it difficult to sit still. She loved to be on the move, to be doing something, discovering something. The only time she liked to sit was when she was writing or reading, and often even then she would pace about her room when she was trying to formulate a pleasing turn of phrase or select the right words for conveying an idea.

"Tomorrow I shall rest," she repeated quietly. If that was what was needed to find Emma's killer, then that was what she would do.

CHAPTER ELEVEN

"Jane, my dear, you look like you haven't slept again," her father said as he entered the drawing room.

It was early and the house was cold and dark. When Jane had risen half an hour ago, she had come downstairs to find even Mrs White was not yet up. She had laid and lit the fire herself, feeling satisfied when the wood had started to crackle and pop in the grate. Now she sat with her dressing gown pulled around her, slippers on her feet, staring into the fire.

Yesterday, she had tried to take Lord Hinchbrooke's advice and rest. She had gone for short walks, spent some time writing, even taken herself to lie down after lunch to try and give all the thoughts in her head time to settle, time to find their place.

She didn't feel as though anything was clearer. If she was honest, she was probably more confused than before and had more questions.

"Are you thinking about the funeral?"

Jane nodded. The funeral and a hundred other things.

"I think it will be well attended. The Roscoes have many friends in the local area. The family has lived here for generations."

Jane felt a lump form in her throat. Emma had been the last of this branch of the Roscoe family. She had no brothers or sisters, there was no one to inherit the house.

"I am relying on you today, Jane," her father said quietly. "I am relying on you to help that poor family through their ordeal."

Jane nodded, wondering if she had the skill and fortitude to do so.

"You must put your own feelings aside today, Jane," her father cautioned her. "I know you feel guilty for not meeting Miss Roscoe on time, but today is not the time or place to let that show."

"I know, Papa," Jane said quietly.

"Good girl." He leaned in and kissed her on the head and then quietly left the room.

The whole house was beginning to stir with creaks and thumps from upstairs as the occupants began to rise in preparation for the day. When Jane heard Mrs White bustle downstairs and go into the kitchen, she rose, ready to help the cook start on breakfast.

Jane was not hungry, she had lost her appetite the last few days, but she knew today could be long and trying and that she should at least try and eat something.

"You look like a ghost," Mrs White said, looking her up and down.

Jane had to smother a smile. Mrs White had been with their family for years and Jane always felt comfortable and happy in her company, as if she were a familiar warm blanket, just waiting to engulf the family with her love. The older woman handed Jane a knife and indicated she should start slicing the bread whilst she heated the pan for eggs.

"You'll need a hearty breakfast today," Mrs White said, not looking up from where she was cracking eggs expertly with one hand. "What a sad day for the village, and her family of course. There is nothing that can prepare you for the pain of losing a child."

Jane glanced up and saw the glint of tears in the cook's eyes, reaching out a hand to squeeze Mrs White's rough fingers in her own. The older woman was a widow who had started working for them when her children were grown, but she had known heartbreak in her younger years. Her husband and her infant twins had been carried off the same winter by a particularly bad fever that had spread to their lungs. She had been left with her two older boys, struggling to survive and cope with her grief at the same time.

"Twenty-one years ago, now," she mused, shaking her head. "And still, I can't think of it without crying. What a silly old woman I am."

Knowing she would be shooed away, Jane wrapped her arms around the cook and hugged her.

"Get on with you," Mrs White said. But Jane saw the little smile on her face before she turned away to see to the eggs.

Three hours later and Jane was jigging from one foot to the next nervously. It wouldn't be long before the first of the mourners arrived at the church with the funeral procession coming behind. They had a long way to travel from the undertakers and Jane hated to think of Emma Roscoe's body being jolted on the back of a cart. It felt undignified and certainly not a fitting end to a short but bright life.

Slowly the church began to fill up. Jane stood by the door, greeting people, exchanging regrets and asking them to have a seat. This wasn't strictly necessary as everyone arriving so far was local and knew the church from the regular Sunday service. Still, it gave her a good view of each mourner as they arrived and stopped her from dwelling on the ceremony to come.

In the backwaters of Hampshire, they did not follow the same rules and customs as in London. Jane knew in the city women often did not attend funerals at all, choosing instead to mourn in private where they would not be observed giving in to their emotions. She found it hard to understand how people would not want to wish their loved ones a final goodbye. Here, everyone was welcome at the church and everyone would be attending to pay their respects to Emma's family.

"Miss Austen," Lord Hinchbrooke said as he entered the church. He was dressed smartly as always but today wore a black cravat in deference to the solemnity of the occasion.

"Lord Hinchbrooke," Jane said, managing a small smile. He moved on without saying anything more, choosing a pew right at the back of the church and tucking himself into it as if trying to be as inconspicuous as possible.

So far Jane knew everyone in the church. Most of Steventon had turned out to the funeral as Emma Roscoe was laid to rest. With her eyes flicking over everyone seated she started to try and compile a list of possible 'S' gentlemen Emma could have been involved with.

Simon Trent, the youngest son of the Trent family. He was in his early twenties and a happy, hardworking young man. He was an officer in the army and as such always had a gaggle of young ladies eager to flutter their eyelashes at him. The young Captain Trent had only been home on leave for a couple of weeks and Jane wondered if that was long enough for Emma to form an attachment to him, unless it had begun before he had left many months ago.

Sebastian Hunter, Steventon's most eligible bachelor. He was a widower, having married the woman selected for him by his family and then lost her and their son in childbirth. A year later it was said he was ready to start searching for a wife again and the gossips of Steventon had been quite overcome by the news. He was objectively handsome with a strong jaw and dark hair, but Jane had always thought there was something a little off about him. Perhaps it was the fact he knew he was so attractive and didn't mind using it to his advantage. Mr Hunter was a possibility, although Jane hoped her friend had possessed more sense than that.

Samuel Tinker, a tenant farmer on the Westworth estate. He was in his mid-twenties and yet to marry, instead focussing all of his time and energy on making his small parcel of land prosper. Jane did not know Mr Tinker well, but he had a soft voice to accompany the well-built physique and she could see how a young woman might fall for such a combination. Normally tenant farmers would not attend a ball at a grand house such as Stanmore Hall, but Jane knew the Westworths had spread the invitations widely across the local society to attend the celebrations. She didn't know if their tenant farmers had been invited but it was worth finding out.

Then there was Sidney Humphries, a married man, but Jane knew this didn't necessarily rule him out. He drank too much and spent his time losing his wife's money at the card tables. Jane couldn't find a single redeemable feature in the man, and she hoped her friend had felt the same.

She paused as the Westworths entered the church. Lady Westworth looked pale and drawn as she walked sedately beside her husband. She managed a small nod of acknowledgement in Jane's direction before Lord Westworth led his wife to a pew near the front. It was a surprise to see the viscount and his wife here. They were normally very private and didn't become involved in the affairs of the village, but Jane supposed they couldn't shy away from the funeral of the young woman who had died in their home. The older brother, Edward Stanmore, was nowhere to be seen, elusive as ever. A horrible thought stirred in Jane's brain. The *S* could of course refer to a surname. Emma Roscoe's gentleman could be Edward Stanmore.

For a moment Jane let the idea wallow in her brain, tossing and turning it over to examine it. Edward Stanmore was much older than Emma, but he had a certain charm about him. He was animated and interesting and Jane could see how a young woman who had never left Hampshire might fall for a man who had led a more exciting life. Plenty of marriages had a similar twenty-year age gap and worked well.

She thought back to when she and Lord Hinchbrooke had questioned Edward Stanmore. He had given no hint that he knew Miss Roscoe, but Jane wasn't sure she trusted what he said.

A murmur passed through the church and Jane glanced out the door, her body stiffening as she saw the procession approaching. There was the horse and cart that carried the coffin first and Mr and Mrs Roscoe walked behind it. Behind them were Emma's aunt and uncle and a boy of about twelve years old, who was probably a cousin. They walked in silence, their expressions sombre, and Jane felt her heart swell with pity.

Carefully, she pushed open the second door, making room for the coffin to be brought in and then she slipped into one of the pews, taking her place beside Cassandra.

As the pallbearers walked into church with the coffin, Jane slipped her hand into Cassandra's and was grateful of the warmth she felt in her sister's grasp. She felt an overwhelming sadness swell up inside her and couldn't bring herself to look at the coffin. Any death was sad, but to be attending the funeral of someone in the prime of their life was a tragedy, especially as it hadn't been an illness or an accident that had taken them from this world so soon.

"Such a waste," Jane murmured, wondering once again what could have happened to make Emma such a threat to someone that they felt the need to murder her.

The service was short and poignant, and Jane couldn't tear her eyes away from the back of Mrs Roscoe's head. She sat clutching her husband's hand with her sister-in-law pressed against her other side. Her head was bent for much of the service but Jane saw the occasional heave of Mrs Roscoe's shoulders as she tried to keep her emotions under control.

When it was over the men from the congregation left the church to walk to the grave whilst the women lingered for a few moments inside. Jane watched as the men trailed past, faces sombre, looking for a clue as to who might have been closer to Emma than the rest. There was nothing, no flicker of deeper grief, no glint of unshed tears. She watched as first Simon Trent walked past, then Sebastian Hunter. Both looked appropriately solemn but neither appeared to have recently lost the woman he loved.

Jane felt her sister's eyes on her and turned.

"I will accompany the Roscoes," Cassandra said, slipping out of the pew. "You do what you have to do, but don't let Father catch you interrogating people and don't be too long."

Jane squeezed her sister's hand in gratitude and waited for the groups of mourners to traipse out of the church. The women were clustering around Mrs Roscoe and her sister-in-law, expressing their sympathies. The congregation had been invited to share in some food and company at the house of Emma's aunt and uncle who lived closer to the church and had offered their hospitality, so Mr and Mrs Roscoe did not have to organise refreshments for everyone in the midst of their grief.

Jane lingered as the church cleared, glancing to the back where Lord Hinchbrooke had sat, but he must have accompanied the men to the graveside. When she was alone she took a moment to herself, breathing in deep breaths. Tears threatened to overwhelm her as she allowed for the reality of the situation. People died every day. Often the old or infirm, but sometimes the young. It was the way of life. But an event like this was a stark reminder that anything could happen and nothing in life was certain.

Slipping from the church she pulled her coat tighter around her as she found a position where she could observe the proceeding at the graveside without being too obvious.

Her focus was directed towards Simon Trent and Sebastian Hunter, both of whom had lingered in the graveyard with the other gentlemen. She hoped to fall into step with them as they walked from the church and somehow ask her questions of them, although she knew it would be hard to contrive the situation to look natural.

Thankfully, Sebastian Hunter was one of the first to leave ten minutes later. Jane had to stamp her feet to warm them up before she started walking, but managed to make it appear she was coming from the church as he rounded the corner.

"Good day, Miss Austen," Mr Hunter said, raising his hat to her. "What sad circumstances we find ourselves in here."

"Indeed, Mr Hunter. I trust the interment went as well as can be expected?"

"It did."

They both fell silent for a moment.

"Did you know Miss Roscoe well, Mr Hunter?" Jane asked, deciding to just jump in and ask before the man spotted someone else to talk to.

"I did, Miss Austen. She was most kind when I lost my wife, as were so many from the local area. Miss Roscoe and her mother called on me in those dark days to see if there was anything I needed and to offer their support."

Jane inclined her head. "That was kind of them."

"It was. They were neighbourly and generous, and I fear the world is a worse place without Miss Roscoe's kindness in it."

"Had you seen her much recently?"

"No. I've been in London these last few months, staying with a friend. I only returned a week ago and I had not seen Miss Roscoe since returning."

"That is a shame," Jane said, shaking her head. "All of this is so terrible." She paused then, glancing over her shoulder to check they were not drawing too much attention from anyone. "Did you see Miss Roscoe at the Westworth's ball?"

A frown appeared for a moment on Mr Hunter's brow as if he suddenly realised he was being questioned. "No," he said slowly, "I do not believe I did. Certainly not to speak to. I was there, of course, but I arrived at about half past nine and went straight to the card tables. Didn't leave the room until there was all that commotion when Miss Roscoe was found." He peered at her then, turning sharply. "You found her, I believe, Miss Austen?"

"Yes, I did."

"That must have been a terrible shock for you."

"It was, Mr Hunter."

He nodded and then started to look around as if done with the conversation. "Please excuse me, Miss Austen, I must have a quiet word with Mr Farrier."

Without waiting for her reply, he bowed and moved away, leaving Jane to feel as though she had done a less than perfect job of questioning him. Still, she had watched his eyes as she had asked about Miss Roscoe and unless he was a very cold and unfeeling man, she didn't think he had been the mysterious *S*. Surely no one could be involved with a young woman who had died and not show any deeper hint of emotion than the passing sadness she had seen in Mr Hunter's eyes.

"You are keeping busy, Miss Austen," Lord Hinchbrooke said, making her jump as he soundlessly moved up beside her.

"I do not think it is Mr Hunter we are looking for," she said, shaking her head. "He thinks a lot of himself, but I can't see him being Miss Roscoe's gentleman."

"Did you ask him about her?"

"Yes. He said he liked her, that she had been kind when his wife passed away, but I did not detect any deeper feeling on his part."

"You don't think he was concealing anything?"

"No." Jane felt the weight of responsibility press down on her as she uttered the word. It was a lot to shoulder, to think that the investigation into Emma's death hinged on her assessment of a man.

"Who else is there?"

"Captain Simon Trent. That is him over there." She discreetly pointed out the young officer. "He is home on leave from the army at the moment and has been for the last few weeks."

"Certainly a possibility. Don't all young women like an officer?"

"That is a gross generalisation."

"But one that is largely true."

Jane tilted her head to the side to consider. "There is always some excitement if a regiment passes through, although I am never sure if it is because they are officers in the army, or if it is purely because it means there are bound to be a large number of unmarried eligible gentlemen."

"What do you think on the matter, Miss Austen?"

"I think the realities of being an officer's wife would soon grow tiresome. My brother Frank is in the navy and he is yet to marry. I often think he is loath to settle down and leave his wife behind for months, even years at a time."

Lord Hinchbrooke seemed to consider this for a moment, his eyes focussing somewhere on the distance.

"Then there is Sidney Humphries, he is married. He was at the church but left with his wife soon after. He has a bit of a reputation as a man who likes his liquor and the card tables a little too much. I would like to think Miss Roscoe was smart enough to stay well clear of the likes of him…"

"But sometimes the heart does not follow the rules of the head," Lord Hinchbrooke murmured.

Jane pondered for a moment, wondering if Lord Hinchbrooke would allow her to ride out with him to question the man. "Then there is Samuel Tinker. He is a tenant farmer on part of the Westworth estate."

"A tenant farmer?"

"Yes, I know he is unlikely to have mixed with Miss Roscoe much, but I thought it best to include him."

"He was not one of the guests at Stanmore Hall, but I agree we should still talk to him."

"You will permit me to accompany you?"

Lord Hinchbrooke suppressed a smile. "I am told I need to be more careful with your reputation, Miss Austen. However, if you decided to take a walk to Mr Tinker's farm this afternoon at two o'clock, I cannot see how we can be criticised."

"Thank you," she said, knowing how easy it would have been for him to say no.

"Shall we see if we can get the celebrated Captain Trent away from the protective bosom of his family?"

Together they slowed their pace so Captain Trent and his father would soon catch them up and when the Trent men were alongside them, Jane stumbled and dropped her reticule.

"Miss Austen, let me get that for you," Captain Trent said, swooping in and picking up the fabric bag.

"Thank you, Captain Trent, how very kind of you," Jane said. "It is lovely to see you back home again. Are you in the area for long?"

"Alas, only one more week and then I will get my orders," he said.

Jane was pleasantly surprised when Lord Hinchbrooke engaged the older Mr Trent in conversation, trusting her to continue with the captain. She walked slowly, allowing the gap between them to widen until she was certain she could talk to Captain Trent without his father overhearing.

"You were away for a long time before this, I believe?"

"Yes. My regiment was sent to Africa." He smiled at her. "Dusty, hot continent but, my lord, it is beautiful. Like nothing you've ever seen before, Miss Austen."

Jane thought of the descriptive letters her brothers sometimes sent home. Neither were prolific writers but over the years she had pressed Frank and Charles for letters about their travels that slowly both had learned to comply or face her endless questioning when they returned home.

"I can only imagine," Jane murmured. She knew as a young woman of the middle gentry she was unlikely to ever travel further than the borders of England. Some did, of course, the lucky few who married strategically, but most women in her social circle barely left the counties they were born in, let alone the country. "Do you hope to go back there?"

"I have a hankering to see the whole world, Miss Austen. I have heard of the treasures of the New World and the bright blue sea of the West Indies. There is so much out there to be discovered."

"You sound contented with your choice in career, Captain Trent."

"I am. I know I am lucky, not many men can say they are truly happy in what they do, but I am. It was the clergy or the army for me and I always knew what direction I wanted my life to go in."

"Then I wish you every happiness." Jane paused, needing to make sure her next question was not seen as positioning herself for a potential wife. "Do you remember my brother Frank?"

"Of course. He is a few years older than me, but I knew him well."

"He wrote to me only the other day with a similar enthusiasm for his job as you describe. The only thing he bemoaned is the lack of opportunity to settle down and have a normal family life." She sent a silent message of repentance to her brother for the little lie. Watching the young man's face she saw no flicker of deceit as he shrugged.

"I know as a man I am privileged to not have to think about that for a few years yet. My sisters are both married despite being younger than me in years, and although they are happy, I do not envy them. Perhaps in five years or ten I will feel differently."

"You are right, the expectations for men and women are vastly different." Jane looked up and let her eyes drift to where Mr Roscoe was walking along next to his brother, eyes cast at the ground. "Did you know Miss Roscoe well, Captain Trent?"

"No," he said, shaking his head. "Well, a little. I actually asked her to dance at the Westworth's ball."

"Oh?" Jane tried to keep the eagerness from her voice.

"Yes. I asked her early in the evening as she was standing in the corner looking a little lost. I felt sorry for the girl. She agreed, seemed quite keen, but then later she didn't turn up. I never imagined…"

"What time was this?" Jane asked sharply, feeling a surge of excitement. So many of the questions they had asked had produced no results, it felt good to hear something positive, something that could be acted upon.

"I must have asked her to dance soon after we arrived, perhaps eight o'clock. Our dance was meant to be at about half past, but I searched the ballroom and couldn't find her. I assumed she had changed her mind."

Carefully, Jane tried to work out the timings. It was a quarter past nine when Emma Roscoe had crashed into her in the ballroom, looking shaken and flustered. If she hadn't been around for the promised dance to Captain Trent at half past eight it must have been then she was either out meeting her mysterious S or overhearing whatever it was she wasn't meant to hear.

"Did you see her later?"

"Not to talk to, although I think I glimpsed her across the room later on."

Jane allowed his words to sink in. It did not seem as though he were hiding a deeper regard for Emma. Captain Trent had an open, honest face and Jane didn't think he was lying to her. She bid him farewell and excused herself, waiting for Lord Hinchbrooke to do the same and fall in beside her.

Silently, she shook her head in response to his questioning look.

"He says he asked Miss Roscoe to dance, but he couldn't find her in the ballroom when they were meant to be taking to the dancefloor."

"That is interesting," Lord Hinchbrooke mused. "But you do not think he is her mysterious gentleman?"

"No. Which is unsettling in itself for all we have left now are the married man, the tenant farmer or..." She trailed off, realising she hadn't mentioned Edward Stanmore as a possible option.

"Or Edward Stanmore, a man old enough to be her father," Lord Hinchbrooke said quietly, holding Jane's eye.

Jane shuddered. People married for all sorts of reasons and she knew many were not as lucky as she to have such a loving and supportive family. If she decided never to marry, she had no doubt her parents would provide her with love and shelter for as long as they lived and then one of her siblings would not hesitate to take her in. In that regard she was very fortunate. Marriages with one or two decades of difference in age were nothing to bat an eyelid at, but more than that and Jane felt there was far too much inequality. Women went into marriage at such a disadvantage anyway, giving up their rights and their possessions and their names to their husbands, it felt even worse when there was a thirty- or forty-year age gap. A marriage of equals was very seldom achieved, but it would be impossible when the wife was barely more than a child and the husband already lived a full life.

"Please don't let it be Edward Stanmore," she murmured.

"I suggest we talk to Mr Tinker next. How about this afternoon?"

Jane nodded and Lord Hinchbrooke walked her to the house of Emma Roscoe's aunt and uncle but paused before he crossed the threshold. "Today is for family and friends," he said quietly. "I will not impose my presence."

Jane nodded, stepping inside alone and turning back to bid him goodbye.

"Until this afternoon, Miss Austen."

"Until this afternoon."

CHAPTER TWELVE

The sky was heavy with clouds and there was a hint of snow in the air as Jane set off across the fields towards Mr Samuel Tinker's farm. She had learned from being out for long periods in the last few days and had multiple layers on under her thick coat, but even so the wind seemed to bite through the fabric and slice at her skin.

As she walked, Jane tried to clear her mind of all the competing facts she had compiled over the last few days. It felt as though there was both too much information and too little at the same time.

Sometimes when she was stuck on a particularly tricky section of dialogue or description with her writing she would take a walk and once she could ensure there was no one else nearby she would start to talk to herself out loud. Sometimes vocalising her thoughts meant she could see where she was going wrong and get over the blockade in her mind.

"Emma was stabbed in the chest by someone unknown in the library at some point between quarter past nine and quarter past ten. The person who stabbed her had retrieved a knife from the kitchen beforehand and brought it to the library." Jane paused, wondering if this meant for certain that they had planned to kill her or if the knife had been brought just to threaten. "Emma had planned to meet someone with an initial *S* at the ball, someone she was close to, even intimate with perhaps. We don't know who this is or if they ever met." She started to walk faster, frustrated by how little they did know. "There were dozens of people at the ball alongside Lord and

Lady Westworth, the long-lost brother Edward Stanmore and all the servants and members of the Westworth household."

Jane let out a growl of frustration. Nowhere could she see a solution. Concentrating instead on putting one foot in front of the other she trudged on, pushing away the fatigue that threatened to overwhelm her.

Samuel Tinker's house was on a ridge overlooking the fields he farmed. It was a large plot of land and the farmhouse was smart and well upkept. As she approached, she saw Lord Hinchbrooke riding up the hill from the other direction. He raised his hat and then dismounted when he saw her. Jane noted that the older man looked tired and worn this afternoon. His movements were stiffer than normal and he looked pale.

"Are you unwell, Lord Hinchbrooke?"

"No, Miss Austen, I am quite well. This case weighs heavily on me, that is all."

She glanced down at his hands and saw them shaking a little, the tremor worsening as he reached out for his horses' reins and started to lead the animal towards the farm.

They hadn't even reached the farmhouse when they were greeted by two sheepdogs, running from one of the barns and barking at the visitors. The dogs came within five feet of them and stopped and Jane realised how well trained the animals must be to encircle any intruders but not attack.

"Good afternoon," Samuel Tinker said as he emerged from one of the sheds. "Heel." He spoke the command softly but firmly and immediately the two dogs moved away and returned to their master.

"You have them well trained, Mr Tinker," Lord Hinchbrooke said.

"They're working dogs. They like discipline and direction." The farmer looked at them enquiringly for a moment and then turned and walked away.

"Might we have a moment of your time, Mr Tinker?" Jane knew the tenant farmer a little. If she saw him around the village or the countryside they would exchange greetings and he attended church on a Sunday. Always, she had found him polite and courteous, which made it all the more strange that he would turn his back on her now.

"I'm fixing the door in the stable," he said. "I need to get it finished before dark."

"We are happy to talk to you as you work," Lord Hinchbrooke suggested, following the farmer before he had chance to answer.

"What can I do for you, my lord?" Mr Tinker asked as he picked up his hammer and began driving a nail into two pieces of wood to join them. He would not meet the magistrate's gaze and as Jane looked at him closer, she wondered if she was imagining the redness around his eyes.

"I am looking into the death of Miss Roscoe," Lord Hinchbrooke said, speaking evenly despite the thud of the hammer piercing the air every few seconds. "I am trying to find out what happened to her."

"Good," Mr Tinker said. "I hear you are a fair man, my lord. I hope you get your man."

"Did you know Miss Roscoe well?"

Jane watched as the young man answered. She noted the way he swallowed discreetly before opening his mouth, as if trying to disguise the emotion he was feeling. "I knew her to talk to, just as I know Miss Austen here."

"Nothing more than that?"

Jane watched Mr Tinker bow his head before answering. "No."

She glanced at Lord Hinchbrooke and took a step forward, wondering if it would be too cruel to trick the truth from this man.

"You see, the thing is, well…" she began, looking suitably flustered. "Oh, dear this is all rather delicate." This caught Mr Tinker's attention and for a moment he stopped hammering, looking up at her. "Miss Roscoe was a friend of mine," Jane said, forcing her voice a little higher than usual to add to the air of panic. "And it has become apparent that there was a man in her life, a man she kept hidden from her parents. There is a note, addressed to a man with the initial *S*."

Mr Tinker continued to look at her with a blank expression on her face. Jane hoped she was right and wasn't revealing too much about Miss Roscoe for no gain.

"You should not discuss things you do not know about, Miss Austen. People's reputations are ruined with gossip like that."

Jane straightened and looked Mr Tinker in the eye. "I think you were the one involved with Miss Roscoe," Jane said. "You are hardworking and kind and have a genial personality. I know Miss Roscoe, and I do not think she would fall for the superficial charms of Sebastian Hunter or be interested in the boyish dreams of Captain Simon Trent." She held Mr Tinker's eye. "She would have chosen a man like you."

For a long moment she did not think Mr Tinker was going to answer her and then his shoulders sagged and he let the hammer drop from his hands. "You'd better come inside."

The farmhouse was immaculately tidy with everything lined up in its place. Mr Tinker led them through to a comfortable sitting room and spent a moment laying and lighting the fire, only straightening when a good blaze was burning in the hearth.

Soon the room was warming up and Jane slipped off her gloves and took off her coat, laying it over the back of a chair.

"Why don't you start at the beginning?" Lord Hinchbrooke said.

Mr Tinker nodded, but for a long time he was silent, his eyes focussed on the flickering flames of the fire. "She had the most beautiful smile," he said quietly. "That was what drew me to her. Her smile and her laugh."

"How did you meet her?"

"I've always known her, or at least known of her, but last winter when she was visiting her aunt and uncle she twisted her ankle in the snow. I came across her limping along the icy road, half frozen to death. Even through her pain and discomfort she had a warm greeting for me."

"You helped her?"

"Yes, I offered her my arm to lean on and for a while she managed to hobble on, but the road was so slippery she stumbled again and I had to carry her."

"It is fortunate you came across her." Jane thought back to the thick snow that had fallen the previous winter and shuddered at the thought of getting caught out in such conditions.

"It was. We were only together for fifteen minutes but I was captivated." He shook his head ruefully. "I had no business falling for her and from that first meeting I tried to put her out of my mind, but I couldn't stop thinking of her."

Jane wondered what it must feel like to experience a love like that. The image of Mr Tom Lefroy flashed into her mind and quickly she suppressed it. Now was not the time to be thinking of the man that set her heart racing.

"I would find reasons, excuses really, to get close to her. Dallying at church so I could walk out behind her as we left or taking walks in the direction of her home in the hope I would meet her along the way." He gave a self-deprecating laugh. "I thought I was being very subtle, but one day Emma commented that we seemed to run into one another rather a lot. I apologised, but she looked at me and I saw in that moment she felt it too."

"You started to court her?" Lord Hinchbrooke asked.

"Not officially. She was betrothed to a man she barely knew, but we started to spend time together. At first, we pretended it was merely a friendship, but soon it grew into something that neither of us could deny."

"What was your plan?" Jane tried to keep the incredulity from her tone. A romance between Emma and Samuel Tinker had been doomed from the very first moment. Her family would not have allowed it, especially when she was promised to someone else.

"I turn a good profit year on year," he said quietly. "I know my place. I know I had no right in falling in love with her, but I will soon have the money to buy my own land. We planned…" He trailed off as if caught up in the memories when all their dreams had been a possibility. "We planned to wait until I owned my own farm and then I would propose. Her family would not have been happy; they were having some money troubles and the union between Emma and her betrothed would have helped them, but she felt they would come around when they saw how well we made a go of things."

"Mrs Roscoe found a note her daughter was writing to you when she thought she would not be able to attend the Westworth ball," Jane said slowly. "Were you invited?"

"No, but we struggled to find time to be together. We had arranged to meet out in the gardens and spend a few minutes walking and talking whilst everyone else was busy in the ballroom." He shrugged. "I know the Westworth estate well and all the servants were preoccupied with the ball. It was easy to slip into the grounds unnoticed."

"Did you meet Miss Roscoe?" Lord Hinchbrooke said, leaning forward in his chair.

"Yes, although only for a few minutes. We took a walk along to the orchard in the darkness and sat on a bench to talk, but nearly as soon as we got there we heard someone approaching."

Jane felt a tingle spread through her body. "Did you see who it was?"

He shook his head. "I motioned to Emma that we should go; I did not want her to get caught and be ruined by the ensuing scandal. I thought she was right behind me, but she must have hung back for when I reached the formal gardens she was thirty seconds behind."

"She heard something," Jane murmured. *This* was what Emma had been so keen to gain Jane's counsel over, not some low-level scandal involving a couple of servants. She had heard something in the gardens and that was what had got her killed.

"Did she say anything to hint at who she might have seen?"

"No, nothing at all."

Jane slumped back in her chair, trying to push away the mounting frustration. The picture was building, but she didn't see how they were ever going to be able to fill in the gaps. "So, you have no idea who Miss Roscoe saw in the gardens when you were leaving the orchard?"

"No."

"Is there anything else you can tell us, Mr Tinker?" Lord Hinchbrooke said, leaning forward in his seat.

The farmer hesitated.

"It is vitally important we know everything, no matter how small, how inconsequential you might think it."

"There has been a man, a stranger, hanging around the area the last few weeks," Samuel said. "I have seen him on a number of occasions and I do not think he is local or staying with anyone who is."

"Where have you seen him?"

"My farm is at the top of the estate and runs down to the parkland of Stanmore Hall. I've seen him near the edge of the parkland a few times, close to the folly."

"Have you approached him?"

"No. As soon as he has spotted me, he has always walked briskly off in the other direction.

"Could he be a gardener or someone who works for the Westworths?"

Mr Tinker shrugged. "Perhaps. It is just his behaviour..." He trailed off. "I find it hard to put a finger on, but he seemed suspicious."

"Thank you, Mr Tinker. If you remember anything else, please send me a note."

"I am sorry for your loss, Mr Tinker," Jane said softly as she rose and followed Lord Hinchbrooke out, pulling on her coat as she left.

"Well," Lord Hinchbrooke said, puffing out his cheeks as they walked away from the farmhouse, "that was a productive interview."

"Most productive," Jane murmured, still trying to get all the information straight in her head. "So, Miss Roscoe did hear someone that night. Do we think it was a couple meeting for an illicit moment of passion in the orchard?"

"That seems the most likely."

"And Miss Roscoe was killed to stop her from revealing the affair."

"It all seems horribly pointless," Lord Hinchbrooke said quietly.

"What do you mean?"

"Someone kills a young woman to protect their reputation or the reputation of their lover. It is cruel and unnecessary and selfish. The world loses a vibrant young woman and only the couple in question benefit."

"People are essentially selfish," Jane said, smiling sadly. "If something was to hurt one hundred people but be of benefit to the one making the decision, much of the time they would choose to benefit themselves."

"Who could this couple be?"

"Not two people who are married to one another, for there would be no need to silence Miss Roscoe then."

Lord Hinchbrooke nodded. "But we have no way of knowing who they are."

For a few minutes they walked in silence, contemplating the new information Mr Tinker had given them.

"Do you think he knew more than he was letting on?"

"No," Lord Hinchbrooke said after a moment. "He loved that young woman; he would want her killer to be caught and punished."

Lord Hinchbrooke looked up at the sky. There was still an hour or so until dusk, but the clouds were low and ominous and it felt as though it might snow. "You should return home, Miss Austen," he said. "Would you like me to escort you?"

She narrowed her eyes. "You're going to take a look at the area where Mr Tinker saw the stranger walking, aren't you?"

"Yes."

"I'm coming with you."

"I can't allow that, Miss Austen."

"Please don't stop me."

"This could be dangerous and I would not want to do anything that could jeopardise your safety."

Jane paused. Lord Hinchbrooke had been most generous in allowing her to assist him in the investigation so far, and she didn't want him to think that she wasn't grateful for that, but she was also completely invested in the case. The thought of the magistrate finding the killer without her felt like she was being pushed out at the most important moment. And if she was completely honest with herself, she also knew this wasn't just about her guilt at not meeting Emma when she said she would. She was enjoying the challenge, pitching her wits against the various witnesses and suspects, looking at the evidence and trying to figure out what had happened. She might be an amateur, but she was a determined one.

"Let me escort you home and then I will check the Westworth's land. Tomorrow, I will let you know what I have found."

"It may be too late. Every minute counts. If this stranger has something to do with Miss Roscoe's murder he could be getting further and further away with every moment that passes."

"You are trying to manipulate me, Miss Austen," Lord Hinchbrooke said, trying to look stern.

"What harm can come of it. We walk down to the edge of the Westworth estate together and take a look around. I will return home before nightfall and you can go on and question the Westworths and their servants to see if they noticed this man hanging around."

"You are a persistent woman, Miss Austen."

"I know. My mother always tells me so."

Lord Hinchbrooke consulted his pocket watch and finally nodded. "It is half past two and you must begin your journey home at half past three, no later. Do you agree?"

"Yes, whatever you say."

"Miss Austen."

"I mean it. At half past three I will march straight home, no protestations."

CHAPTER THIRTEEN

Jane and Lord Hinchbrooke walked side by side in silence for some time, the magistrate leading his horse beside him. They skirted the edge of the fields, heading downhill towards the Westworth estate.

"Mr Tinker has a good view of the rest of the estate from his farm," Jane said. From up here you could see the vastness of the lands belonging to Stanmore Hall stretching out in front of them. The main house was resplendent in the middle, but the gardens and wider estate stretched on for miles in each direction.

"There's the folly," Lord Hinchbrooke said as they began the final gentle descent into the estate.

They had to climb over a low wall to gain access and Lord Hinchbrooke paused to tie his horse to a nearby tree. Jane picked up her skirts and clambered over, landing squarely on her feet, turning back in time to see Lord Hinchbrooke struggle over the wall.

For a moment she regarded him, trying to work out his age. His hair was thick and silvery but his skin was not particularly wrinkled. He had an air of assurance about him, as if he knew who he was and what his role was in life. She would place him perhaps in his late forties or early fifties.

She glanced down at his hands. At present, with him in motion, there was no sign of the tremor that plagued him so much of the time. Initially she had thought it was just the tremor that troubled him, but the more time she spent with Lord Hinchbrooke the more she began to understand about some of the struggles he faced. Although he hid it well the viscount had a certain stiffness about his movements and sometimes a slowness. It was as if he knew what he wanted to do, but it took a little longer than normal for his muscles to respond.

Jane had seen something similar before in one of her father's parishioners, but that was a man well into his eighth decade who had been overcome by stiffness in his muscles and tremors in his hands.

"The doctors say I am unusual," he said, catching the direction of her gaze. "Most people who develop my condition are older."

"They have told you what it is?"

"A shaking palsy. I am told it will get worse."

Jane nodded. It seemed to be the way with these things to build up gradually.

"For now, I can walk, I can ride. There is nothing wrong with my mind. I have to remind myself to be thankful for all of this."

"Are you in pain?"

"No. Only from the indignity of not being able to do everything I could a year ago."

"I think you do remarkably well."

"You are kind to say so, Miss Austen. I made a promise to myself that I would continue to be useful whilst I could."

She wondered how many of the other little habits she had noticed were due to the disease taking hold. She knew his handwriting was affected; she had noted the tiny scrawl, barely readable, in his notebook when she had first offered herself as his scribe. Then there was his quiet, even voice, calm when events would normally prompt otherwise. Apart from the few frustrated glares at his hands when they didn't work as they were meant to or the groans of impatience as the stiffness in his muscles slowed him down, she had never heard Lord Hinchbrooke complain. She marvelled at his determination to continue on, regardless of the discomfort he felt or the difficulties he faced.

They headed straight for the folly, a white stone structure with commanding views over the estate. It was built in the style of an ancient Greek temple with ornate pillars framing the entrance.

"What is it used for?"

"Nothing," Lord Hinchbrooke said, smiling at her expression. "It is a point of interest in the estate, something the eye is drawn to."

"But surely it could have some practical purpose too."

"Sometimes these sorts of structures are used to host tea parties or as a shelter from the rain on the furthest reaches of the estate, but I do not think this folly has any purpose other than to look pretty."

There were three wide stone steps leading up to the heavy wooden doors at the front of the building and as far as Jane could see there was no other entrance.

"Stand back, Miss Austen," Lord Hinchbrooke murmured.

He gripped the chunky metal ring that served as a handle and twisted, pushing the door in at the same time. It opened smoothly, without a sound, and Lord Hinchbrooke stepped inside.

Unable to contain her curiosity, Jane followed the magistrate up the steps and into the darkness of the folly. It was gloomy inside with only the light from one small window to illuminate the square space. It consisted of just one room with a stone floor and bare walls. A bench had been fitted along one side and as Jane peered at it, she realised there seemed to be a bundle set at one end and something hanging down to the floor.

"My entreaty for you to stay back fell on deaf ears I see," Lord Hinchbrooke murmured.

"There's no one here."

"You didn't know that before you stepped inside. Really, Miss Austen, you should have a care for your own safety."

"What about yours?"

"It is my job, my responsibility."

"I would wager most magistrates have an assistant to do this sort of thing for them," Jane said, smiling as she caught the flicker of guilt across Lord Hinchbrooke's face. "You and I are not so different, my lord."

Carefully she propped open the door to allow more light into the room and then together they approached the bench. Close up, it became apparent the bundle was a small cloth bag, filled with something soft. There was also a blanket bundled up and placed on top of it.

"Someone has been sleeping here," Jane said in surprise. She thought of the freezing temperatures outside and glanced around the folly. It was well built but even so it was not intended for habitation. A draught whistled in around the window and the air had a chill about it.

"I suppose it is a better option than sleeping outside in weather like this."

"Do you think this person does not have a home?"

"There are many who are desperate enough to find even a little shelter."

In silence they regarded the sorry display of a bed and Jane shuddered at the thought of this being the best choice for someone.

"Of course, there could be another explanation," Lord Hinchbrooke said, his brow furrowing. "This person could have something to do with Miss Roscoe's death."

"How so?"

"The household was distracted by the sheer number of guests. Many of the downstairs rooms were in darkness and not being used for the ball. It would be a good time for a thief to creep in and help themselves to a few items of value."

"And Miss Roscoe disturbed them in the library," Jane said, following Lord Hinchbrooke's train of thought.

"This could be nothing more than a burglary gone wrong — a man who was caught helping himself to something of value and stabbed Miss Roscoe to escape."

Jane shook her head. "It doesn't explain why he risked going into the kitchen and taking the knife when he could have been seen by one of the servants. Surely if he was a thief his whole reason for choosing that time was to avoid the risk of being spotted."

"Very true, and it does seem a little excessive. If he was disturbed by Miss Roscoe he could have fled. I doubt she would have chased him and by the time she raised the alarm he would have disappeared into the gardens."

Jane approached the small cloth bag, not wishing to put her hand inside but knowing it could provide vital evidence. If the contents had dried blood on them then they would have their answer.

"Please, allow me, Miss Austen," Lord Hinchbrooke said. "It is not clear how long this person has been living a life on the streets, but I wouldn't be surprised if his clothes were filthy and riddled with fleas."

Jane didn't protest, taking a step back at the mention of fleas. She watched as Lord Hinchbrooke pulled the items from the bag and spread them across the floor. There were two shirts and two pairs of trousers, as well as assorted undergarments. Despite initial appearances the clothes were not in bad disrepair and were relatively clean and well-mended.

"No blood," Lord Hinchbrooke observed.

"And it does not look like he has been on the streets for long."

"No, it doesn't. The clothes are crumpled and have been worn, but they are not threadbare or even dirty."

Lord Hinchbrooke began patting down the pockets, stopping as he felt a small bulge at the top of one leg. Reaching in he pulled out a coin purse, the coins jangling inside. He handed it carefully to Jane and continued to check the clothes.

With her fingers trembling Jane pulled open the threads at the top of the purse, peering inside. There was not much money there, just a few shillings, a penny and a coin Jane did not recognise. She pulled it out and held it up to the light.

"What is it?"

"It's foreign."

She handed it over to Lord Hinchbrooke, who raised an eyebrow.

"It's a rupee."

"Indian?" Jane said, puzzled.

Lord Hinchbrooke nodded, checking the remaining pockets for anything more.

"That doesn't make sense — why would a vagrant have an Indian coin in his purse?"

"It doesn't make sense at all. Unless he was once a soldier I suppose, or a sailor — someone who had been to India…" He paused and Jane's eyes came up to meet his. The obvious connection to the case was Edward Stanmore.

"I think we need to talk to Mr Stanmore again," Lord Hinchbrooke said eventually.

"Do you think these are his clothes?"

"No. Why would he stash them out here in the folly? I am sure there are more private places to keep anything he doesn't want anyone else seeing in the house, but it is too much of a coincidence to find a rupee in the pockets of these clothes whilst Mr Stanmore spent the last two decades in India."

"If the clothes aren't Mr Stanmore's, then could they belong to someone who has followed Mr Stanmore home from India? A friend or acquaintance would have been put up in the house," Jane said slowly. "There would be no need for them to sleep out in the folly."

"Unless it was someone Mr Stanmore didn't want his brother or sister-in-law to meet."

"If we question Mr Stanmore, he is going to deny any knowledge of the clothes or the person they belong to," Jane said, biting her lip. "Surely there must be a better way. I feel certain whoever it is sleeping out here is more likely to talk than Mr Stanmore. He is protected by his position, his family. If he says he doesn't know who the man is, we have to accept his word."

"And he will then be privy to our discovery and be able to warn whoever it is staying here to keep their distance," Lord Hinchbrooke agreed. "I may be able to arrange some local lads to help me watch the folly and see if we can catch this mysterious visitor as he returns. Questioning him would hopefully be revealing." Taking his pocket watch from his waistcoat he glanced at the time. "It is nearly time for you to return home, Miss Austen."

"You can't do everything by yourself," she said, squaring her shoulders as if preparing for a fight. "You cannot rally a group of men to help you watch the folly and also be here to ensure the man does not return in the meantime."

"Before you go any further, please do not consider suggesting you stay here whilst I gather some helpers."

"I can hardly summon assistance, I'm not the magistrate."

"This man may be our killer, Miss Austen. If he is then he has already taken the life of one innocent young lady — he will not shy away from taking a second."

Jane shuddered at the thought, knowing Lord Hinchbrooke was right. "But…"

"I am not a domineering man, but on this I must insist. You will return home and I will go and find some help. If the man returns whilst I am gone then we will have to hope he is still here when I come back."

Jane opened her mouth to protest again but saw the determined slant of the magistrate's brows. "I will return home," Jane said.

"Good. Do you want my horse?"

"No. There is enough light for me to make it home before sunset and you will be back here faster if you are on horseback."

For a moment Lord Hinchbrooke regarded her warily, as if not quite believing she had capitulated so easily. "Let us go," he said eventually, placing the bundle of clothing back in the cloth bag and rearranging the scene to look as it had when they'd found it.

Bracing herself against the cold wind, Jane bent her head as they stepped out of the folly. The sky was darkening, threatening rain or perhaps even snow and part of her yearned to be at home in the drawing room, sitting in her favourite chair by the fire with her family. On afternoons like this she would read them passages from her writing, watching their faces carefully for their reaction. Her mother would beam with pride, Cassandra would listen enraptured and her father would nod along to phrases he particularly like. She enjoyed it most when her brother Henry visited. He would sit beside her, arms folded and eyes closed, really taking in the words. Often, he would say nothing at all, just nod his approval, but if there was something he felt she could express better he would point it out without any hesitation or fear of hurting her feelings.

If she was sensible, she would walk over the fields to her home and in forty minutes be ensconced by the fire, sipping a cup of tea. Jane watched Lord Hinchbrooke mount and as he was about to ride off called up to him.

"Mr Tinker is close by," she said as he turned in his seat. "You could be at his farm long before you could muster a group of men from anywhere else. I know he is not completely cleared from suspicion, but perhaps in this matter he could help."

"A good idea, Miss Austen. I will ride to him and ask him to keep watch whilst I rally some more helpers. Now get on your way home."

Jane made a start up the field beyond the perimeter wall of the Westworth estate, walking at a sedate pace. Once or twice, Lord Hinchbrooke turned back as if to ensure she was really leaving. Only after he was out of sight over the brow of the hill did she pause and glance back over her shoulder.

The folly stood in the late afternoon light, beckoning her nearer. She felt loathe to leave it unobserved, unguarded. Although she did not fool herself that she would be a physical match for any man, she could at least observe. Surely if she was hidden somewhere close by she could watch and wait until Mr Tinker or Lord Hinchbrooke returned. Then she could sneak away and no one would be any the wiser.

Ignoring the voice of protest in her head, Jane turned back, climbing over the perimeter wall. "Twenty minutes," she murmured to herself. "Twenty minutes and Mr Tinker will appear and I can sneak away knowing we did not miss this man."

The garden would be lush and green in spring and summer, but a few months of cold weather had stripped the leaves from the trees leaving the branches bare. Thankfully there were a few evergreen bushes dotted around and Jane selected one of these to hide herself behind. She was aware the unknown man might approach from any direction so it was a bit of a gamble to decide what side to place herself on, but after a few moment's contemplation she picked a spot and made herself comfortable. At first, she crouched, but after five minutes her leg muscles began screaming in protest so she stood, reasoning she needed to be ready to move quickly if the man returned.

Jane did not have a watch so she could only judge the amount of time that had passed by how cold and stiff her body was becoming in the wind. She was beginning to curse her decision to stay when she heard a soft rustle behind her. She spun quickly, her eyes flitting over the garden, unable to see anything out of place. Her heart hammered inside her chest and she felt breathless, as if she had been running across the fields rather than standing still.

Turning back to the folly Jane attempted to slow her breathing, telling herself it was the impending darkness that was making her nervous. As she turned around, fixing her eyes on the building, she heard a rustle again and then a more definite crunch.

There was a searing pain in her skull and then Jane felt her knees buckle underneath her.

CHAPTER FOURTEEN

"Miss Austen?" It sounded like the voice was coming to her through water, muffled and distorted.

Jane forced her eyes open, squinting as everything seemed bright even though it was dusk.

"Can you hear me?"

Struggling to sit up, Jane gasped as a bolt of pain shot through her head. She lay back down, defeated for a moment, before trying again. This time she managed to prop herself up onto her elbows and start to take in the scene around her.

Mr Tinker was leaning over her, concern etched on his face and his coat draped over the lower part of her body to keep her warm.

"Did you see him?" she asked.

Mr Tinker frowned and then motioned to a spot to her left. "Better than that," he said quietly, "I caught him."

Jane put a tentative hand to her head, feeling the point of impact and touching it to see if there was any blood. She winced, finding the start of a lump with her fingers, but the skin was not torn and there was not the anticipated slickness of blood.

"What happened?" she said, peering over to the man Mr Tinker had bound with the reins from his horse.

"I was riding down to the estate from my farm after Lord Hinchbrooke paid me a visit. He directed me to the folly to watch for the man who had been staying there. As I was approaching, I saw this cretin creeping through the bushes. I couldn't make out what he was doing at first because you were hidden from my view." He shook his head, an expression of regret on his face. "I would have called out to warn you if I had known you were hiding in the undergrowth."

"He hit me with a branch?" Jane saw a discarded tree branch nearby and marvelled that she had only been stunned for a few minutes.

"Yes. You went down immediately and he was so distracted by what was going on that he didn't hear me approach."

Jane noticed the swelling over Mr Tinker's fist and the start of a black eye. "It looks like he fought you."

"He did," the farmer said with a grimace. "But he lost."

"Thank you."

"You shouldn't have been here, Miss Austen; it was not a wise thing to do."

"I know." Jane closed her eyes, thinking how lucky she had been. If Mr Tinker had been a few minutes later, if he had stopped to change his coat or if it had taken a little longer to saddle his horse, she might be dead right now.

"Lord Hinchbrooke should return with his reinforcements soon, but shall we get you somewhere a little more comfortable?"

There weren't many options and Jane shuddered at the thought of stepping inside the folly, into the darkness, with her attacker still outside.

She sat up further, planning on getting to her feet, pausing when her head protested at the rapid movement. After everything had settled she tried again, slower this time, and made it upright. She turned towards the man sitting with his head bowed and ankles tied.

"Don't do it, Miss Austen," Mr Tinker said, his eyes fixed on the man.

"Don't you want to know whether he was the one?"

Samuel Tinker turned to her with fire in his eyes and a flash of anger on his face. "Of course I do, more than anything, but if I hear his confession, I am liable to lose control," he said. "If he tells me he stabbed Emma to stop her from raising the alarm whilst he robbed the family silver, I do not think I could stop myself from beating him until there was nothing left."

Jane laid a hand on the farmer's arm, feeling the tension in the firm muscles. He was holding his whole body taut, thrumming with energy and it was clear he was struggling to keep that energy contained. "Do you have the time, Mr Tinker?"

"Sorry, no. It was a quarter to four when I left so it must be a little after four now."

Jane grimaced. Her father was lenient with her and her sister, allowing them to choose their own society and how they spent their time. He had been keen they attended school and gained an education, but more than that, he encouraged them to follow their passions. Over the years Jane had brushed against the boundaries of his leniency a few times. Once when her dear friend Mrs Elliott had organised a dinner party that had stretched long into the night. Jane had been supposed to be staying with Mrs Elliott, but at half past midnight she had been inspired by a new idea and had needed to write it down. After roaming the Elliott household with her hosts long since in bed, she had set off home in the middle of the night to fetch her prized notebook so she could jot down her idea before any of it could leave her.

Jane had been young and foolish, her head spinning from too much wine that she wasn't used to drinking. Halfway home she had realised what a silly idea her midnight trek had been, but by then it was too late. Her father had been astounded when he found her alone at the door at such an hour and in the weeks that followed she had received many lectures on *appropriate behaviour for young ladies*, *the consequences of reckless behaviour*, and her favourite, *notable young women who have been ruined by less.*

This would be another occasion that would have her family worried and her reputation hanging by a thread. Soon it would be dark and here she was alone in the far reaches of the Westworth estate with only a tenant farmer and a criminal for company.

"I do not think I can make this any worse," Jane murmured to herself and with a resoluteness she did not feel, approached the man tied at the ankles.

"Miss Austen," Lord Hinchbrooke's voice boomed out. "Whatever it is you think you are about to do, step away."

The magistrate had ridden up from the direction of the house, the sound of his approach shielded by the whistling of the wind which was beginning to pick up. He dismounted, sliding from the horse and taking in the scene with a deep frown. "What on earth has happened here?"

"I found this ruffian sneaking up on Miss Austen," Mr Tinker said with a shake of his head. "I couldn't get to her in time, but managed to catch him after."

"You're hurt, Miss Austen?"

"A bump to the head only."

Lord Hinchbrooke looked her over with concern in his eyes. "I thought we had agreed you would return home?"

"We did."

"Did you have any intention of obeying my instructions?"

Jane thought about lying but knew the magistrate was too sharp to see through her. "No."

He sighed; the bone-weary sigh of a man burdened with something he is struggling to shoulder. "We will discuss this further, Miss Austen; make no mistake." He paused, looking between her and the tied-up man. "Tell me what happened."

"I thought I would wait until you returned, or Mr Tinker arrived, just in case the man from the folly showed up."

"What did you plan to do if he did?"

"Watch him, ensure he did not flee."

"I am glad I am not your father, Miss Austen; I think I would be halfway towards my grave with worry."

"I thought I heard something at one point, but could not see anything, then there was a crunching in the undergrowth behind me and before I could turn around I felt a terrible pain in my head."

"Did he knock you unconscious?"

"I think so. I was certainly stunned, but I do not know how long for."

"I saw the whole thing, but I was too far away to warn Miss Austen. I raced down here on my horse and thankfully was able to capture that man." Mr Tinker indicated behind them.

"I am grateful to you, Mr Tinker, for your quick thinking. Has he said anything?"

"No. Although I haven't asked him anything."

"I think it best I question this man this evening and we shall see what he has to say."

Jane's eyes flicked to his and Lord Hinchbrooke sighed. "I should send you home with instructions to not leave the house until this matter is over and done with," he said quietly, "but I am not that cruel. We shall question him at Stanmore Hall, once word has been sent to your family that you have been delayed."

"I can help you get him to Stanmore Hall," Mr Tinker said, subconsciously rubbing his bruised fist.

"Thank you, Mr Tinker, that is kind of you."

The walk through the estate was longer than Jane had anticipated. The folly really was at the furthest reaches of the gardens, tucked away down a winding path. They walked in silence, Lord Hinchbrooke leading the way, followed by the bound man who had shuffled along for a few moments until the magistrate had deigned to untie his feet for the walk to Stanmore Hall, with Mr Tinker pulling him along by the arm. Jane brought up the rear, happy with her position and with the distance she could keep from her assailant.

As they walked, Jane wondered if they had their murderer. Although not every piece of the puzzle seemed to fit yet, it was unlikely this man would have reacted so violently to seeing her waiting for him if he had not committed a crime already. An innocent vagrant would have no reason to see her as a threat and hit her over the head with a branch. He might not want to return to the folly whilst being watched, but he wouldn't have directly attacked her.

Twenty-five minutes later they arrived at the front door of Stanmore Hall. As Lord Hinchbrooke knocked on the door, Mr Tinker excused himself to return to his farm, and Jane wondered what a spectacle they must make; a viscount, a bound man and the daughter of the local rector, all traipsing together as the light rapidly began to fail.

The footman who opened the door blinked in surprise at their little party and quickly retreated to find someone with more authority.

"Come in," Lord Westworth said, a frown on his face as he approached the door. "Is this the scoundrel?"

"He may be," Lord Hinchbrooke said. "I will take him to the jail in Winchester tonight but wanted to question him before we set out on the journey to ensure I am not missing anything, given it is such a long ride. I know it is an imposition to use your house for this purpose…"

Lord Westworth interrupted with a shake of his head. "I'm just relieved you've caught him. Perhaps now we may be able to put this blasted matter to bed." He turned to the footman. "Stoke the fire in the drawing room and ask Jones to stand guard with you."

"Miss Austen's family will be worried," Lord Hinchbrooke said, his frustration hidden as he spoke to Lord Westworth. "Perhaps you could be kind enough to send a messenger to let them know she is safe and will be escorted home soon?"

"Of course. Our carriage will be at your disposal, Miss Austen," Lord Westworth said, frowning as he looked at her directly. Jane could only imagine what she looked like after spending time lying in the undergrowth.

There was a flurry of activity with the man being taken into the drawing room, handled roughly by the footmen. So far, he had not uttered a single word, but had only looked defiantly out from hooded eyes, glaring at anyone who dared to make eye contact.

"Where did you find him?" Lord Westworth peered at his back as he disappeared into the drawing room.

"In the folly at the eastern border of your estate."

"He had been sleeping there?"

"Yes, so it appears. He had a bundle of clothes with him, although it would have been extremely uncomfortable in these freezing temperatures we've been having."

"It's a surprise he survived so long out there."

Lord Hinchbrooke inclined his head and then caught Jane's eye, looking at her thoughtfully. She wondered if she might be banished from the investigation for her lack of care for her own safety, but the magistrate seemed to accept her need to see this through and gave her a subtle nod of acceptance.

As he stepped forwards, she followed him and together they walked into the drawing room after their captive.

"Please take a seat, Mr…?" Lord Hinchbrooke said, shutting the door firmly behind him once the footmen had left. For a second the man hesitated, then seemed to decide there was no point in denying himself a comfortable seat for a few moments. He must know soon enough he would be locked in a cold and uncomfortable cell where there would be no upholstered armchair for him to rest on.

He did not offer up his name, instead staring into the fire as if it were inviting him in.

"My name is Lord Hinchbrooke, I am magistrate for this area. What is your name?"

The man remained silent, his eyes not wavering from the fire. His body was stiff and upright and Jane could see his hands were clenched together in his lap.

"I am sure you are aware this is a serious situation," Lord Hinchbrooke said softly, his voice not showing any of the frustration he must surely feel. "There has been a murder and you have been caught hanging around the place the murder was committed. It would be better for you to cooperate. Tell me your name and your business here in Steventon."

Still there was silence and Lord Hinchbrooke leaned forward in his chair.

"Of course, this murder may have nothing to do with you and if that is the case then I would urge you to tell me everything now so we can work on getting to the truth of the matter."

This time there was not even a flicker of acknowledgement in the man's eyes. He remained distant and aloof and Jane wondered if he truly understood the gravity of the situation.

Here he was, a stranger in Steventon. A man no one knew and no one could vouch for. He had trespassed on Lord Westworth's estate, stayed without permission in the folly. In itself this was a crime, but it was nothing compared to murder.

"Can I tell you about my friend?" Jane said quietly, not waiting for a response. "Miss Roscoe was the sweetest, kindest young woman you could hope to meet. She would think nothing of walking for two hours to visit a sick or elderly acquaintance to bring them some bread and cheese in their hour of need or stopping off at the house of a new mother to watch the baby whilst the mother caught up on her household chores." Jane paused, making sure the man was listening. Even though he wasn't looking at her she could see from the frown on his brow he was taking in her words. "Miss Roscoe was eighteen years old and in love. She had her whole life ahead of her." Jane brushed a tear from her cheek, not wanting to let this man see her cry. "Now she is dead. Never will she marry or have children of her own, never again will she spread happiness and charity throughout the community. Never will she grow to realise her great potential, to fulfil the plans she had made for her life as she became an adult. All I wish is to know what happened to her, to find out the truth."

Jane stood and approached the man, trying to hide her own fear and trepidation. He had not hesitated to hit her over the back of the head with a tree branch. It would be beyond foolish to try and hurt her here whilst under guard at Lord Westworth's house, but the situation was dire and he might strike out.

"Please," she said, kneeling down in front of him, low enough so she could meet his eye.

For a moment his gaze flicked to hers and she saw the mixture of panic and desperation there, quickly hidden behind a veil of nonchalance. Despite her plea he still did not speak and after thirty seconds Jane stood up and returned to her seat.

"At least tell me your name," Lord Hinchbrooke said, and Jane marvelled at his ability to keep completely calm in the face of such a stubborn refusal to communicate. "I have been doing this a few years now," the magistrate said slowly, his eyes not wavering from his prisoner. "And I know how these things go. It is hard to defend yourself against an allegation such as this. Murder is a serious business and it is treated accordingly in the courts. A man who refuses to speak, to offer his name, to give even a brief explanation as to why he was in the vicinity of the crime, he will not fare well."

When it became apparent that nothing was going to persuade the man to open his mouth Lord Hinchbrooke stood and beckoned to Jane, motioning she should follow him from the room.

"We are getting nowhere," Jane said, letting the exasperation seep into her voice once the door was firmly closed behind them.

"I agree it feels pointless, but the decision to remain silent in itself is telling."

"It isn't telling me anything," Jane grumbled. She was damp from lying on the cold earth and her head was beginning to throb. Her neck felt stiff and a shooting pain travelled across her shoulders and into her arms with even the slightest movement of her head. In truth she wished she was at home, tucked up in bed with Cassandra bringing her a bowl of soup or a comforting cup of tea. This surprised her, for over the last few days she had wanted to be as close to the investigation as possible, poised and ready for any developments that might occur.

"He is guilty of something, or at the very least he knows something, otherwise why stay quiet."

Jane pondered this for a moment and realised the magistrate was right. If he was unconnected with Emma's murder, a vagrant passing through, caught at the wrong time in the wrong place, he would be quick to offer up an explanation, anything that might save him from appearing guilty and being charged with murder.

"We cannot forget the rupee we found in his belongings," Lord Hinchbrooke said.

"Perhaps…" Jane began slowly, wondering if it was too bold to offer forth her next suggestion. "Perhaps we could ask Mr Stanmore to come down to the drawing room and see his reaction to the man in custody?"

"To see if the India link is more than coincidence," Lord Hinchbrooke finished the thought for her.

"You don't believe in coincidences?" Jane said with a smile.

"No, I don't." Lord Hinchbrooke pulled aside one of the footmen standing guard and asked him to go and fetch Mr Stanmore urgently, but to say Lord Hinchbrooke had not said what it was in relation to.

They waited, Lord Hinchbrooke much more patiently than Jane. She could not stop herself from pacing backwards and forwards along the length of the hall, looking up with each creak of the stairs or shuffle of feet.

A couple of minutes later Mr Stanmore appeared, striding down the stairs as if he didn't have a care in the world. "I hear you've caught the murderer," he said, nodding in approval. "Good work."

Lord Hinchbrooke inclined his head but did not say anything, instead motioning for Mr Stanmore to follow him into the drawing room. Jane slipped in behind the two men, her eyes locked on Mr Stanmore's face.

"Is this him?" Mr Stanmore said, regarding the dishevelled captive with an air of distaste. Jane saw no flicker of recognition, no hint of panic, and her spirit sank. She had thought because of the Indian coin found in the vagrant's possessions he would have a connection to Mr Stanmore, and perhaps that connection would explain a little about who he was and why he was at Stanmore Hall. Of course, it was possible for an unsavoury character to have chosen the folly as his shelter at random and crept into Stanmore Hall to see what there was to steal. Emma could have disturbed him, but it didn't explain why he had a knife from the kitchen or what it was she had overheard.

Jane turned to Lord Hinchbrooke and saw the magistrate's eyes had been locked not on Lord Stanmore but on their captive.

"I see it now," he said quietly.

"What do you see?" Mr Stanmore asked, his voice nonchalant.

Jane frowned, perhaps he was trying to be a little too casual.

"The family resemblance. I thought this man looked familiar when I first laid eyes on him, but I couldn't quite place where I might have seen him before. Of course, I hadn't, but I'd seen someone who looked enough like him that it felt as though we had met before."

Mr Stanmore took a long, hard look at the man who had been living in the folly and then gave a humourless laugh. "I am trying my hardest not to be too insulted, Lord

Hinchbrooke, but you have just compared me to a vagrant, a homeless criminal."

Jane peered at the two men. There was perhaps a similarity in the shape of the eyes and the eyebrows, the same straight nose. It was hard to tell as one was neatly coiffed and the other looked like he was in dire need of a good bath and a shave. Still, she knew her role here and had enough faith in Lord Hinchbrooke to agree with him until she could question him in private.

"I see it now," she murmured, taking a step forward and allowing her eyes to flit between the two men. "It's the eyes, and perhaps the nose. There's even a hint of similarity in the shape of the mouth. Brothers would you say? Or cousins?"

"Brothers would be my guess."

Jane almost shouted in triumph as the man they had caught by the folly flicked an uneasy look at Mr Stanmore. It was so quick she almost missed it, but Lord Hinchbrooke nodded in satisfaction and she knew he has seen it too.

"You know this man, don't you?" Lord Hinchbrooke said, taking a step towards their captive. "You know him well. Consider his silence, his willingness to let you answer for every crime that has been committed here whilst he stands untouched."

"This is ridiculous," Mr Stanmore said. "I refuse to be insulted thus in my own home."

"Lord Westworth's home," Jane corrected quietly.

"Do not test my patience, Miss Austen." Mr Stanmore took a step towards the door. "I am not going to continue to engage with whatever it is you are trying to do. I suggest you focus on getting to the truth rather than accusing me of being related to a vagrant, or whatever this charade is."

He stormed out of the room and Lord Hinchbrooke let him go.

Jane sank down on the sofa in front of the prisoner. "He's older, isn't he? I have older brothers and an older sister. When we are all together, I feel like my life is not my own. They feel like they have a right to tell me what to do and how to do it. Coming from a parent is one thing, but a sibling? No, it is too much."

"I do not know that man." It was the first time their prisoner had spoken and Jane was surprised by his voice. It was deep and gravelly and hoarse from little use.

"Sibling fidelity is honourable," Lord Hinchbrooke said, "but you are likely going to swing for this murder. If there is more to it than a burglary gone wrong it would help your cause to be honest."

The prisoner pressed his lips together and looked away. It would seem he had said all he was going to.

"Come, Miss Austen, it is time you were getting home," Lord Hinchbrooke said, stepping out of the room and waiting for her to follow. "I will get this man to jail and hopefully tomorrow he will be more inclined to talk."

"What about Mr Stanmore?" Jane asked quietly, aware of the servants close by.

"We shall see what happens. He will have to have strong nerves to stay here now he knows of my suspicions that he is connected to our prisoner. His instincts will tell him to flee."

"Do you truly think they are brothers?"

"There is something highly suspicious going on here at Stanmore Hall and I don't think we have yet got to the bottom of it. I am convinced it has something to do with Mr Stanmore's return, but whether they are brothers…" He shrugged. "It was a ruse designed to inflame and heighten emotions. Now we wait to see what happens next."

As she collected her coat and gloves Jane felt overcome by a wave of exhaustion. Emotionally it had been a draining few days and although they had a suspect there was much yet left unexplained.

"Do you want me to accompany you home?" Lord Hinchbrooke asked, looking concerned as she swayed a little on her feet.

"No, thank you. See to your prisoner. All I need to do is sit in Lord Westworth's coach as it takes me home."

"I will send news of any updates, Miss Austen. Thank you for all your help."

Jane left the house, approaching the carriage and trying to ignore the pull back. Perhaps it was because everything wasn't wrapped up satisfactorily yet, but she didn't feel the relief she thought she would with the culprit in custody.

CHAPTER FIFTEEN

"Jane, you look terrible," Cassandra said as she rolled over in bed, her eyes flickering open in the early morning light.

"Go back to sleep," Jane murmured.

"And leave you like this. Have you slept at all?"

Shaking her head, Jane flopped back on the pillow. It had been days since her last proper night's sleep and it was taking a toll on her mind and body. Forming a coherent thought was like wading through treacle and her body was aching even though she had not done any excessive physical exercise.

Her fingers danced over the small lump at the back of her head. It had throbbed during the night, another thing to keep her awake, to remind her of the events of the last couple of days.

"Come here," Cassandra said, wrapping her arms around Jane and holding her. She sang, a quiet lullaby their mother had sung to them if there was a storm when they were children.

"What am I going to do without you, Cassandra?"

"You'll be fine. There will not be anyone stealing the blankets at night or snoring in the early hours keeping you awake."

Most of the time Jane tried to ignore the fact that her sister was engaged. One day soon she would be married, going off to run her own household and bring beautiful bouncing babies into the world. Although she would never begrudge Cassandra her happiness, Jane knew it would make her own life change beyond recognition.

"Anyway," Cassandra said with a sleepy yawn, "soon you will find a husband yourself and everything will be as it should."

Unbidden, an image of Mr Tom Lefroy popped into Jane's mind. She had been trying not to think of him, trying not to hope or dream. It felt wrong, to wonder about their future when Emma Roscoe was cold in the ground, but Jane knew one day she would have to try and put her guilt behind her and allow herself to live a normal life.

She waited until Cassandra had dropped back off to sleep before she rose, dressing quietly and then slipping downstairs. Today would be difficult, waiting for news that might never come. Lord Hinchbrooke would be busy with his prisoner and although she didn't doubt he would send her an update at some point, she knew it would not be at the top of his list of priorities.

After breakfast she helped to prepare the vegetables for lunch and when the work was done slipped out into the garden. It was still cold, almost unbearably so, but she didn't feel any great need to hurry back inside. She quite enjoyed the cold burn in her chest as the freezing air settled in her lungs and the sharp sting of the wind on her cheeks.

Her mother had just called her to come inside when there was a clatter of hooves on the road outside. Jane hurried through the side gate, eager to see if it was a messenger bearing news from Lord Hinchbrooke.

"We have a development, Miss Austen," Lord Hinchbrooke said, stepping down from his carriage. He looked older today, wearied and worn, and she saw he was finding even simple movements difficult. The past couple of days must have been a physical strain on the magistrate and Jane saw the wince of pain as he tried to get his muscles to obey his silent commands.

"What's happened? Has the prisoner escaped?"

"Nothing so dramatic. He is safe and secure in a cell at Winchester jail."

The front door opened and Jane's mother stepped out, looking from Jane to the magistrate.

"Good morning, Lord Hinchbrooke, please come inside. We can get you some tea to warm you up."

"Thank you, Mrs Austen, that is very kind of you." He glanced at Jane and she could tell he knew he needed to tread carefully with her mother when mentioning Jane's involvement in helping him investigate the recent murder. "But I regret I have been summoned to Stanmore Hall and must make haste there."

"Of course, my lord. Your duty comes first," Mrs Austen said.

Jane folded her hands in front of her, trying to look demure and innocent whilst also doing her best to convey how important it would be for her to accompany the magistrate.

"There are a few things I think I may need to clarify in the timeline of events with Miss Austen," Lord Hinchbrooke said slowly. "I wonder if she might accompany me to Stanmore Hall. I will, of course, ensure she is escorted home after."

"I am not sure that would be wise," Mrs Austen said. "The terrible events have had such an impact on Jane, perhaps it is better she keeps her distance now."

"Mother," Jane began, but was surprised when Cassandra came sailing out of the house, slipping into her coat as she did.

"I will accompany Jane, Mother. That way, once Lord Hinchbrooke has finished with his questions, I can see to it she comes back home and is not too overwhelmed."

Jane turned to her mother, trying not to look too keen.

"Very well," Mrs Austen said. "Be sure to stay together and listen to your sister, Jane."

"Yes, Mother."

Before Mrs Austen could change her mind Jane grabbed hold of Cassandra's hand and pulled her up into the carriage, watching as Lord Hinchbrooke raised his hat to her mother before climbing up behind them.

For a moment, as the carriage picked up speed, they sat in silence. Only once they were far enough away from the rectory that they could not be called back did Jane speak.

"What is happening?"

"Lady Westworth sent a message this morning, asking me to attend Stanmore Hall. A maid has found something, but she did not elaborate as to what."

"Did the prisoner say anything once you took him to the jail?"

"No, not even his name. I am hoping whatever this maid has found will shed some light on the matter or it is going to be hard to get to the truth, even when this goes to trial."

"You think you have the right man, Lord Hinchbrooke?" Cassandra said, her fingers pulling at the fabric of her dress nervously.

"I am certain this man is involved somehow and it is difficult to think of him as anything but guilty when he will not speak in his own defence."

"Thank you for calling for me," Jane said quietly, "and thank you for coming with me, Cassandra. I know Mother would not have let me come on my own."

"I know how restless you have been these past few days," Cassandra said quietly. "I hope if this matter can be laid to rest you will be able to let go of the guilt you feel."

Jane reached out and squeezed Cassandra's hand. Her sister was just as eager as she to see justice done for Emma Roscoe, but if it were Cassandra's choice, they would patiently await news at home rather than inserting themselves right into the middle of the investigation.

"I wonder," Cassandra said as the carriage rattled along the bumpy road, "why you called for my sister, Lord Hinchbrooke? I know why she is so eager to assist you, but I cannot fathom what it is that motivates you to include her in your enquiries."

Jane nudged her sister in the ribs, but it was too late, the question was already out there, hanging in the air, unable to be taken back. Of course, she had wondered the same over the past few days. Despite Lord Hinchbrooke's condition he was still perfectly capable of carrying out the more physical aspects of his investigation, and even if he had not been it wouldn't be her, a mere young miss barely out of the schoolroom, he would turn to. She had told herself perhaps it was her wit and intelligence, her quick conversation he admired and felt was an asset to him, but she knew this was unlikely the reason he let her accompany him. In truth she had decided not to question it too closely, aware she might not like any answer she received.

Lord Hinchbrooke cleared his throat and waited until she looked up at him to speak.

"Many years ago, when I was a studying at university, a friend of mine was stabbed in a tavern after hours. We had paid the innkeeper to lock the doors and keep serving us well into the early hours of the morning." He shook his head, taking a deep breath before continuing. "The only people in the tavern were our friends, a dozen or so people who were also studying at Cambridge, and of course the innkeeper, but he had stayed behind the bar all night."

"One of your friends had stabbed him?"

"Yes. I felt terrible; I had arranged the party, invited the group of gentlemen, encouraged everyone to drink their fill. It was a celebration of the end of our time at university you see, and everyone was rip-roaring drunk."

"You felt guilty?"

"As if I had stabbed him myself. For weeks I was obsessed with what had happened, I kept going back to the tavern, questioning my friends, pushing away the people I had lived the past four years with." The magistrate stared out of the carriage window, reliving events as if it were yesterday.

"What happened? Did you find out who had killed your friend?"

"No. Never. I had my suspicions, but the crime was never solved, no one was brought to justice."

"And you've carried it with you ever since."

"I have. So, you see, Miss Austen, I understand what it is like to be personally invested in finding the truth, in bringing justice to a cruel world, and I know how it haunts you if a crime like this is not solved."

"Thank you for understanding," Jane said, looking across at the older man. It was rare to find someone so attuned to the feelings of others, and so willing to act in a way that made allowances for that.

The carriage turned into the long drive leading up to Stanmore Hall. The grounds were quiet, with no one in sight. Everything looked pristine and Jane wondered how many gardeners it took to maintain an estate like this.

Lord Westworth came bursting out the door to meet them before the carriage had rolled to a stop, looking agitated. "Come in, come in," he said, barely acknowledging Jane or her sister, so eager was he to get the magistrate inside.

"What has happened?"

"I never thought it would lead to this," Lord Westworth said, shaking his head. "I can't quite believe it."

Cassandra squeezed Jane's hand as they moved from the hall to the drawing room and then slipped away, no doubt to find a quiet corner to sit herself in whilst the events of the morning unfolded.

"Tell me what has happened."

"First I will get my wife, so you do not get the story second hand."

Lord Hinchbrooke sank down into an armchair as they waited and Jane perched on an upright chair. The magistrate looked exhausted and Jane could see he struggled to keep his posture erect as the fatigue overcame him.

"Thank you for coming, Lord Hinchbrooke," Lady Westworth said as she sailed into the room. Her face was pale and drawn and there was a hint of red around her eyes as if she had been crying. "I have Rebecca, one of our housemaids waiting outside, but she is nervous and I said I would speak to you first."

"There has been a development," Lord Westworth said, his expression grim. "One I barely can bring myself to believe."

"Tell me," Lord Hinchbrooke said.

"Early this morning, Rebecca went into Mr Stanmore's bedroom. She lays the fires every morning upstairs before the rest of the household is awake," Lady Westworth said, reaching out for her husband's hand. He squeezed it reassuringly and Jane realised it was the first sign of affection she had seen between them. "Mr Stanmore often rises early to ride or walk, even when it is freezing outside, so whilst the bedroom was empty Rebecca decided to quickly straighten things out a little. There was a shirt over the back of a chair and she returned it to the wardrobe." Lady Westworth paused and Jane could see they were coming to the important bit of the story. "As she was about to close the wardrobe door something in the corner caught her eye. It was another shirt but screwed up and crammed into the corner behind a box. Of course, she took it out, thinking she would see it was laundered and returned, but what she found was a shirt covered in blood."

"In Mr Stanmore's wardrobe?"

"Yes."

"Do you have the shirt?"

"I will get someone to fetch it."

Lady Westworth pulled the bell cord in the corner to summon a footman and instructed him to bring the shirt in question.

"What happened after the maid found the shirt?"

"She brought it to me. Thankfully Mr Stanmore was still out riding and I could show my husband before he came back."

Lord Westworth nodded, taking up the tale. "It looked mighty suspicious, there was no denying it. Of course, there could be an innocent explanation for blood on a shirt, but that much? And if it were something innocent why hide it?"

"Mr Stanmore returned home?"

"Yes, I confronted him and he became damn shifty. Started yelling and saying no one had any right to poke through his wardrobe. Denied the shirt was his at first, but once I made him look at it he accepted the shirt was his but said he hadn't a clue how the blood had come to be there." Lord Westworth shook his head. "I said he'd better stay put until we could get you to come and sort everything out, but he refused to stay."

"He's gone?" Jane asked, unable to stay quiet any longer.

"No, I summoned a couple of our footmen and we managed to subdue him. Currently he's locked in one of the storerooms downstairs. I wanted to keep him somewhere he couldn't easily escape out of a window."

At that moment the footman returned with the shirt and immediately Jane felt her stomach heave. Normally she wasn't squeamish, but the thought this was likely Emma's blood she was looking at made her stomach roil.

Lord Hinchbrooke stood and took the shirt from the footman, moving stiffly over to the window to examine it properly. Jane moved with him, watching as he opened out the shirt, revealing the rust brown colour of dried blood in a bloom in the middle. There were some drops of blood on the sleeves as well and a few splatters leading out from the middle.

"That is a lot of blood," Jane said quietly. "More than you would get from a shaving cut."

"The maid is waiting?"

"Yes," said Lady Westworth. "Shall I bring her in?"

"Please."

The young woman looked petrified as she entered the room and her eyes widened as they settled on the shirt.

"It is Rebecca, is it not?" Lord Hinchbrooke said in his kindest voice.

The young woman nodded.

"Please come and sit down, I think you have had a terrible shock today."

She sat, her hands clenched before her and her eyes flitting about the room.

"I understand you found this shirt whilst tidying up Mr Stanmore's room?"

"Yes, my lord."

"Can you tell me exactly what happened?"

The maid nodded but didn't speak for a minute, her eyes seeking out reassurance from somewhere in the room. Lady Westworth gave the young woman a little nod.

"My first job of the morning is to clean and set the fires for the day. Mostly I do this while everyone is sleeping, but Mr Stanmore is always an early riser." She paused, biting her lip. "When I went in, the room was a bit of a mess and I thought I would tidy up a little. Mr Stanmore doesn't have a valet and I thought I would take anything that needed washing or mending downstairs with me."

"He doesn't have a valet?" This question was directed to Lord Westworth who shook his head.

"He didn't want one. When I found him in India, he told me he had never had a personal servant and he wasn't about to start at this point in his life."

Jane edged forward in her seat, wondering if the lack of valet was significant.

"I folded up a few things, straightened out the bedsheets that were hanging on the floor. His room would be properly seen to later in the morning, but I thought I would make it a little more presentable whilst I was there." Rebecca paused and looked up at Lord Hinchbrooke.

"Go on."

"I opened the wardrobe to put something away and before I closed the doors a flash of white caught my eye in the corner. It was tucked away behind some boxes as if hidden. When I pulled it out, I found that shirt."

All eyes turned to the bloodstained shirt still in Lord Hinchbrooke's hands.

"Do you go into Mr Stanmore's room every day, Rebecca?" the magistrate asked.

"Yes, my lord, always to set the fire and sometimes to clean and make the bed later in the morning."

"When did you last open his wardrobe?"

The maid frowned and shook her head. "I don't know, my lord."

"I am trying to work out when this shirt was stuffed into the back of the wardrobe — if you had perhaps noticed it or not noticed it any other day."

"I couldn't say, my lord."

"Thank you for your help," Lord Hinchbrooke said, smiling reassuringly at the young woman.

"Yes, well done, Rebecca," Lady Westworth said. "Take the rest of the day off. Go and see your family but make sure you are back before dinner tonight."

"Yes, my lady. Thank you, my lady." Like a scared rabbit, the maid scuttled out of the room.

"Well, what do you think?" Lord Westworth said as the door closed behind her.

"It is interesting," Lord Hinchbrooke said. "Certainly, it is the most convincing piece of physical evidence we have found in this case."

"I can barely believe it," Lord Westworth said, and Jane noticed Lady Westworth lay a hand on her husband's arm. "I find myself wary of this man all of a sudden, when he has lived in our home for the past two months."

"You are doubting that Mr Stanmore is your brother?"

The silence stretched out before them as Lord Westworth struggled to find the right words. "The man I saw earlier today, the half-crazed, defiant character, *that* did not ring true to me," he said eventually. "There is something very wrong going on here."

"I think perhaps it is time I ask Mr Stanmore for the truth in the face of this new evidence." Lord Hinchbrooke regarded Lord and Lady Westworth. "I am sure you are as eager as I to get to the bottom of this, but I beg your indulgence a little longer. I think it would be best if I asked you to wait outside whilst I question him. He may feel less threatened than if we are all here staring at him."

"You will give me a frank and honest account of everything he has to say for himself?" Lord Westworth said after a moment's pause.

"Yes."

He nodded and offered his arm to his wife and reluctantly they both made their way to the door. "I will see he is brought up. There will be two footmen outside if you need them."

Lord Hinchbrooke looked over at Jane as they were left alone in the drawing room and gave her a reassuring smile. "I think finally we may be peeling away the layers of deception and getting to the truth."

"I think you may be right," Jane said.

CHAPTER SIXTEEN

Mr Stanmore came calmly, flanked by two footmen. His hair was dishevelled and his cheeks flushed, but he was not ranting or raving. As he entered the drawing room he took a moment to straighten his shirt and run his fingers through his hair, making his appearance a little more acceptable.

"Lord Hinchbrooke, Miss Austen," he said, nodding in greeting. The door closed softly behind him and Lord Hinchbrooke motioned for the man to have a seat.

"I understand it has been an eventful morning," Lord Hinchbrooke said.

"Indeed. I have at least learned the level of trust my brother has in me."

"I think perhaps now is the time for the truth, Mr Stanmore," the magistrate said, his voice low but steely.

For a long moment Jane thought the gentleman might refuse to say any more like the prisoner in jail in Winchester, but after a few seconds of contemplation he nodded and spread out his hands as if inviting Lord Hinchbrooke's questions.

"You have seen the shirt found in your wardrobe?" Lord Hinchbrooke asked.

"Yes."

"Can you tell me how it came to be there?"

"Devilled if I know," Mr Stanmore said, shrugging.

"Is it your shirt, Mr Stanmore?"

"I believe so."

"How did it come to be covered in blood?"

"I don't know."

"You haven't cut yourself and used the shirt to soak up the blood?"

"No, unfortunately not."

"Given the events of the past week I think it is safe to say the blood is likely to be Miss Roscoe's, and her killer was probably wearing the shirt in question when he stabbed her."

"I would assume you are right, but it wasn't me."

Lord Hinchbrooke regarded the man for a moment and then shook his head. "You're lying to me, Mr Stanmore; you've been lying to me all along. Now is the time to tell the truth. Lay to rest every deception and let us see what we can salvage from the truth."

There was a heavy silence and Jane felt the tension building in the room.

"You can sit there looking at me for as long as you want, *my lord*, it isn't going to make me say something."

Jane shifted in her seat. Gone was the polite if stiff man she had strolled with in the gardens a few days ago and she wondered if Lord Hinchbrooke was right, if this was all an act. "You're not Mr Stanmore, are you?" She spoke quietly, but both men turned to her and gave her their full attention. "You're not Mr Stanmore, Lord Westworth isn't your brother, and you never spent years in India not knowing who you were."

"What makes you say that, Miss Austen?" Mr Stanmore replied.

"All along something has felt off, as if you were an actor in a play. You always delivered your lines on time, spoke the words you were supposed to, but there was an emptiness behind it all. You don't belong here."

Mr Stanmore raised an eyebrow. "I think it is you who does not belong here, Miss Austen."

"You're right, I don't. This isn't my world, the world of grand drawing rooms and dozens of servants and seven courses to every meal." She paused and looked Mr Stanmore squarely in the eye. "I do not belong here, but it makes it easier for me to see that neither do you."

Mr Stanmore regarded her with a mildly bored expression.

"That bloodstained shirt was found in your room," Jane said, indicating the fabric folded next to Lord Hinchbrooke. "You are going to be charged with murder whether you tell the truth or not, but a judge and jury will not look kindly on a man who has continued to lie and deceive. *If* you are innocent of this crime, the best way to prove it is to lay out the whole truth, to be completely honest, so there is no deception left. Only that way will we be able to see what has happened and clear your name if you did not stab Miss Roscoe."

For a long moment Jane thought the man was going to just sit there, staring at her with that sardonic half-smile of his. She could see him weighing up his options and tried not to hold her breath, hoping at last they might get to the truth.

"You're right, I don't belong here," he said quietly after a whole minute of silence.

Jane felt her heart skip a beat. Finally, they were about to get some answers. Her eyes kept flicking back to the bloody shirt and she wondered if in half an hour the whole mystery would be laid to rest.

"My name is Phillip Lanbridge."

"I think you should start at the beginning, Mr Lanbridge," Lord Hinchbrooke said, "And tell us the whole story."

"The whole story," Mr Lanbridge repeated with a shake of his head and a smile that didn't reach his eyes. "What is the point? Someone is trying to pin this murder on me; my life story isn't going to help."

"It will help us understand," Jane said. "At the moment it seems madness to impersonate a man who was missing for twenty years, but I feel you had your reasons."

"If you want the whole story we have to go back many years, to when I was little more than a boy."

Jane and Lord Hinchbrooke sat silently, waiting for Mr Lanbridge to gather his thoughts.

"I expect you have heard some of the rumours about the Stanmore family. They are rich, obscenely so, but that wealth was not all made in ways that would be considered moral or just. Twenty-six years ago, my father was persuaded to invest his money in a venture of the late Lord Westworth. He wanted to branch out into shipping and he persuaded my father and a few other investors to back his company. There was a lot of money to be made, he said, and they were going into it at just the right moment.

"My father ploughed all our money into it, more than he could really afford to, but Lord Westworth was an old friend and he trusted him." Mr Lanbridge snorted. "It all went wrong quickly. There were some unanticipated storms, a few spoiled consignments. Soon the company folded and the money my father invested was lost."

"And Lord Westworth?" Jane asked, her brow furrowed. The family had lived on the land for many generations and had never appeared to struggle for money.

"Somehow he protected his investment by sacrificing his old friends. He had been very careful, very clever, and had his lawyers draw up documents that meant he lost very little whereas his investors were left destitute." Mr Lanbridge shook his head as he continued. "All my family was left with was a parcel of land in India. In a final insult Lord Westworth offered to buy it from my father for less than it was worth, but he was forced to agree for a quick sale. That money was all he had to support his family."

"That's terrible," Jane said quietly. She knew people could be heartless, but to act so dreadfully and then abandon an old friend was beyond awful.

"My father passed away a couple of years after and my brother and I set off into the world with hardly a penny to our names. In an absurd twist of fate, we ended up on a ship sailing for India with young Edward Stanmore.

"At first we could not believe the cruelty of fate. Stanmore was heading to India to inspect the land that his father had bought from ours. It was inconceivable."

"What happened?"

"We were young, battered by the downfall of our family, but we were not bad men. We befriended Stanmore but kept our identities secret. At first, we thought we might perhaps be able to trick this foolish young man into giving us our land back somehow, certainly nothing more nefarious."

"What *did* happen?" Lord Hinchbrooke said, leaning forward in his chair.

"We offered to accompany Stanmore on his trip across India, to act as his guide. My brother had visited the country once before and thought he could remember enough of the journey to be convincing."

A sense of impending doom seemed to be mounting from the story and Jane had to resist the urge to get up and start pacing the room. She hated the tension, but didn't want to do anything to throw Mr Lanbridge off his stride.

"Halfway into the journey Stanmore took ill. He became delirious with a high temperature and soon it became apparent he was not going to survive. We debated trying to transport him back to Surat, to seek medical attention, but by that time it was too late. He died a hundred miles from Bombay."

"You didn't kill him?" The question slipped out before Jane could stop it.

"No, of course not."

"But you didn't save him either," Lord Hinchbrooke said quietly.

"No. It probably wouldn't have made much difference. He died quickly, there was no time to get him to a doctor. We buried him and then we got on with our lives."

"That was twenty years ago," Lord Hinchbrooke said. "How did you come to be here?"

"Two years ago, my brother came to me. He was destitute and desperate. He'd lost his wife and wanted to give his children a better future than he'd managed to scrape together for them so far. He suggested we extort some money from the new Lord Westworth, perhaps ask him for a payment in return for the truth about what had happened to his brother."

Jane watched as the man in front of her shifted in his seat. She could see that despite being caught, despite the stress of the last year, he still enjoyed the thought of getting revenge on the family who had so carelessly ruined his father's life.

"We had got to know Edward well; we knew of his childhood, of his family, his education. I thought I could mimic some of his characteristics, enough to convince a man who had last seen his brother decades ago, when he was but a child."

"And the story about the concussion and memory loss?"

"Something to cover any gaps. Of course, Lord Westworth was highly suspicious at first, but little by little I succeeded in breaking down those doubts."

"What was the plan?" Jane said softly, not wanting to break his flow now he was talking so openly. "To claim the title off Lord Westworth?"

"No, nothing so ostentatious. In a year or two, Lord Westworth and I would agree on a suitable settlement. Perhaps a country house and a generous annual income. Unlike the late Lord Westworth, I have no desire to destroy this family, only to reclaim what is rightfully mine."

"And the man I have in jail in Winchester?" asked Lord Hinchbrooke.

"My brother, Oliver. We agreed he would stay close in case anything happened. At first he took rooms nearby, but the money ran out, so we had to come up with another solution. He decided to make the best of it and sleep in the folly."

It was a fascinating story and Jane would love to have heard every little detail, but she couldn't stop thinking about Emma Roscoe and the fact that this seemingly cultured man, or perhaps his brother, had stuck a knife into her as if she were worth nothing.

"Which of you killed Miss Roscoe?" Jane said, her voice quiet but firm.

His reaction seemed one of genuine surprise and Jane had to remind herself he was a consummate actor. "No, you have it wrong. Neither of us killed Miss Roscoe. I have been completely honest with you. I admit the deception, I admit the plan of trying to extort money from Lord Westworth, but I had nothing to do with the death of Miss Roscoe."

Lord Hinchbrooke sat back in his chair and steepled his fingers together. "I can see a scenario," he began, speaking slowly as if following a train of thought in the moment, "of you sneaking out to meet your brother on the night of the ball. I expect it was pre-arranged, you knew Lord and Lady

196

Westworth and their servants would be preoccupied with the guests arriving, it was a safe time to tell everyone you had a headache and slip away for half an hour."

"No," Mr Lanbridge said, shaking his head vehemently.

"You went out to the orchard and met with your brother as arranged, but whilst you were there you were seen or perhaps overheard by Miss Roscoe."

Jane nodded; Mr Tinker had told of how Miss Roscoe had hung back as they made their way back to the house. It would have been confusing for her to see the brothers greeting one another. No wonder she had returned to the ball so flustered.

"The orchard?" Mr Lanbridge said, and then shook his head again. "No, it didn't happen like that. It didn't happen at all. I didn't even know who Miss Roscoe was, I'd never met her."

"It wouldn't matter. You would have recognised her from the sighting in the orchard and could have watched for her at the ball. Then, when she went to the library to meet Miss Austen, you took advantage of her being alone and stabbed her with a knife from the kitchen."

"No. It's not true."

He sounded so earnest Jane almost believed him, but she knew he had a talent for deception, having fooled a man like Lord Westworth for many months.

"You have a motive," Lord Hinchbrooke said quietly. "At a trial that would be enough, but we also have the bloodied shirt secreted in the wardrobe of your room."

"Someone must have put it there."

The magistrate motioned to shirt beside him. "Take a look at the shirt and tell me if it is yours."

"Lord Westworth showed it to me earlier."

"Take another look."

They watched as Mr Lanbridge rose and took hold of the shirt. Jane could see his hands were shaking as he realised the implication of this bit of evidence. It would be this that sent him to the gallows.

"Is it your shirt, Mr Lanbridge?"

"Yes. At least, I think so."

"Do you have an explanation for the blood?"

"No."

"Talk me through your movements on night of the murder." Lord Hinchbrooke leaned forward in his chair and Jane found herself doing the same.

Mr Lanbridge hesitated and Jane knew immediately that he was constructing a lie. Perhaps with some truth added in, but whatever came next was not the whole tale.

"As I said, I had a headache. I spent the evening in my room, trying to recover from that and then came down to the ball on hearing the commotion."

"You did not venture out of your room before that?"

"No, I did not."

"Believe me when I say the evidence against you is already enough to convict you for this crime, but if I can find one single person who can swear they saw you that evening before Miss Roscoe's body was found then it will be the bow on top of a well-presented case."

Mr Lanbridge nodded.

"If that is how you wish to leave things," Lord Hinchbrooke said quietly, "then I will arrange for you to be transported to jail. You will be reunited with your brother."

"You are making a mistake, my lord," Mr Lanbridge said, his expression sincere.

"Let us see what the courts think."

Lord Hinchbrooke stood and motioned for Jane to follow him from the room. She did so gladly, not wanting to be in the presence of such a devious man any longer.

Outside, the magistrate said a few words to the footmen and they stepped inside the drawing room to wait with the prisoner.

"What happened?" Lord Westworth said, hurrying from his study.

"I will be transporting Mr Lanbridge to jail to await trial for murder."

Lord Westworth shook his head in disbelief. "Lanbridge, eh?"

"You had your suspicions I think, Lord Westworth?"

"Not about the murder."

"But about his identity?"

"These last few days…" Lord Westworth said and then trailed off with a sigh. "I think I was very easily deceived."

"It is easy to be fooled when the lie is something we desperately want."

Lady Westworth descended the stairs and came to stand next to her husband. She looked pale, shaken from the events of the last few days. "I will be pleased to have an end to this terrible ordeal," she said, "and I hope the truth will give some comfort to Miss Roscoe's family. I always think not knowing is the worst kind of torture."

"Indeed. Can I ask one final indulgence?" Lord Hinchbrooke waited for the viscount to nod before continuing. "I would like to return Miss Austen and her sister home and collect a couple of my men for the transfer of the prisoner to jail. Your footmen seem to be very capable, are you happy for me to leave Mr Lanbridge in your custody for an hour, perhaps two?"

"Of course. I will see he is well guarded," Lord Westworth said, bowing his head.

"Thank you."

They collected Cassandra on the way out and all ascended the steps to the carriage in silence.

"It is resolved then?" Cassandra asked, leaning forward.

"It is resolved. The man claiming to be Edward Stanmore is not the real Edward Stanmore, he is Mr Lanbridge, a man trying to con his way into some of the Stanmore family money," Jane said, feeling a little overwhelmed from the morning's events. "He has not admitted to the murder, but has admitted the truth about the deception around his identity."

"You believe him to be the murderer though?"

"Yes," Lord Hinchbrooke said. "I do. I think Miss Roscoe overheard some discussion between Mr Lanbridge and his brother, the ruffian we have already in custody, and she must have realised he was not who he claimed to be. When Mr Lanbridge realised the scheme he had dedicated this past year to was about to unravel, he killed Miss Roscoe to stop her from telling anyone what she had heard."

Jane nodded. It all made sense. Yet she couldn't shake a nagging feeling that it wasn't quite as simple as that. There was something that didn't sit right.

"Why would he leave the shirt in his own wardrobe?" Jane said after a few moments.

Lord Hinchbrooke frowned and then shrugged. "You would not believe the stupid things people do, Miss Austen. They think they are untouchable, that they have got away with the crime, that they have outwitted everyone."

"Mr Lanbridge managed to deceive Lord Westworth for almost a year as to his identity, he was thorough, meticulous, and yet he leaves an incriminating piece of evidence in his own wardrobe." She shook her head, she couldn't quite believe it, no matter what Lord Hinchbrooke said. "It is hardly as if his bedroom was a private place. Even without a valet, the maids come in to clean and straighten things a couple of times a day. It was inevitable the shirt would be found."

"Perhaps he stashed it there temporarily and was planning on getting rid of it when there was not quite so much scrutiny around the house."

Jane was not convinced. It seemed such a big mistake for a man who had made hardly any others.

"It sounds like we should be thankful he did not get rid of it," Cassandra said. She was looking out of the window and Jane could see the strain on her face. In her focus on trying to find the murderer, Jane hadn't stopped to think how Cassandra might be feeling. She pressed her lips together and reached out for Cassandra's hand. She squeezed it, trying to convey the love and affection she felt.

"Let us hope we can lay the matter to rest," Lord Hinchbrooke said. "I would dearly love to be able to tell Miss Roscoe's family they can grieve their daughter without the shadow of an unknown killer looming over them."

"And Mr Tinker," Jane said quietly.

"Yes, and Mr Tinker."

They all fell silent, swayed by the rocking of the carriage, and Jane felt a great weariness descend on her. She felt as though she could sleep for days and wondered if it would be frowned upon to take to her bed this afternoon and not get up until the morning.

"Shall I call on you in a few days, Miss Austen?" Lord Hinchbrooke said as he helped Jane and Cassandra down from the carriage. "There are some formalities, things I need to prepare for this case to go before the Crown Court, but I will be able to spare some time in a few days for us to discuss how things are going."

"Yes, I would like that. What about the Roscoes?"

"I will pay them a visit once Mr Lanbridge is secure in a cell in jail."

"Good." Jane paused and then reached out for the magistrate's hand. "Thank you," she said softly. "I know this is not what is normally done, I know how many exceptions you have made for me, and I will not forget the kindness you have shown me."

"Look after yourself, Miss Austen, get some rest and try to think of something else other than this case and poor Miss Roscoe."

"I will."

CHAPTER SEVENTEEN

"Come, Jane, this is the event you have been looking forward to for weeks," Mrs Austen said, giving her youngest daughter an encouraging smile. "It will do you good to get out and stop moping around the house."

"I have hardly been moping," Jane muttered. The last few days she had been particularly industrious, drafting and re-drafting a chapter of *Elinor and Marianne*, screwing up the sheets of paper she wasn't satisfied with in a rare show of wastefulness.

"Mr Lefroy will be there," Cassandra reminded her sister with a smile.

Not wanting to show quite how much she was looking forward to seeing Mr Lefroy again, Jane continued scowling.

"Now, Jane, your mother is right. This matter with Miss Roscoe is terrible, but it cannot be your focus for evermore. It will make you ill, obsessing over it. Tonight at least try to put it from your mind." Mr Austen held up his hands to ward off the rebuke that was forming on Jane's lips. "I am well aware that Miss Roscoe will not be enjoying the Templeton's Christmas ball tonight and that her life was so tragically cut short, but perhaps that should instead prompt us to give thanks that we are still here, able to enjoy earthly pursuits for a little longer."

Jane closed her mouth and slumped back in her seat. It was impossible to argue with her father when he was so reasonable.

"Come, let me look at you," Mrs Austen said, prompting Jane to sit up straight. The truth was she was excited for the ball tonight.

"You look lovely, Jane," Cassandra said, squeezing her sister's hand and giving her a reassuring smile as the carriage slowed to a halt. It was just the four of them inside, with none of the Austen sons home for Christmas this year. It meant the house was unnaturally quiet, but her mother had promised a wonderful Christmas day feast and they would swap presents in front of the fire after the Christmas day service.

The carriage had been borrowed from Mrs Elliott, a close friend of Jane's. She had opted to stay at home as she had guests in residence, but had offered the carriage for Jane and her family to use for the ball.

The Templeton's house was lit outside by a dozen lanterns burning bright and Jane was struck to the similarities to the Westworth ball a few weeks earlier. She alighted the carriage behind her mother and father and together the family group entered the grand house.

Mrs Templeton was standing in the hall, greeting guests and directing them to the drawing room to the left. The house was large, but nowhere near as imposing as the Westworth's and instead of a separate ballroom the drawing room had been cleared of furniture and the big double doors that led into the dining room opened. It created a huge space and as yet there were not too many people inside.

"Miss Austen," a deep voice came from inside the drawing room.

"Mr Lefroy." Jane felt the familiar flutter of nerves as she spun and saw the young man standing to the left just inside the room. He headed directly for her, greeting Mr and Mrs Austen and Cassandra before stepping in to talk more intimately with her.

"There's Mrs Marwood," Mrs Austen said, gripping her husband determinedly by the arm and guiding him away. Cassandra shrugged and then followed her parents.

"That was artfully done," Mr Lefroy observed.

"I wonder," Jane mused, "if there is a pamphlet that is sent to all parents when they have their first child as to how to cause the most embarrassment through the different stages of their children's lives."

"At least they trust you to decide who you want to spend your time with."

"That is very true." She turned to Mr Lefroy, noting the casual way his hair flopped over his forehead.

"How many dances can I claim until it is thought too scandalous?"

"Two. Although I will be upset if we dance less than four together."

"The gossips will talk."

"The gossips always talk," Jane said, feeling reckless. Tonight, she wanted to forget about the events of the last few weeks, to dance until her chest was heaving and the blood pounding in her ears. She wanted to twirl and clap until all thoughts of Mr Lanbridge and his brother had left her and she could think of nothing but the next step of the dance or the face of her partner opposite her.

"I think we have a while until the dancing begins," Mr Lefroy said, offering her his arm. "Whilst the drawing room is quiet would you care to stroll around the perimeter with me?"

"That sounds lovely, Mr Lefroy."

As they walked Jane's eyes flitted over the rest of the guests, noting many of the same people that had been at the Westworth's ball. She was struck at how small their community was, how intertwined all the people were.

"I see you have stolen Miss Austen already," Mrs Anne Lefroy said as she spotted them. Jane immediately noticed that the older woman looked anxious.

"We are debating which dances we shall partner for," Mr Lefroy said, and Jane watched his aunt's face as he spoke. There was a pinched, concerned look that pulled at her mouth and Jane wondered if they were the cause of it.

"I am sure Miss Austen will have many young gentlemen clamouring for her attention tonight, Tom. You must allow her to dance with them too."

Jane felt a tension flow between aunt and nephew as Mr Lefroy murmured something too quiet for her to hear.

"You are wearing your pink dress trimmed with lace, Mrs Lefroy," Jane commented, trying to break through the tension. "It is one of my favourites and you look very well in it."

"Thank you, Miss Austen, it is kind of you to say."

A stilted silence followed and for a moment Jane felt like bursting into loud laughter it felt so unnatural. It wasn't in her nature to run from the difficult things in life, so she stood her ground, but felt a great relief when Mrs Lefroy murmured an excuse and moved on.

"What was that about?" Jane asked, turning to Mr Lefroy.

Mr Lefroy shook his head. "It doesn't matter. What matters is tonight, the hours I get to spend with you."

"It was very strange; I wonder if I have done something to offend her."

"I promise it isn't you."

Jane frowned, looking up at Mr Lefroy. He seemed to be suggesting it was he who had upset his aunt, which she struggled to believe as Mrs Lefroy only ever spoke of him in warm terms.

"Please forget about it," Mr Lefroy said, summoning a smile. "Tell me instead what has developed in your investigation with the magistrate. I hear rumours of an arrest."

"Lord Hinchbrooke has made two arrests," Jane said, allowing herself to be distracted. She welcomed the opportunity to talk of recent events with someone who had fresh eyes. There was something about the case that nagged at her, though what that something was she couldn't quite grasp.

"He is confident he has the right people?"

"He is."

"But you are not?"

Jane sighed and shook her head. "I don't know. It all fits, the two men had good motive to murder Miss Roscoe if she overheard their plan to swindle money from Lord Westworth, and they had the opportunity to do so. There is evidence of a bloodstained shirt which seems to tie everything together."

"And yet you are not convinced."

Jane sighed. "Imagine you have just committed a brutal murder; you have stabbed a young woman through the heart and whilst you have been unobserved, there is a ball going on in the rooms around you."

Mr Lefroy nodded. "Am I clear-headed and calm?"

"Yes, I think so. There is an element of planning to this, the killer brought the knife with them." She paused, trying to formulate the question she wanted to ask. "You have blood on your shirt, a lot of blood. What do you do?"

"I would hurry somewhere more private and change."

"Yes, what then?"

"Then I would destroy the shirt. Perhaps burn it if there was a fire, or place it somewhere private to get rid of later if there was no other opportunity."

"I thought the same."

"That isn't what the killer did?"

"No," Jane said, shaking her head. "He screwed it up and placed it in a wardrobe."

"Perhaps he was confident he could get rid of it later?"

"That's what Lord Hinchbrooke said."

Mr Lefroy paused, waiting for Jane to turn and look at him. "I suppose I should tell you that Lord Hinchbrooke is the expert," he said slowly, "and I do not dispute he is a good magistrate and the best person to investigate such a heinous crime, but sometimes you have to trust your own instincts. You know human nature, Miss Austen; you understand people and the funny ways they think and act. If you think there is something amiss with the conclusions Lord Hinchbrooke has come to then you have to speak out."

"I have no proof, nothing beyond the judgement that a man who had been otherwise so meticulous would not leave a damning piece of evidence to be found so easily."

"Then perhaps you need to revisit what you have been told by everyone. The details are what prove or disprove a story, see what doesn't match up."

Jane nodded, wondering how she was going to persuade her father that visiting a possible murderer in jail was an acceptable way for a young lady to spend her time.

"I am aware I have not known you for long, Miss Austen, but I feel as though I understand you. You are not going to be content with things as they are. It may be best to admit to yourself you need to know more, whatever the consequences, and just get on with it."

"Do your tutors teach you to speak so plainly?"

"No," Mr Lefroy said. "When studying law, it is made clear that the archaic language is there to act as a barrier between common man and the lofty matters of the law. My plain speaking is reserved for those I hold in truly high regard."

Jane felt the heat flood to her cheeks and had to turn away, glad there was only the muted candlelight to illuminate the room.

He let her consider his words, remaining silent for a few moments, until the first notes of music drifted through the room. "They will be calling the first dance soon," he said softly. "I would be honoured if you would agree to dance with me."

"Of course, Mr Lefroy, nothing would make me happier."

For the next fifteen minutes Jane did her very best to enjoy the moment. She laughed and twirled and stomped, clapped and paraded and smiled. She acknowledged the shadow of guilt she still carried about Emma's death and tried to put it to one side.

As the music slowed and the last notes faded away Jane drew in deep gulps of air. She enjoyed dancing, enjoyed the pure physicality of it, and Mr Lefroy was an energetic partner. Some gentlemen would ask her to dance and then half-heartedly drag their feet to the steps, but not Mr Lefroy. He had leapt around with her, laughing and joking and not seeming to care people were staring at them.

"You looked as though you enjoyed that, Jane," Cassandra said as she glided over to them. She had not been dancing but was one of the crowd of onlookers, although Jane did not doubt she would take to the dance floor later in the evening. Despite her engagement Cassandra was always popular amongst the local young men, she asked just the right number of questions, smiled encouragingly and made people feel at ease.

"It was wonderful," Jane said, finally getting her breath back.

"Good. You look happy." Cassandra smiled at Mr Lefroy, but Jane saw there was something in her eyes, something troubling. "Would you mind terribly if I borrowed my sister for a moment, Mr Lefroy?"

"Of course. I will see if my aunt needs anything. Until later this evening, Miss Austen."

Jane watched as Mr Lefroy slipped through the people gathered in little groups along the length of the drawing room. He moved quickly and she reminded herself he was used to navigating the busy streets of London.

"Walk with me, Jane," Cassandra said, linking her arm through her sister's.

"What has happened?"

"Nothing."

"You're acting strangely."

"Nothing has happened, but I do need to talk to you."

"You're worrying me."

"Perhaps we should sit down."

Jane allowed Cassandra to lead her to a row of chairs pushed back against the wall. A few were taken by some of the older women attending the ball, but there was enough space for them to sit in relative privacy.

"What is it, Cassandra?"

"What has Mr Lefroy said to you about his intentions, Jane?"

"What?"

"Has he promised you anything?"

Jane shook her head. "No, nothing."

Cassandra bit her lip, seeming to find it difficult to choose the right words. "Mrs Anne Lefroy is concerned by the attention he is paying you."

Jane balked. "She doesn't think I am suitable?"

The look of pity and kindness in Cassandra's eyes was almost enough to make Jane burst into tears, but she rallied quickly. No one here tonight would ever have the satisfaction of seeing her lose her composure.

"You know Mrs Lefroy thinks you are wonderful."

"I don't understand then."

"She is worried for you. There are expectations from certain members of his family that Mr Lefroy will marry well."

"Better than a rector's daughter from rural Hampshire."

Cassandra considered for a moment and then must have decided complete honesty was the best way to get through such a difficult conversation. "Yes."

"I see."

"Mrs Lefroy cares about you, Jane, she is worried the two of you are getting too attached."

"I have spoken to him a handful of times only," Jane said, trying to retain her composure.

"Yes, you have, but I can see the light in your eyes, that spark when you talk to Mr Lefroy. It is as if you come alive when you are with him."

"He has promised me nothing, and I know that means I should expect nothing."

"That may be so, but I can see you dreaming."

Jane shook her head, not sure if she was trying to deny what they both knew to be true or just wanting her sister to stop talking. Mr Lefroy *hadn't* promised her anything. He had offered good company, scintillating conversation and a partner for the dances that Jane had so enjoyed. Still, no one could deny there was a spark between them, a fizz and crackle every time their eyes met. When they had been dancing Jane had felt as though they were the only two in existence, her eyes locked on his, her thoughts consumed by him.

"You do not need to concern yourself, Cassandra. I will be realistic in my expectations."

"Jane, you know I would like nothing more than to see you settled and happy."

"For that to happen a suitable gentleman has to want the same." Jane held up her hand as she saw the flare of pity in her sister's eyes. "I am perfectly able to accept the truth of the situation, Cassandra, I will not pine for something that cannot be."

"Mrs Lefroy is distraught; she thinks her nephew has deceived you as to his intentions."

"He has not."

"Perhaps when Mr Lefroy has returned to his studies in London you might call on her and reassure her your friendship is unaffected."

"Of course I will."

Cassandra fell silent and for once there was an awkwardness between them. Jane looked around, trying to find some excuse to leave, to escape the press of the drawing room and be on her own for a few minutes.

Thankfully an acquaintance moved to greet them and after a couple of perfunctory remarks Jane made her excuses and left Cassandra to chat politely.

Trying to maintain her composure Jane hurried from the drawing room, cursing the equally packed grand hallway and dining room. There was a door to the left of the stairs that was shut and as she tried the handle she gave thanks it turned and she was able to slip inside.

The room was dark, disorientating so, and Jane had to wait for a moment to allow her eyes to adjust enough to make out the outlines of the furniture. It seemed to be a study and immediately her thoughts went back to the last room she had slipped into alone whilst a ball went on around her. Before she could stop herself her eyes were flitting over the floor, looking for anything that shouldn't be there. Of course there was no unmoving leg, no dead body, no dress with a bloom of blood.

Jane frowned; something was tugging at her mind, but she couldn't quite grasp hold of it — only a sense that she was missing something.

With a sigh she sat down, almost collapsing into one of the chairs. Only ten minutes ago she had felt as though she were soaring through the sky. Now she had crashed back down to earth and it was not a pleasant feeling.

"Hopes and dreams are what make us human," she murmured to herself. She told Cassandra most things, but never would she admit quite how infatuated she was with Mr Lefroy. Of course, he had promised her nothing and she now knew of his familial obligations, but still there was a part of her that was defiant and hopeful.

Closing her eyes, Jane tried to clear all thoughts of Mr Lefroy and dancing from her mind. The incongruous detail was still nagging at her and she knew she needed to pull at it to find out whether it was something worth pursuing. Perhaps it would be enough to stop her obsessing over Mr Lefroy.

Slowly, allowing her mind to linger wherever it wanted, she went over everything that had happened during the last couple of weeks, starting with the Westworth's ball and finishing with the arrests of the Lanbridge brothers. Of course, the shirt bothered her, but she had to accept that people did make mistakes and perhaps that was Mr Lanbridge's hubris, his feeling of being untouchable, that had meant he kept the shirt too long.

There was a noise outside the door and Jane's eyes flew open. She knew what it was that was niggling her.

"She didn't shout out," Jane said. Even though the library was set a little apart from the rest of the rooms that had been in use during the ball, Emma would have been heard if she had screamed. The music and chatter were not that loud to mask a cry of terror.

Emma hadn't known Mr Lanbridge. She had never been introduced to him as Mr Edward Stanmore. If he had entered the library whilst she was waiting there for Jane, surely Emma would have called out. Any young woman would be wary of a strange man in a darkened room, it didn't make sense she would have just stood there and waited for him to approach her. There was no sign of a struggle, no sign that Emma had tried to get away from her attacker.

She must have known whoever it was who stabbed her.

Standing abruptly, Jane felt the urge to act, to do something to prove her point but after a moment she had to acknowledge now wasn't the time. The Lanbridge brothers were being held in the jail in Winchester two hours ride away. Nothing would be achieved tonight, and storming through the middle of the ball declaring she did not think the right people had been arrested for Emma Roscoe's murder would cause panic. People would think her hysterical.

Taking a minute to compose herself, she straightened her dress and ensured her expression was serene before she stepped back out into the hallway. With her head bent and her movements swift she hurried back into the drawing room, hoping her demeanour would discourage any acquaintances from trying to engage her in conversation.

"Cassandra, we have to leave," she said, gripping hold of her sister's arm as she found her close to the dancefloor. The second dance was about to be called and Cassandra was with a gentleman Jane did not recognise.

"Is something amiss?"

"My head is pounding," she lied, smiling as sweetly as possible at Cassandra's companion. "I feel unwell."

Cassandra looked at her and apologised to the young man she was with. "Has something happened?"

"No," Jane said, wishing there weren't so many people in close proximity.

"I shall find our parents," Cassandra said, finally picking up on the air of urgency in Jane's voice.

"Thank you. I think I will wait in the hall."

Five minutes later Cassandra reappeared, her face a picture of concern. Mr and Mrs Austen were nowhere in sight, but Jane expected they were finding their host and hostess to apologise for their early departure.

"Mama and Papa will be here shortly," Cassandra said, before disappearing again to ask a footman to arrange for their carriage to be brought around. When she was back she took Jane's arm. "Did something happen with Mr Lefroy?"

"No."

"Oh, Jane, I am sorry."

"Nothing happened."

"You don't have to tell me."

"I haven't seen him since you dragged me away from him."

"Then what is all this?"

Jane leaned in closer and lowered her voice. "I was thinking about the arrests Lord Hinchbrooke has made and I think there has been a mistake."

"Jane, you need to stop."

Jane blinked. She knew it wasn't normal for a young woman to get involved in the investigation of a crime, it wasn't even considered proper for a young woman to show so much interest in something violent and unsavoury like this, but Cassandra had thus far been supportive.

"This isn't healthy, dwelling on it like this."

"I'm not dwelling."

"Lord Hinchbrooke, an experienced magistrate, is confident he has the right people in jail for the crime. They are awaiting trial and will be judged and sentenced for what they have done. There is nothing more for you to do, except mourn poor Emma and try to move on with your life."

"You don't understand…"

"I do, Jane. I understand your sense of guilt, this need to be doing something so you aren't left dwelling on what might have been if you had left the ballroom a few minutes earlier, but you need to accept what has happened. You can't change it."

"I am aware of that, Cassandra. That isn't what this is about."

Cassandra was prevented from saying anything further by the appearance of their parents in the hall.

"You do look pale, my dear," Mrs Austen said, taking Jane's hands in her own. "Perhaps it was a mistake coming to a social event when everything has been so hectic and trying recently."

"Perhaps," Jane murmured, pleased when her father announced the carriage was ready and they stepped out into the cold December air.

CHAPTER EIGHTEEN

The morning was grey and grim, the sky heavy with clouds, and already there had been a torrential downpour on the carriage ride to Winchester.

"We shouldn't be here," Cassandra fretted, wringing her hands together as they peered out the window of the carriage. The Winchester jail was situated in the middle of the town, a small, squat building that looked as though it had been built as a fortress. The walls were thick and the few windows were high and small with bars over them to prevent any possibility of escape.

Even from here Jane fancied she could smell the stench of men being held in crude conditions, the reek of human waste and despair mixed into one.

"I will not be long."

"Do not think for one second I am letting you go in there alone, Jane Austen."

Jane smothered a smile. Most people thought of her sister as the meek and mild one, the young woman who was obedient and happy. They never got to see this side of Cassandra, never experienced the steely will that was hidden underneath the layers of politeness and pleasantness.

"I doubt it will be an enjoyable experience," Jane said, wanting to spare her sister if she could.

"It will be no worse for me than for you."

"I suppose that is true." Jane hesitated, knowing she should stop delaying and go and see if they could gain access to the prisoner.

"I wonder if we should have asked Lord Hinchbrooke first," Cassandra said, following Jane's gaze.

"I have no real evidence, just a gut feeling, that we don't know the whole truth yet. Let us try and if we cannot bribe our way in then we can go to Lord Hinchbrooke." Before she could talk herself out of it Jane opened the door to the carriage and got out, waiting for Cassandra to join her before starting across the road.

The door to the prison was thick and old and Jane wondered if the accommodation for the local criminals had changed since medieval times. She banged loudly on the wood and was surprised to see a small hatch in the door open almost immediately.

"Yes?"

"My name is Miss Jane Austen; I am here to see Mr Lanbridge."

The hatch closed and for a moment there was silence. For the first time Jane doubted her plan, wondering if the guards might simply refuse to let them in. After thirty seconds there was the scraping of metal across wood and the door opened just enough for them to slip through the gap.

They entered into an archway with an open courtyard beyond. To one side was another heavy wooden door that looked as though it led to the guards' station, although the man in front of them must have been standing right by the door to respond so quickly.

"No visitors allowed," the guard said, scratching his oversized belly and regarding the two women in front of him with narrowed eyes.

"I only want a few minutes with him," Jane said, summoning her friendliest smile. She held out a few coins in her fingers. "I know it is an inconvenience, having to open up the cell, but I would really appreciate your help."

The guard took the coins, inspecting them and then giving a curt nod. Jane had debated how much to use as a bribe and settled on a middling amount that would persuade the guard to allow the visit without making it too obvious how desperate she was to talk to Mr Lanbridge.

"Which one do you want to see?"

"The one who came in second."

"Follow me."

Picking up their skirts to try and avoid some of the filth that lay on the ground Jane and Cassandra trailed the guard across the courtyard. He paused to open another door on the opposite side and ushered them into a dim corridor where the stench was even worse.

The jail wasn't big, but it did have a few separate cells and as they passed the wooden doors Jane realised these were all individual. The large communal cell used for the poor must have been situated elsewhere in the building.

"In here," the guard said, selecting a key from the hook at his waist and opening the door. "You've got five minutes."

Although Jane had been bracing herself against the shock of the conditions, she couldn't help the sharp intake of breath as they stepped into the cell. It was small, claustrophobically so, with light coming from a tiny window high up in the wall. In one corner was a straw mattress laying directly on the floor and in another a bucket that she assumed was for the collection of bodily functions.

She had last seen Mr Lanbridge a week previously, but even in that short time he had become unrecognisable. His hair was wild and matted, his clothes dulled with filth and his skin had a grey sheen to it.

"Miss Austen," he said, standing slowly as if it took his muscles longer to respond than normal.

"Mr Lanbridge." She trailed off, not able to bring herself to ask if he was well. A week in jail had almost broken the man, she dreaded to think what state he would be in by the time of the trial.

There was movement in the straw mattress and Cassandra yelped as a fat rat darted out and ran over her shoes.

"Sorry about that," Mr Lanbridge said, as though the conditions were his fault. "The rats like the warmth of the mattress."

"You do not look well, Mr Lanbridge," Jane said, unable to stop her eyes from darting around the cell looking for more rats. "Are they feeding you?"

"A ration of gruel and stale bread a day."

"Is that all?"

"Unless you have money to pay for more."

"Did you pay for an individual cell?" Jane had read about the communal cells and knew the risk of dying before trial was even higher if kept in with other prisoners. Disease spread quickly through prisons, claiming the lives of those already weakened by despair and lack of food.

"No, Lord Hinchbrooke insisted my brother and I were kept separately, I assume so we do not have the chance to confer before our trial." He stretched his neck to one side then the other. "Please do not think I am unhappy for a visit to break up the awful monotony of the days, but what are you doing here, Miss Austen?"

Jane cleared her throat, knowing she had to tread carefully if she were to get to the truth. She did not doubt Mr Lanbridge would protest his innocence whether he had stabbed Emma or not, he was facing months in squalid conditions followed by a trip to the gallows. Any sensible person with an ounce of self-preservation would declare their innocence no matter the truth.

"Miss Roscoe was my friend," Jane said. "I have known her my whole life. Every ball I went to, every summer picnic, every trip to town she would be there, smiling with a few friendly words."

"I am sorry for your loss, Miss Austen."

"I know nothing can bring her back, but more than anything I want to know what happened, what really happened."

"I can't help you with that," Mr Lanbridge said quietly, and Jane saw the flicker of his eyes. He knew something he wasn't saying, something that might change the outcome of this case.

"Did you kill her?"

"No."

"Do you know who did?"

There was the slightest pause, a momentary hesitation — enough for Jane to know she was on the right path.

"If you didn't kill her, what happened that night? Did Miss Roscoe overhear you with your brother in the orchard?"

"No."

"But you did go out to meet him?"

There was that hesitation again. Jane marvelled at how quickly he covered it.

"No," he said again, shaking his head. "My brother was nowhere near the house on the night of the ball." He paused, then added, "The night of the murder."

Jane screwed up her eyes for a moment, trying to place things in the right order in her mind. There were things that she and Lord Hinchbrooke had accepted as fact even though they had not been confirmed by witnesses. One of them was that Mr Lanbridge had gone to meet his brother in the orchard and it was this meeting Emma Roscoe had overheard.

She decided to bluff a little. A little white lie here and there was often necessary for a harmonious life in a busy household, so Jane was proficient at fibbing about minor things such as who had left the window open and allowed the heat to escape or what had happened to the plate of biscuits left to cool on the worktop in the kitchen. What she wasn't as practised at was telling the big lies, lies that deceived and tricked.

"You were seen leaving the house, Mr Lanbridge," she said, remembering to hold his gaze and not look away too quickly. "A witness will swear they saw you leave the house when you told us that you were upstairs with a headache."

For a long moment she thought he had seen through the lie, but as Mr Lanbridge lowered his head into his hands she found herself holding her breath.

"I did leave for a few minutes," he said slowly. "But I did not meet my brother."

"You went to the orchard?"

He scrutinised her face and then nodded abruptly. "Yes. I wanted some fresh air, so I went for a stroll. My path led me to the orchard."

"You weren't alone."

"My brother was nowhere near the house that night. I did not meet him."

"If it wasn't your brother…"

Mr Lanbridge shook his head. "You can try and pin this murder on me, but I refuse to drag anyone else into it."

"So, there was someone else?"

"That is all I am going to say on the matter, Miss Austen."

He sank down the wall, sitting on the edge of the straw mattress. It took him a while to get comfortable and Jane wondered if he would make it to trial. She wasn't sure of the dates, but a murder would need to be prosecuted by the Crown

Courts and that meant waiting for the assizes in a few months. He would be a shell of his former self by then.

"There is one more thing I don't understand, Mr Lanbridge," Jane said, crouching down so her face was on a level with his. Down low the stench was even worse and she was mindful to keep her balance as she did not wish to topple into the filth on the ground.

"It seems you will ask whether I give you permission or not, Miss Austen. What do you wish to know?"

"Why did you keep the shirt with the blood on it in your wardrobe?"

"Do you think I am a foolish man?"

"Not at all."

"I did not stab your friend, and if I had I certainly would not have placed the bloodied shirt I had worn whilst doing so in my own wardrobe. It is beyond madness."

"If you had killed Miss Roscoe and then noticed your shirt was covered with blood, what would you have done?"

"It was a cold night, the fire was burning in my room, I would have burned it. Or perhaps buried it when I went for a ride the next morning."

"You saw the shirt, was it one of yours?"

"Yes."

"Do you have any explanation for the blood."

"No."

"If you did not put the shirt there, then who did?"

Mr Lanbridge looked at her and frowned as she forced him to consider who might be trying to implicate him. Slowly he shook his head, murmuring under his breath, "Surely not."

"You know, don't you?"

"No. Now if that is everything, Miss Austen, I am a very busy man." With that he flopped back on the straw mattress and rolled over to face the wall.

Jane observed him for a moment and then went and knocked loudly on the cell door, hoping the guard would be able to hear her and let them out. She had the sudden urge to be free of the small cell, to be out in the fresh air with no rustling of rodents and stench of filth.

After a few seconds the guard approached and let them out, giving the prisoner a cursory glance.

"Before we go," Jane said as they walked back down the corridor towards the courtyard, "I would really appreciate it if I could speak with the other Mr Lanbridge briefly."

"He's in the communal cell."

"I do not mind."

The guard leered at her and then shook his head. "Wouldn't be safe. It isn't worth risking my job over."

Jane cursed herself for handing over all her money earlier without holding some back. To her surprise Cassandra stepped forward with some coins from her purse.

"Please," she said softly. "We will be quick."

The guard eyed the coins, unable to take his eyes off them for a moment and then nodded.

"Two minutes," he said, leading them back into the courtyard and then into a parallel corridor, unlocking and locking doors as he went. The smell down here was worse and every so often there was a faint moan, but whether of despair or pain it was impossible to know.

At the end of the corridor was another identical door which the guard paused in front of and banged loudly.

"Lanbridge, you have visitors. The rest of you stand away from the door. If anyone approaches, I will beat you until both your legs break."

He unlocked the door and Jane got her first glimpse inside the communal cell. It was dark and ominous and she shuddered as she looked into the shadows, knowing thoughts of what could be lurking there would haunt her for weeks.

"There he is," the guard pointed out, making no move to leave. Jane was glad, she didn't think she wanted to be locked inside here as they had with the other Mr Lanbridge. "Two minutes and that is it."

Mr Oliver Lanbridge was struggling to his feet, using the wall to steady himself. He looked dishevelled and unkempt, his hair matted and his beard already substantial. His eyes brightened in recognition of her for a moment and then despair seemed to settle on him again.

"Hello, Mr Lanbridge," Jane said quietly, taking a step towards him. As she moved she noted the other shapes in the cell. From this vantage point she could see three other prisoners, all men by the looks of it, all emaciated and dirty. It was impossible to tell what age they were, all had hunched backs and long, straggly hair.

None of them seemed overly interested in her or Cassandra, not enough to move them from their positions propped up against the walls.

"Miss Austen," Oliver Lanbridge said respectfully, his voice croaky through misuse.

"Are you well?" Jane knew it was a stupid question as soon as it passed her lips and she saw an amused smile pull at the corner of Oliver Lanbridge's mouth.

"As well as can be expected, Miss Austen," he said mildly. "I hope your head has recovered. I apologise for my actions. I panicked."

"Thank you."

"Have you seen my brother?"

"Yes."

"How does he fare?"

"He…" Jane hesitated, knowing the truth would be hard to bear. "He has his own cell." It was the best she could do.

Oliver Lanbridge grunted acknowledgement.

"I am trying to get to the truth, Mr Lanbridge," Jane said quietly. "I have no interest in the wrong people being punished for Miss Roscoe's death, I just want to know what happened."

"I did not kill your friend."

"That night, the night of the ball, the night Miss Roscoe was killed, did you meet your brother near the house?"

"No. Phillip told me to stay away. We knew the house would be heaving with people and as always happens at these events couples would slip off into the gardens for some privacy. Phillip said to stay hidden, to stay away for the night. I went nowhere near the house."

"You didn't even venture into the gardens? Perhaps the orchard?"

"I stayed at the folly. It was a damn cold night and I got next to no sleep, but I did not move from my makeshift home."

"We know your brother went into the gardens to meet someone," Jane said, lowering her voice further. "If it was not you, then who was it?"

Oliver Lanbridge blinked and shook his head. "No one. He wouldn't have been going to meet anyone."

"Time's up," the guard said, jangling his keys.

"Are you sure?" Jane persisted; her eyes fixed on Oliver Lanbridge's.

"I was in the folly on the other side of the estate, what need would my brother have to be out in the gardens?"

"Come Jane," Cassandra said, pulling on her sister's arm gently. "It is time to go before the good will of the prison guard is exhausted."

Jane allowed herself to be led away, turning her head as they reached the door. "Is there anything I can do for you, Mr Lanbridge?"

The man hesitated and then seemed to swallow his pride. "I have a second cousin in Bath. Mr Peter Kitts, he lives on Milsom Street. Write to him, ask if he will send money for my food and accommodation."

"I will do it today, Mr Lanbridge."

The door closed behind her and the guard turned the key.

"That was kind, Jane," Cassandra said, "especially after he attacked you."

"I do believe in the law and punishment," Jane said quietly, "but I do not think we should lose sight of our humanity in the process."

The guard grunted but didn't say anything, leading them out through a series of doors until they were in the street. Jane turned to thank him but already the heavy wooden door was swinging shut and the guard had disappeared back into the darkness.

"That was one of the worst things you've ever made me do," Cassandra said, shuddering as they stepped away from the jail.

"Only one of the worst?"

"It was horrific. Those poor men, how does anyone survive long enough to go to trial?"

"It's barbaric," Jane agreed, "especially if the man arrested is innocent."

"You think the Lanbridge brothers are innocent now?"

"Well, at least one of them is. They hardly could both have wielded the knife that killed Emma."

"True."

"I believed Mr Lanbridge when he said he wasn't going to meet his brother Oliver."

"Who was he going to meet then?"

"I don't know. We have no proof he was outside in the orchard even."

"They *are* criminals, Jane. This scheme to trick Lord Westworth into believing Mr Lanbridge was his long-lost brother, wheedling money from him, taking a dead man's identity. What are a couple more lies to men like that? You're overthinking this."

Jane turned to her sister and for the first time didn't try to suppress the raw emotion in her eyes. "I can't *stop* thinking about it, Cassandra. It plagues my thoughts every waking hour. I find myself picking over each piece of information, wondering if I have interpreted it wrong. Can you imagine…?" she trailed off.

"Can I imagine sending an innocent man to the gallows?"

Jane nodded, glad her sister was so attuned to her thoughts.

"I do not mean to belittle the role you have played in this, but it is not your responsibility to determine the guilt or innocence of these men. It is not even Lord Hinchbrooke's in this case. A judge will come, a jury. They will listen to the evidence and decide whether there is enough to convict Mr Lanbridge or his brother."

"You have heard how quick these trials are, how perfunctory. Many people think if the local magistrate is convinced he has the right person in jail that is evidence enough."

"What does Lord Hinchbrooke think? You've been impressed by his search for the truth — you should tell him your doubts and see how he reacts. He has been nothing but supportive up to now."

Jane bit her lip, knowing Cassandra was right. She should have gone to Lord Hinchbrooke first, asked him to arrange this little interview. "Do you think Mrs Elliott will object if we return her carriage a little later than planned?"

Cassandra glanced up at the clock just visible on the cathedral tower and shook her head. "I am sure another hour will make little difference. Mrs Elliott has guests visiting and she is hardly likely to want her carriage today."

"Thank you," Jane said quietly, starting across the street toward the waiting carriage. There was the risk their parents might question why they had been gone for so long when they had only been meant to be delivering the carriage back to Mrs Elliott and perhaps staying for tea, but the clouds had cleared to make way for bright sunshine, and she reasoned they could be convinced that she and Cassandra had taken a longer route back along the country lanes.

CHAPTER NINETEEN

"Miss Austen, you look as though you have had a shock. Is something amiss?" Lord Hinchbrooke emerged from a doorway as they were ushered into the grand hall. Petersfield House was large and imposing on the outside, but there was a sense of warmth and hospitality as soon as they stepped over the threshold.

Lord Hinchbrooke looked more relaxed and better rested than the last time Jane had seen him. He was dressed casually, with his shirt sleeves rolled up to his elbow and his cravat discarded, leaving the neck of his shirt open. He looked younger too and Jane realised how heavily his duties as a magistrate must weigh on him when there was a matter of such importance to look into.

"It is lovely to see you again, Miss Austen," Lord Hinchbrooke said, turning to Cassandra.

"I am sorry for calling uninvited," Jane said, knowing her mother would scold her if she ever found out she called on a viscount without the correct etiquette being followed.

"Nonsense," Lord Hinchbrooke said with a smile, "you are always welcome here, Miss Austen, think of it as an open invitation to call whenever you please."

"You are too kind, Lord Hinchbrooke."

"Now, why don't you join me in the library? It is my favourite room in the house and wonderfully warm with the fire burning. We shall have tea and cake and you can tell me what is bothering you."

Already Jane felt swept up by the magistrate's calm manner and kindness and as they walked towards the library she saw Cassandra relax as well.

"I have a confession to make," Jane said as she settled into the armchair Lord Hinchbrooke had guided her towards. She had slipped off her coat and gloves in the hall and now she loosened the shawl she had been wearing around her shoulders. The room was toasty and Jane could see why it was the magistrate's favourite. There must easily be a thousand books in the room, perhaps more. Shelf upon shelf was lined with beautifully bound volumes of different sizes. It would be a dream to sit here for a day, leafing through all the information contained in the pages of these books.

"You visited the Lanbridge brothers in prison," Lord Hinchbrooke said, his expression serene.

"How did you know?"

"There is a certain aroma I associate with that place," he shuddered. "On you it is subtle, but I can smell it all the same."

Cassandra looked down at her boots aghast and Jane reminded herself not to linger downstairs when they reached home in case her mother picked up on the same smell.

"The conditions there are horrific," Jane said quietly. She could still see the emaciated prisoners hunched near the walls in the communal cell.

"I know. It is something I have tried to tackle many times, but without a complete overhale of our justice system I think it will be close to impossible to change." He shook his head in frustration. "I understand the idea of punishment, of making criminals suffer to deter others from committing crimes and to ensure there is a balance, a sort of emotional restitution for the victims, but the people in the jails are often petty criminals, those awaiting trial for stealing a paltry amount or causing unrest in some minor way. Many do not even reach trial; they die from disease or malnutrition beforehand."

"You do not think this can be changed?"

"Who would pay? The wealthier prisoners pay for better conditions, for more food, but the poor have nothing to give. What law-abiding citizen is going to pay for prison reforms, to improve the conditions so criminals can be held in comfort."

"No one."

"It is not a problem I have a solution to," Lord Hinchbrooke said, "but every time I visit that jail…" he trailed off and shook his head.

"I am sorry I went without talking to you first."

"I am not surprised, Miss Austen, nor am I angry. I understand you need to see this case through to the end, to see justice is done for Miss Roscoe." He paused and looked at her, his expression sharp. "What did you find out?"

Jane took her time choosing her words, deciding on what to tell Lord Hinchbrooke and how to phrase it. He was a fair man, but with the arrests of the Lanbridge brothers he obviously felt his job was done. She didn't want to annoy him when he had been so helpful.

"I kept coming back to the shirt," Jane said slowly. "The thought that any intelligent person would have got rid of it, or at least hidden it better, and we know the Lanbridge's are intelligent enough to scam Lord Westworth for the past year."

"That is true, although I still believe that intelligent people sometimes do stupid things, especially when under immense pressure."

"I wanted to ask Mr Lanbridge about it, and I wanted to ask him what had happened that night, look him in the eye whilst I did so."

"And what did he say?"

"He said he didn't murder Miss Roscoe. He also said he didn't meet his brother that night so there was nothing for Miss Roscoe to overhear between them. I believed him, or at least partly believed him. Mr Oliver Lanbridge was adamant he didn't leave the folly on the night of the murder; he stayed away because he knew there would be a lot of people attending the ball."

"What do you think happened?"

"There was a hesitation when I asked Mr Lanbridge who could have been out in the orchard that night, and I have a suspicion that instead of meeting his brother he was meeting someone else."

"What did he say about the shirt?"

"He said if he had stabbed Miss Roscoe and seen the blood on his shirt, he would have burned it, or at least buried it the next day when he went out for his morning ride across the estate."

Lord Hinchbrooke nodded slowly.

"I have been thinking about this shirt as well, Miss Austen. Do you know what it is that bothers me the most?"

"The timing," Jane said quietly.

"Exactly. Mr Lanbridge had days to dispose of it if he knew it was there, and the maid — Rebecca, was it? — said herself she often tidied the room twice a day. Why had she not noticed it before?"

"Because it was not there before."

"It is a thought, isn't it? That someone planted the shirt in order to implicate Mr Lanbridge as the murderer. Especially when the truth about his identity was unravelling, it would convince us of his guilt."

"If that is true," Jane said slowly, her mind working to catch up, "then there are only a select few people who would have access to the room of Mr Lanbridge."

"Indeed. Lord Westworth, Lady Westworth and the servants at Stanmore Hall. Anyone else would be noted and unlikely to be able to gain entry to an upstairs room."

Jane felt a frisson of excitement and as she looked over at the magistrate she saw a similar sentiment in his eyes.

"Do you have time to come to Stanmore Hall, Miss Austen? There are a few people I would like to question and I have need of your skills as my scribe again."

Jane looked at Cassandra, begging her with her eyes to acquiesce.

Cassandra sighed. "If I could borrow some stationery to write a note to our parents explaining our absence might there be someone to deliver it?"

"Of course," Lord Hinchbrooke said, directing Cassandra to a desk in the corner of the room.

"Thank you," Jane whispered to her sister as Cassandra began writing.

"At least it is not a filthy jail this time," Cassandra murmured.

The journey to Stanmore Hall was short in distance but today it seemed to take forever. First there was a long stretch of thick mud on the road that Lord Hinchbrooke's carriage almost got stuck in. They had to get down and walk a short distance to allow the horses to pull the carriage through without the extra weight before they could climb back up into the carriage and continue on with their journey. A few minutes later they had to slow to a stop again as the wrought-iron gates to Stanmore Hall were closed. Closer inspection showed they were not locked, but merely pulled together to deter visitors.

"I plan to bend the truth a little when I confront Lord Westworth," Lord Hinchbrooke said as they approached the house. "Will you be able to maintain a neutral expression?" He asked the question of Jane, but his eyes flicked to Cassandra.

"I think I will remain in the carriage," Cassandra said, silencing Jane's protests with a wave of her hand. "Lord Hinchbrooke is correct, I am not adept at hiding my emotions and I do not wish to jeopardise the search for the truth. I have my coat and gloves and I do not think I will be too cold sheltered here in the carriage."

Lord Hinchbrooke nodded and Jane didn't protest. Cassandra was right, she was too innocent, too guileless to not react to a lie, even if pre-warned it was going to be uttered.

"Come, Miss Austen, let us see what the Westworths have to say for themselves."

He stepped down from the carriage and reached back to help Jane down and together they made their way to the house.

"I hope you will forgive me," Jane said, suddenly feeling nervous, "I have planned a little deception too."

"Oh?"

"When we were at the jail, I got the distinct impression Mr Lanbridge was hiding something, that he may have gone to meet someone other than his brother Oliver in the orchard that night."

"What have you done, Miss Austen?"

Before Jane could answer, the door of Stanmore Hall opened and the young footman peered out, looking perplexed to see them.

"No doubt Lord Westworth has rallied his staff and promised things will return to normal now the Lanbridge brothers have been arrested," Lord Hinchbrooke murmured quietly to Jane, so only she could hear. "It is what I would do if this were my household." As the footman ushered them inside then turned away to fetch his master, Lord Hinchbrooke said, "I trust your judgement, Miss Austen, but next time a little more warning of any surprises would be nice."

"Lord Hinchbrooke," Lord Westworth said as he emerged into the hall, "and Miss Austen, I have to say I am surprised to see you. Do you need to have a look through Mr Lanbridge's possessions?"

"Not exactly, Lord Westworth," the magistrate said. "There are a few loose threads I still need to pull together before the matter goes to trial. You understand the need to be thorough with these things?"

"Of course, we don't want the jury to be tricked by Mr Lanbridge's eloquence and gift of deception. As always, I am happy to assist you in any way needed."

"Thank you. We may have a few questions for Lady Westworth, is she around as well?"

"My wife is indisposed," Lord Westworth said, shaking his head with a sigh. "The last few days have taken a toll on her health and the doctor has suggested she rest undisturbed in bed for a while. Perhaps a week, maybe two."

"I am sorry to hear that," Jane said. "I cannot imagine the strain Miss Roscoe's death and the subsequent investigation must have put on Lady Westworth. Please give her my warmest regards."

"That is kind, Miss Austen. Shall we go through to the drawing room and hopefully I will be able to assist you with anything you need?" Lord Westworth seemed jovial, relaxed, as he ushered them through to the drawing room and called for tea, discussing the weather and the impending Christmas festivities whilst they waited.

Once the door was firmly closed behind the maid that had brought the tea Lord Hinchbrooke cleared his throat.

"Have you been made aware of the extent of Mr Lanbridge's deception?" Lord Hinchbrooke asked softly.

"Indeed. There was a journal in amongst his things and it outlined the whole awful plan, from when my brother died near Bombay to the way they would deceive me into thinking Mr Lanbridge was Edward."

"I thought you might try and visit Mr Lanbridge in jail, to get some answers from him?"

"There was no need, the journal answered everything. I was shocked, of course, but I do not wish to spend any more time on a reprobate such as Mr Lanbridge."

"May I see the journal?"

"Of course, I'll have it brought down." Lord Westworth jumped to his feet and pulled the bell cord in the corner of the room, instructing the footman to collect the journal from Mr Lanbridge's possessions.

In less than a minute the footman reappeared, handing over a leather-bound book to Lord Hinchbrooke. Jane itched to get her hands on it, to open up the pages and see what Mr Lanbridge had committed to paper.

"It must be a relief to finally know," Lord Hinchbrooke said as he leafed through. "All those years of not knowing what had happened to your brother, now at least you have the truth, even if it is not the happy miracle you had hoped for."

"It is a weight off my mind."

"When did you realise Mr Lanbridge was not your brother?"

Lord Westworth blinked and then his eyes narrowed just a fraction. "Well, the whole business with the shirt being found in his wardrobe and him acting mighty suspicious in the day or two before his arrest."

"You suspected before then though," Lord Hinchbrooke said, the words formed as a statement rather than a question.

For a long moment Lord Westworth held the magistrate's eye and Jane realised she was holding her breath, waiting to see what path the viscount would choose.

"I did," Lord Westworth said slowly.

"In fact, you knew this whole time, didn't you?"

The magistrate was taking a gamble here. It would be easier to let Lord Westworth tell them when he suspected, but she wondered if even now he would tell them the truth.

"What makes you think that?"

"I have a brother, Lord Westworth, ten years younger and a complete rapscallion. Even if someone mimicked his ways, copied his idiosyncrasies and I had not seen him for twenty years, I would not be taken in by a fraud. I don't think you would be either." Lord Hinchbrooke gave a knowing smile. "The masses think we have it easy with our inherited wealth and privilege, but they do not know what it takes to successfully run an estate, to hold the future of your tenants in your hands. You have a thriving estate, Lord Westworth, it wouldn't be that way if you were easily duped."

"I knew the moment I laid eyes on him," Lord Westworth said, and Jane felt herself leaning forward in her seat. This wasn't what she had expected when she had pushed Lord Hinchbrooke to come to Stanmore Hall. She had been fixated on the shirt, but she could see now that this matter had been playing on the magistrate's mind.

"Tell me the story," Lord Hinchbrooke said, relaxing back in his chair as if he and Lord Westworth were at their gentleman's club discussing tales from their youth.

"I knew Edward must have been dead. A man might go missing for a year, even two or three when a voyage to the other side of the earth is involved, but twenty, that's ridiculous."

"You were suspicious of the letter you received from the man Hooper saying he had seen your brother alive?"

"I was. I knew it was a hoax."

"Yet you travelled to India anyway."

"I was curious. Why now? Why after all this time would someone claim to be Edward?" He shifted in his seat. "Do you know how much heartache it caused my mother, never knowing what had happened? It broke her, sent her into fits of deep melancholy and drove her to an early grave."

"Terrible," Jane murmured. With two brothers in the navy Jane knew the horrible tension that mounted when waiting for news, especially if a letter was delayed along the way, which happened often. She couldn't imagine the torture of not knowing what had happened to someone she loved for years on end.

"What happened when you arrived?"

"I knew straight away that it wasn't Edward, but Lanbridge was as convincing as an imposter could be. I realised he must at the very least have known my brother and there was a possibility he had been there when he died."

"You wanted answers."

"If I had revealed that I knew the whole thing was a hoax, Phillip Lanbridge would have fled and I would never get the truth."

"How did you think it would end?" Jane asked, unable to stop the question from escaping.

"I knew there would come the moment he had been working towards this whole time, the pinnacle. I suspected he would ask for money and at that point I would reveal I knew he was an imposter. A year of his life spent on this scheme… I hoped he would accept a pay-off in return for the truth, finally."

"It was risky."

Lord Westworth shrugged. "Not really. What could he do to me? Officially Edward Stanmore has been declared dead so he couldn't poach the title and the money, and I was confident I could prove he wasn't actually my brother."

"Who else knew?" Jane said, wondering if Lord Westworth had confided in anyone else.

"My solicitor. He's a sensible chap, advised me to leave the past in the past. Apart from him, no one."

"Not even your wife?"

"Not even my wife. She only found out a few days ago. She's livid with me of course for keeping it from her, but really there was no need for her to know the truth."

Jane felt a pang of pity for Lady Westworth, whose husband hadn't seen fit to inform her of the true identity of the man staying in their house, treated like family.

"Thank you for being so candid," Lord Hinchbrooke said, putting his teacup down on the table. "It is helpful to understand the whole story when building a case to present to the judge and jury."

"I trust the details will be kept from the public. The family name has suffered enough. Scandal this salacious would excite the gossips for years to come."

Lord Hinchbrooke inclined his head, but Jane noted he did not make any promises.

"Lord Hinchbrooke," Jane said, opening the notebook he had given her, pen poised as usual, "you wanted to ask about the night of the ball."

"Ah yes," the magistrate said, as if it were merely an afterthought. "We are trying to place everyone in the hour or so before Miss Roscoe's death. Tell me, did you leave the ballroom at any time?"

Lord Westworth considered for a moment. "I went to the drawing room where the cards were set up and talked to the gentlemen there for a few minutes, but apart from that, no, I did not."

"Did you step out into the gardens at all?"

"No."

"Not to visit the orchard?"

"No, not to go anywhere. I was inside the whole time."

"Did you see anyone else leave the house and go into the gardens?"

"No, but I wouldn't have noticed in particular. I was focussed on greeting guests, not who was slipping away."

"How about Lady Westworth?" Jane said.

"She was greeting our guests too; you must remember, Miss Austen."

"Of course," Jane hesitated, "but most of the guests arrived before my family. Did Lady Westworth stay in the ballroom after that?"

"I doubt she stayed solely in the ballroom. It is a difficult job hosting a ball, so my dear wife often tells me. You have to be in five different places at once, greeting guests, calling the dances, ensuring everyone is having a good time, liaising with the servants in the kitchen."

"So, she could have slipped out?"

"She would have been missed. Everyone's eyes are always searching for the hostess. If she was not there for any length of time then it would be noted."

"And did you see Mr Phillip Lanbridge at all that night?"

"No. Only once Miss Roscoe had been found dead. He complained of headaches, debilitating ones, although now I wonder if that was just part of his deception."

"There is the matter of the bloody shirt," Lord Hinchbrooke said.

"Yes, pretty damning, isn't it? Hard to protest your innocence when the victim's blood is all over your shirt."

Jane felt a bitter taste in her mouth as Lord Westworth spoke so casually about Miss Roscoe's death. For him it was all over, all wrapped up. The man pretending to be his brother had been exposed, he knew the truth about his brother's death and the murder that had occurred in his country home had been solved. Soon he would be sitting in his London club regaling his friends with tales of the last few months, unaffected by it all.

"Strange he would hide it in the wardrobe when the maid saw to his room every day, don't you think?"

"He thought he had got away with so much already, he had an idea he couldn't be caught."

"That is an interesting theory."

Jane snapped her notebook closed. As much as she had wanted to come here, to press Lord and Lady Westworth on the anomalies of the case, now she had the urge to flee. Lord Westworth and his cheery demeanour made her realise how little Emma Roscoe meant to him. She was an unfortunate victim, nothing more.

"Thank you for your time, Lord Westworth," the magistrate said as he rose from his chair. "It would be helpful to speak to Lady Westworth in the coming few days. Perhaps you might send a message when she has recovered enough to talk?"

"Of course."

As they moved to the door there was a clatter of hooves outside and Jane watched the footman open the door to a young man on horseback.

"Sorry to disturb you, my lord," the man said, brandishing a note. "An important message from the jail in Winchester."

"Thank you," Lord Hinchbrooke said, taking the note and cursing quietly as his hand shook so much he could barely unfold it. She was pleased when the young messenger on horseback turned and rode away, only glancing at her for a second before he did so.

"You said you left your spectacles at home, my lord," Jane said, moving up beside him. Lord Hinchbrooke flashed her a grateful look and handed over the note.

Quickly Jane skimmed the contents. It was written on a scrap of paper, yellowed with age. The writing was looping and elaborate, but she didn't need to read the words to know what it said. She had put pen to paper earlier today and produced this very note, slipping a few coins to one of the men in Lord Hinchbrooke's pay to act as messenger for this deception.

"It is from Mr Lanbridge," she said, "Mr Phillip Lanbridge. He asks to see you tomorrow afternoon, he says he has been thinking things over and would like to tell you the truth."

Lord Hinchbrooke exhaled and shook his head. "This will be the third story Mr Lanbridge has spun, I wonder if it will be the truth or more lies."

"Surely it is impossible to believe anything that comes out of that man's mouth," Lord Westworth said, peering over Jane's shoulder as if trying to catch a glimpse of the words.

Jane quickly folded the note up. "As you say, it may be further deception, but I think we should hear what he has to say. He may be ready to tell us who he was meeting in the orchard on the night of the ball."

"He may indeed," Lord Hinchbrooke said, catching Jane's eye. "I will ensure I make time to visit him tomorrow afternoon."

"Please let me know if there is anything further you need," Lord Westworth said, stepping away.

Jane felt Lord Hinchbrooke's hand on her arm and she allowed herself to be guided to the carriage, but as she stepped up she glanced back over her shoulder. At one of the first floor windows she caught a glimpse of a figure watching them. It was there for just a second and then it was gone.

For five minutes they sat in complete silence in the carriage, Jane and Lord Hinchbrooke both deep in thought. Cassandra gripped Jane's hand but did not ask what had occurred. Only as they left the Westworth estate did Lord Hinchbrooke speak.

"I assume that was of your doing, Miss Austen?"

"I am sorry for the presumption," Jane said quietly.

"It was a very clever idea."

"You are not angry?"

Lord Hinchbrooke sighed. "We have been going round in circles with this case for weeks. I would like to know once and for all if Mr Phillip Lanbridge is a murderer or if he is merely a lying conman. Your deception may settle the matter."

"What deception?" Cassandra asked, her interest piqued.

"I paid one of Lord Hinchbrooke's men to deliver a message supposedly from the jail, from Mr Lanbridge, wanting to speak to Lord Hinchbrooke."

"Why on earth did you do that?"

"The way I see it there are two possibilities: either Mr Lanbridge killed Miss Roscoe out of fear she had uncovered the truth of his identity and would reveal it, putting an end to his scheme of revenge."

"Or?"

"Or someone in that house is the real murderer. Lord or Lady Westworth or one of the servants. *That* person is the one Mr Lanbridge met in the orchard and *that* person will be dependent on Mr Lanbridge keeping their secret."

"You're baiting them?" Cassandra's eyes widened and she shook her head in disbelief.

"Everyone at Stanmore Hall will know by the end of the day that Lord Hinchbrooke has received a note from Mr Lanbridge. The footman will spread the gossip around the servants' hall tonight and Lord Westworth is sure to tell Lady Westworth. I am hoping to provoke a reaction."

"You think someone will try to reach out to Mr Lanbridge before Lord Hinchbrooke speaks to him tomorrow?"

"If Mr Lanbridge knows something of their guilt, then yes, I do." Jane turned to Lord Hinchbrooke. "It will mean someone standing watch at the jail, to see who turns up."

"I will go there this evening and brief the guards. I am sure I will be able to acquire a room in the local inn and be ready in case anything happens tonight or tomorrow."

"Can I…?" Jane began and both Lord Hinchbrooke and Cassandra said "No," in unison.

"You don't know what I was going to ask," Jane muttered.

"I understand your desire to be there, but I am determined to end this matter without ruining your reputation completely, Miss Austen," Lord Hinchbrooke said kindly.

"Perhaps we can ride to Winchester tomorrow morning?" Cassandra said, surprising Jane. "We may not be there when events unfold, but you will get your answers."

"That sounds like a good compromise," agreed the magistrate. "Remember, nothing at all might happen, it is a gamble, a ruse that may not provoke any response."

Jane nodded, knowing she would not get a better offer than that.

"I will send my carriage for you," Lord Hinchbrooke said, settling back on the seat and closing his eyes. After a moment he roused and sat forward again. "What did you think of Lord Westworth?"

"He seemed confident, jubilant."

"He has no motive that I can see," Lord Hinchbrooke said, shaking his head.

"He knew about Mr Lanbridge's deception. What if this has all been orchestrated to punish him?"

Jane could see Lord Hinchbrooke consider the suggestion for a long moment, but it felt thin even to her.

"And Miss Roscoe was chosen at random? It would a be a cold man who could murder an innocent young woman for no other reason than to implicate another."

"What about Lady Westworth then?"

Lord Hinchbrooke looked thoughtful. "I am not sure I believe this story of her being indisposed today. The murder unsettled her, but on all our other visits she has been remarkably composed. Why take to her bed now?"

"What reason would she have, though, to murder Miss Roscoe or frame Mr Lanbridge?"

"It could have been her in the orchard. Lord Westworth said she was expected to float all over during the ball, it would mean her absence would not be noted if she slipped out for a few minutes."

"And she is one of the few people the servants would not notice if she came to the kitchen and took a knife."

"That is true, Miss Austen. Any of the guests would have been spotted. Just as the placing of the shirt in Mr Lanbridge's room narrows our pool of suspects, so does the knife from the kitchen."

They fell silent, contemplating the possibilities, wondering if tomorrow might reveal the truth.

CHAPTER TWENTY

"My dears, where on earth have you been?" Mrs Austen said as Jane and Cassandra entered the house, both shrugging off their coats and wearied from the excitement of the day.

Wondering how much to tell her mother Jane opened her mouth but was saved by Cassandra peering past her.

"Do we have a visitor, mama?"

"Yes, we do. Mr Lefroy has come to call on Jane. He has waited ever such a long time, but not once has he grumbled or shown signs he might leave."

Despite her preoccupation with what might happen at the jail tomorrow morning Jane felt a frisson of excitement.

Mr Lefroy stood as she entered the room, his eyes searching for hers and locking on to them with his customary warmth. Jane knew the warning Mrs Anne Lefroy had given, but she couldn't see anything but affection in his expression and she felt some of the doubts she had fostered melt away.

"Hello, Miss Austen," Mr Lefroy said, and Jane wondered how even the mere sound of his voice could send such shivers down her spine.

"Hello, Mr Lefroy."

"I hope you will forgive the impertinence of my coming to call unannounced for the second time?"

"There is nothing to forgive, Mr Lefroy. You must excuse my appearance; my sister and I have been out for much of the day."

"You look radiant, Miss Austen, as always."

"Cassandra, there is something I need your help with. We shall be just next door, Jane, if you need us," Mrs Austen said, leaving the room but ensuring the door remained wide open for the sake of propriety.

"I apologise for my mother," Jane said, shaking her head once they were alone. "She has quite despaired of me finding a husband and now any time a gentleman pays a call she forgets how to act like a sensible person."

"Your mother is charming. She was telling me of her youth spent in Oxford with your grandfather. It must have been quite a thrilling existence, sneaking into the lectures and learning from the tutors who are experts in their subjects."

"My mother the rebel, it is a role I have a hard time associating with her now. I think all mothers are cursed to be underestimated by their daughters."

Mr Lefroy glanced at the door and lowered his voice, leaning in closer to Jane. She sensed he wanted to reach out for her hand, but wary that her family could return at any moment he held off.

"I know my aunt spoke with you at the ball, Miss Austen, or at least expressed her concerns to your sister." He paused, pressing his lips together as if trying to find the right words. "I understand her motives and appreciate her predicament. She is a woman stuck between loyalty to her family and respect for you, tossed like a boat in a storm until she doesn't know which way to turn. If I was any sort of decent gentleman, I would have had the courage to speak to you myself."

"Then what she said was true?" Jane felt her pulse quickening as he spoke. She pushed down any hope of a proposal, any hope of a future together. It wasn't what she had set out looking for and she shouldn't miss what she had never had.

Mr Lefroy stood and stalked over to the window, turning his face away. Jane watched him run a hand through his hair, his whole posture stiff and on edge, tension radiating from him.

"Do you remember when we met, Miss Austen? The exact moment?"

"Of course."

"I wasn't looking where I was going. I almost bumped into you and as I turned my head to look at you, to see you for the first time, I felt as though the light of a thousand angels was shining down upon us. Even though I did not know your name or anything about you, I knew every moment I spent with you would be one that enriched my life." He said the words looking out of the window, as if he couldn't look at her and tell her exactly how he felt at the same time. "Normally I am a sensible man, a man of ethics and morals, but these last few weeks I would have discarded every last piece of myself to spend one more moment with you."

Jane stood and took a couple of steps towards him, but Mr Lefroy held out a hand to stop her. They were standing a few feet apart and more than anything Jane wanted to cross it, but she knew it had to be his decision. If there were reasons they could not continue their friendship, their courtship, then the rational part of her knew it would be better to find out now, even though the rest of her was screaming silently for him to shut up, to not end things yet.

"How can two people who barely know each other be so attuned?" he asked softly, his eyes seeking hers.

"Some people believe you are made for one other in this world. One person who fits you perfectly, who balances every part of you."

"You might spend your life searching for that one person," Mr Lefroy said quietly.

"Or they might bump into you at a ball only a few miles from home."

Mr Lefroy took a step forward and then another until he and Jane were standing only inches apart. She looked up at him, knowing the next few minutes would change her life irrevocably in one way or another.

"Why is life so cruel?" Mr Lefroy said, his lips barely moving. "Does it have to be?"

For a long moment there was silence and Jane knew that was her answer. She did not doubt the depth of his feelings or the validity of hers, but some things had to take priority over the desires of the heart.

"I never meant to hint at something that could never be, Miss Austen," Mr Lefroy said. "Please believe me when I say I hold you in the highest regard. I only wish…" he trailed off.

"Things could be different?"

"Yes."

Jane could feel her whole body begin to tremble and she did not want to show such emotion in front of Mr Lefroy. He had made his decision and now they both had to live with it.

"Will you permit me to explain?" Mr Lefroy reached out for her hand, but she stepped away before he could take it.

"It isn't necessary, Mr Lefroy," Jane said, turning slightly so he wouldn't see the glint of tears in her eyes. "You do not owe me an explanation. You never promised me anything."

"My family have certain expectations…"

Jane held up a hand, halting him. "Please stop. I do not need to hear how I am not worthy enough to be your wife."

"Miss Austen, I do not think that."

There were so many things she could say, but Jane knew none of it would make any difference. Their acquaintance had been short and intense. She had only met the man on a handful

251

of occasions but the spark between them was white hot. She should have known not to build her dreams on something so fleeting.

"We barely know each other, Mr Lefroy," Jane said, moving towards the door. She needed this to be over, for Mr Lefroy to leave and allow her to collapse into Cassandra's arms. In a week or perhaps two the initial sting of rejection would fade and she would be able to see this for what it was — a short infatuation that would soon be a distant memory.

"Miss Austen, please."

"Please excuse me, Mr Lefroy." Without another word she left, making sure she walked calmly up the stairs, refusing to flee and fling herself on her bed.

A minute later Cassandra entered the room, took one look at Jane and wrapped her in her arms.

"Oh, Jane, I'm sorry."

"There's nothing to be sorry about."

"Of course there is. Is Mr Lefroy leaving Hampshire?"

"I do not know."

"What happened?"

Jane shook her head and rested her head on her sister's shoulder. "I feel a complete fool," she whispered. Never would she admit such a thing to anyone else, but Cassandra was privy to all her innermost thoughts and experienced every mood alongside her, there was no point keeping it from her sister.

"You should never feel foolish for caring for someone."

"We danced a few times, spent a few hours in one another's company. Laughed and talked, but there was nothing more. He never promised me anything, never even hinted there might be anything to our friendship past these few weeks he was visiting Steventon. And yet…"

Cassandra remained quiet, listening and stroking Jane's hair.

"And yet I built it up in my mind into something it was not. I dreamed about being Mrs Tom Lefroy, of running his household and of the children we might have together. I dreamed of a life, a future, with him." She shook her head, feeling a deep ache of embarrassment and sadness. "All because we laughed together and he wanted to spend time with me."

"Anyone could see you were well matched, Jane."

"Not well enough. I feel so foolish to allow myself to think all of this when we barely knew one another."

"It is no crime to dream. You should not punish yourself for that."

Falling silent, Jane sniffed and allowed the tears to cascade down her cheeks. No one else would see her cry about this, but right now she needed to rid herself of all the pain that was building inside her.

Cassandra held her tight in her arms and rocked gently, as their mother had done when they were small and had fallen and grazed a knee or bumped an elbow.

"Rest now, Jane. Tomorrow, hopefully the truth of who killed Emma Roscoe will come out and then after a few days of being surrounded by family and love things will not seem so bad."

CHAPTER TWENTY-ONE

Jane saw Lord Hinchbrooke before he saw her and for a moment it struck her how much he had aged over the course of the last few weeks. He was sitting at a table near the window, his hands resting in his lap, but every time he went to lift the glass in front of him his hand displayed the characteristic tremor. She wondered if he had questioned doctors over the prognosis of his disease.

"Miss Austen," Lord Hinchbrooke said, looking up at Jane and nodding politely to Cassandra. He clasped his hands together and stood, his movements slow and a frown upon his face. "You look terrible."

"I think you missed your etiquette lessons the day they taught you never to insult a young lady before she has had her first cup of tea of the day," Jane murmured.

"Forgive me. You do not look terrible of course, all I meant was you look as though you haven't slept. For weeks."

"I haven't, not really."

"Me neither," Lord Hinchbrooke said quietly. It was a surprising admission from the magistrate and Jane wondered if he felt all the cases he became involved in so deeply. "I promise you that once the perpetrator is brought to justice, once you are sure the right man is in prison, it gets better."

"I hope so," Jane said. Last night she had tossed and turned until she had woken even heavy sleeper Cassandra, plagued by regrets about Mr Lefroy and worries that they might never get to the truth of what happened to Emma Roscoe. She hadn't touched her manuscript in days and more than anything she wanted peace, both within herself and with the world.

"Have you been here all night?" Cassandra asked.

He was set up in a seat by the window in the local tavern, obscured from view outside by the grime on the windows. The view across to the jail was obstructed only by the occasional carriage passing by and Lord Hinchbrooke kept returning his gaze to the window.

It was not a time for taking risks. The carriage that had brought Jane and Cassandra here had been instructed to take them into the courtyard at the back of the tavern and they had slinked in through the rear door.

"Yes. There are some young men I know and trust, who have helped me before in similar situations. They have taken up posts with a good view of the jail."

"And you spoke to the guards?" said Jane.

Lord Hinchbrooke smiled. "It is not my first time apprehending a suspect, Miss Austen. I have spoken to the guards and instructed them to act as they would normally, but not to let anyone leave."

Jane ignored the gentle teasing. "They will take anyone who visits down to the cell?"

"They will. I hope they might overhear what is said."

Jane sighed and sat down in a chair across the table to Lord Hinchbrooke. "I wonder if anyone will come or if this is all for naught. Perhaps the murderer is already locked away in the jail after all."

"Perhaps, but it is worth a few hours to find out," Lord Hinchbrooke said. "Please do make yourself comfortable, Miss Austen." He looked up at Cassandra and motioned for her to take a seat.

Cassandra sat down, tucking her skirts round her and looking around the tavern with interest.

"Did anything happen overnight?" Jane asked the magistrate.

"No, although I did not expect it to. The guards are unlikely to let any visitor in overnight and it would be much more of a risk. Better to come in the morning when it is less likely to be noted or remarked upon."

"It is a gamble though. If someone is trying to beat you here to speak to Mr Lanbridge, they do not know when you might come."

"That is true."

They fell silent, all eyes locked on the prison across the road.

For half an hour they watched, Jane trying not to fidget too much in her chair. It was monotonous work and soon she found that although she was looking, she wasn't really seeing what was happening in the street. It meant it took a few seconds to realise when a carriage pulled up outside the jail and a figure got out. They were too far away to see who it was, just a flash of black material as the person hurried from the carriage and into the jail.

"Watch the jail door," Lord Hinchbrooke told Jane and Cassandra. After what felt like an eternity, a guard came out and walked a few steps into the street before disappearing back into the darkness of the jail.

"What was he doing?" asked Jane.

"I told the guards that if anyone comes asking to see Mr Lanbridge to send a signal by stepping out of the jail. This is it."

Lord Hinchbrooke manoeuvred himself to his feet and motioned for Jane to follow. "Are you coming, Miss Austen?" he asked Cassandra as they neared the door.

"No. This is for you and Jane to finish together."

Jane didn't protest, she was already halfway out the tavern and into the street. With Lord Hinchbrooke by her side, his movements stiff after sitting for so long in one position, they approached the jail. The door was opened before they could knock, a guard ushering them in. This man was young and had a gleam in his eye, as if excited by all the intrigue of the morning.

"This way," he said with no preamble, unlocking doors with lightning speed.

"Who is it? Who is the visitor?" Jane said, but already the guard and Lord Hinchbrooke were hurrying away. She followed, not wanting to get left behind, retracing the steps she and Cassandra had taken on their visit to Phillip Lanbridge in his cell.

As they approached it felt as though time slowed down. Every step was like wading through honey, every breath made her chest feel as though it were being crushed under rock. Until now she had never quite believed they would find the perpetrator, but the last piece of the puzzle was finally slotting into place.

The guard slotted the key into the lock of Mr Lanbridge's cell, but before he could turn it there was a cry of surprise from inside. Lord Hinchbrooke lunged forward but stumbled and Jane held out an arm to steady him. The guard saw the desperation on their faces and turned the key, flinging open the door of the cell.

At first Jane's mind could not quite comprehend what she was seeing, and it took her a few seconds to jump into action.

Mr Lanbridge was lying on the straw mattress, an expression of shock and agony on his face. A bloom of red was spreading along the arm of his shirtsleeve. It looked as though he had held up his arm to ward off a blow and taken a wound to his upper arm.

Standing in the corner of the cell, a knife in her hand, was Lady Westworth. She was pale and shaking her head, although whether this was frustration at having been interrupted before she could finish the job, or aghast at what she had done, it was impossible to know.

With one eye on Lady Westworth, aware she could strike again at any moment, Jane edged into the cell and knelt down in front of Mr Lanbridge. He was holding his arm, trying to stop the flow of blood, but it was seeping out through his fingers.

Carefully, Jane ripped open his shirt, exposing the wound. It was deep and long and she knew that if he had been struck in the chest it would have been fatal.

"Hold your arm above your head," she instructed, using some of his ripped shirt to put pressure on the wound. "I need your cravat, Lord Hinchbrooke."

The magistrate's hands shook as he took off his cravat, but he managed to complete the task and hand it over to Jane.

Trying to be as gentle as possible Jane tied the cravat around Mr Lanbridge's arm above the cut. She pulled it tight, ignoring his cry of protest.

"It needs to be tight, Mr Lanbridge," she said quietly, "or you'll lose all your blood onto this filthy cell floor."

"Lady Westworth, I need you to put down the knife," Lord Hinchbrooke said now, his voice surprisingly calm. He sounded as if he were enquiring about her health, not trying to stop her from injuring anyone else.

Jane glanced up and saw Lady Westworth's eyes darting around furiously, as if searching for a way out, but still her fingers clutched the knife.

"Put down the knife, Lady Westworth," Lord Hinchbrooke said, taking a tiny step closer.

"I need something more to bind this wound with, and a doctor to see to it properly," Jane said, pleased to see the flow of blood had lessened a little.

"The guard is going to go now," Lord Hinchbrooke said calmly to Lady Westworth. "He will fetch some cloth for the wound and send for a doctor."

The prison guard, who had been staring open-mouthed at the scene inside the cell, hesitated, then gave a curt nod and dashed off.

"Put down the knife, Lady Westworth, and we can work together to sort this out."

Jane was surprised when Mr Lanbridge struggled to his feet, still clutching his arm.

"Give him the knife, Hen," Mr Lanbridge said, a softness to his voice Jane had not heard before. "We're in a prison and all the doors are locked. There is no way out."

Lady Westworth looked at the knife in her hands as if she had never seen it before and then up at Mr Lanbridge.

"I can't believe…" she said, unable to finish the sentence.

"It is fine. I'm fine, just drop the knife."

There was a long pause and then Lady Westworth let the knife slide out of her fingers and clatter to the ground. Lord Hinchbrooke moved as quickly as he could to retrieve it, picking it up and then stepping back away from the viscountess.

Slowly Lady Westworth collapsed to the ground, not seeming to notice the filthy conditions as the expensive fabric of her dress soaked up the grime.

"What now?" Mr Lanbridge said, his face pale and his voice a little weaker than usual.

"The doctor should be here any moment," Jane said, hoping it was true. As she guided him back to the mattress, she saw how much blood had soaked into the bedding. With a competent surgeon and some luck, he would survive, but the sooner he was treated the better, and of course there was always the risk of infection.

"What will happen to Henrietta — Lady Westworth?"

"Come, my lady," Lord Hinchbrooke said, moving over to the woman who was openly sobbing now and lifting her up to her feet. "I would like to hear your story. I would like you to tell me everything that has happened."

"She won't survive in here," Mr Lanbridge said softly, looking around the cell. Even though she had stabbed him, and likely tried to push suspicion onto him for murder, he still seemed to care for her comfort.

Two guards returned with a smartly dressed man in tow and they led Mr Lanbridge from the cell. Jane looked around her, shocked by the events of the last few minutes.

Slowly she followed the path Lord Hinchbrooke had taken with Lady Westworth, escorted by another guard who locked the heavy doors behind her. Only when she was standing on the pavement outside the jail did she pause and take a deep breath. To one side Lord Hinchbrooke was arranging to have Lady Westworth taken to his home where he would question her. She knew this consideration was to be expected for the aristocracy, they couldn't be hauled into a jail cell like the common people, and she wondered if Lady Westworth would be held accountable for what she had done or if it would be hushed up and swept away.

"My men will take Lady Westworth to my house and I am sending a messenger asking her husband to attend immediately. Are you willing to scribe for me one last time, Miss Austen? It would be good to have a record of what everyone has to say. I think it will be difficult to see justice done and the wrongs of the last few weeks righted."

"I would not be anywhere else, Lord Hinchbrooke."

"Good. Fetch your sister from the tavern and we will ride in my carriage and meet my men at the house with Lady Westworth." He paused, looking at her in concern. "Are you hurt?"

She glanced down, seeing a few spots of blood on her dress. It would be the devil to get out, but she supposed it was a small price to pay for having preserved a man's life. "No, it is Mr Lanbridge's blood."

"You did a good job with him. Thank you."

"Hopefully the poor man will recover quickly."

"What a morning," Lord Hinchbrooke said and closed his eyes for a moment. Jane saw him start to overbalance and quickly grabbed his arm, but the magistrate had righted himself. "Thank you, Miss Austen. What am I going to do without you once we have laid this matter to rest?"

Jane went to get Cassandra and find Lord Hinchbrooke's carriage, whilst the magistrate ensured everyone was where they needed to be.

CHAPTER TWENTY-TWO

It was late afternoon by the time everyone was gathered in the library at Petersfield House. The light was rapidly fading outside and an intermittent drizzle blurred the view of the deer park beyond the garden. Jane sat in the chair behind Lord Hinchbrooke's desk. She had felt self-conscious and tried to protest she would be more comfortable somewhere more discreet, but the magistrate had refused to let her move.

"We are here because of you, Miss Austen. Your tenacity, your determination. Do not hide from what you have achieved, revel in it, be proud of it."

So here she was, sitting at the desk, notebook open on a blank page, ready to take down every word Lady Westworth had to say.

Cassandra sat to her right, providing a comforting presence in a room full of hostility. Lady Westworth was in an armchair by the window, ignoring her husband.

Standing in the corner, uncomfortable with the company in the room, was Samuel Tinker. His face was pale and drawn and he looked as though he had lost weight in the days since Emma Roscoe's death.

Finally, the two Lanbridge brothers were perched on upright chairs, both looking as though they had spent the last month living on the streets without access to clean water or soap; of course their reality had been much worse.

"I think we are all here," Lord Hinchbrooke said, looking around the room. "I decided not to invite the Roscoes, they have been through enough these last few weeks. Tomorrow, I will visit them and let them know everything that has occurred."

"Are we to be set free?" Oliver Lanbridge said, his voice croaky with disuse.

"All in good time, Mr Lanbridge. Please make yourself comfortable and we will get to your part in this matter very soon." The magistrate turned to Jane and smiled a fatherly smile. "You all know Miss Austen, who has been helping me on this quest for the truth. She started as my scribe, an assistant, but I can honestly say I doubt we would be here today without her. I wonder, Miss Austen, would you like to give us a quick summary of events and everything we have learned? You have been making notes, after all."

Jane stood and smoothed down her skirts, feeling all eyes on her. "Good afternoon," she said, meeting everyone's eye in turn. Only Cassandra smiled back encouragingly.

"Is this really necessary?" Lord Westworth asked, sighing loudly. "I want to take my wife home."

Lord Hinchbrooke looked as though he were going to step in, but Jane spoke first. "I beg your indulgence, my lord, for a few minutes only. You may not have known Miss Roscoe well, but as an influential member of our local community I am sure you are as invested in finding who murdered her as the rest of us."

"You've already found the murderers. Those two ruffians sitting over there." Lord Westworth pointed at the Lanbridge brothers. "They tried to con me out of my family's money and then they killed Miss Roscoe to protect their deception."

"It is a theory, Lord Westworth," Jane said calmly, "but it doesn't quite fit all the facts. Permit me to start at the beginning, or at least the beginning for me. Cast your minds back to the night of the ball."

She was silent for a moment, allowing them all to remember that terrible night. Jane glanced at Lady Westworth but could not read her expression.

"It was a night of celebration. A ball thrown for Lord Westworth's long-lost brother, Edward Stanmore, to allow the local people to celebrate his homecoming. Of course, it was also a night of duplicity. We now know that the man claiming to be Edward Stanmore was in fact Mr Phillip Lanbridge, who for the past twelve months had been impersonating a man he knew had died twenty years earlier."

"Villain," Lord Westworth muttered.

"Your family owed mine," Phillip Lanbridge began, but his brother put a warning hand on his arm and he settled back in his chair silently.

"There was yet more deceit, for Lord Westworth had not in fact been taken in by the charade. He knew Mr Lanbridge was not his brother, he knew it was a ruse."

Both Lanbridge brothers' heads snapped towards Lord Westworth, who was smiling.

"I knew as soon as I laid eyes on you. You may have studied my brother all those years ago, remember a few of the phrases he liked to use and some of his mannerisms, but it was clear from the very first moment that you were not him."

"If you knew, why would you go along with it for so long?"

"I could see you had known my brother and known him well. Even after all these years I needed to know what had happened to him. I would have endured ten years of your deception if it meant finally getting to the truth."

"All that time…" Phillip Lanbridge shook his head, thinking of the months wasted on a ruse that would never pay off.

"Let us go back to the night of the ball," Jane said. "Lord and Lady Westworth are greeting their guests and Mr

Lanbridge, in the guise of Edward Stanmore, is upstairs, ostensibly with a headache."

"I did have a headache," Phillip Lanbridge muttered.

"Miss Roscoe collides with me in the ballroom, visibly upset. She does not feel she can discuss what has upset her with so many people around, so she asks me to meet her at ten o'clock in the library." Jane paused, taking in the faces of everyone in the room. "Miss Roscoe arrived at the ball with her aunt and uncle and according to them drifted off to talk to friends soon after. They lost track of her for a short while but were not unduly alarmed."

"She was with me," Samuel Tinker said, drawing all eyes to him.

"Yes, she was, Mr Tinker. As you had arranged previously, Miss Roscoe sneaked from the ball to meet you in the orchard whilst everyone was preoccupied with the festivities."

"We had barely any time together," he said quietly. "If I had known that was to be the last time I ever saw her…" He trailed off, unable to finish the sentence.

"You were disturbed by someone approaching and you decided it best if you left. As you crept away, Miss Roscoe lingered for a few moments and was visibly shaken when she emerged." Jane paused, waiting for Mr Tinker to nod. "It must have been an instinctive decision to wait, to see who was there, a decision that sealed her fate."

The room was quiet now, everyone engrossed in her story, all knowing some part of it, but no one aware of the whole complicated tangle.

"Miss Roscoe observed someone — or some persons — in the orchard, but she was also seen. The killer saw she was flustered, knew she could not keep such a momentous secret to herself, and they followed her to the library, where Miss

Roscoe had arranged to meet me, to unburden herself." Jane felt the guilt welling up inside her, that knowledge that if she had been on time to their meeting the killer might not have had the opportunity to silence Emma. "With a knife taken from the kitchen, they stabbed Miss Roscoe and left her to die, safe in the knowledge that no one else knew their secret."

"Who was it?" Mr Tinker said. "I need to know."

"Mr Lanbridge," Jane said, turning to the elder of the two brothers. "You were out in the orchard that evening. You had arranged to meet someone there and used the pretence of a headache to excuse yourself from the first part of the ball. At first, I was convinced it must be your brother you went to see, to discuss the next stage of your plan, but he told us that you had advised him to stay well away from the house as it would be so busy with guests."

"That's right," Oliver Lanbridge confirmed, nodding his head vehemently as if it might clear his brother's name.

"It was true, there would be more people around, but I think you wanted your brother out of the way for another reason. You had arranged to meet Lady Westworth."

Jane watched the reactions of everyone in the room. Mr Tinker's eyes widened in disbelief and Oliver Lanbridge shook his head. Lady Westworth looked down at her lap, but Lord Westworth did not feign surprise either.

"For the past few months, you have been having an affair with Lady Westworth and on the night of the ball you arranged to meet her in the orchard for a few stolen moments together whilst her husband's attention was fixed elsewhere."

Phillip Lanbridge glanced at Lady Westworth, but she did not look up.

"That's not true," Oliver Lanbridge said, shaking his head vehemently. "Tell her it isn't true, Phillip."

Phillip Lanbridge turned to his brother. "I'm sorry, Oliver, I should have told you."

"Why would you do that? After everything we've been through — all the time we've spent on this. The nights I've spent in that damn freezing folly when our money ran out, all the sacrifices I've made, and all the time you were having an affair with the viscountess."

Phillip Lanbridge shrugged. "It just happened. We were both lonely, we both hated her husband. I didn't set out thinking there would be any intimacy between us."

Jane glanced at Lord Westworth. He had barely reacted to the revelation, as if he had known all along. She was only just realising what a sharp, observant man he was.

"Miss Roscoe saw Mr Lanbridge and Lady Westworth in an intimate embrace in the orchard, which was what had her so flustered. And you saw Emma, didn't you, Lady Westworth?"

"Yes," Lady Westworth said quietly, finally raising her head. "Our eyes met and in that moment, I knew she could ruin everything."

"Quiet, Henrietta," Lord Westworth snapped, placing a hand on her shoulder, and Jane could see his fingers pressing into the flesh.

Lady Westworth pulled away, standing and walking over to the window, and despite everything Jane knew she suddenly felt sorry for the woman. She looked small, broken, not the composed, elegant viscountess the world thought they knew.

"I saw her bump into you in the ballroom, Miss Austen," Lady Westworth said now, "and I heard her arrange to meet you. I knew that once she had spoken to you everything was over. At some point, somehow, news of our affair would get out."

"So, you decided to silence Miss Roscoe before she could tell anyone."

"No, it wasn't a conscious decision."

"Yet you must have gone to the kitchen and taken the knife. You were the only one who could have walked in there without the servants questioning it, and with everyone busy with the ball no one would have noticed you slip a knife into the folds of your skirt."

For a long moment Lady Westworth didn't answer. When she did, her voice was quiet. "I didn't take the knife thinking I would stab Miss Roscoe, not consciously. I was in the kitchen talking to Mrs Lamb and the knife was there on the side. My mind was in a blur and when Mrs Lamb turned her back, I slipped the knife off the kitchen counter before I could even properly think it through."

Mr Tinker rose form his chair and before anyone could react, he launched himself at Lady Westworth. "How could you kill her?" He gripped her by the shoulders and started shaking her, the tears flowing freely down his cheeks. Despite his wound, Phillip Lanbridge was the first one to move. He gripped hold of Mr Tinker, pulling him back. It didn't take much effort, Jane had the impression Mr Tinker didn't want to hurt Lady Westworth, but the cold, calm way she spoke about the murder of the woman he loved must have made his pain even worse.

Lady Westworth took a step back as Phillip Lanbridge wrestled Samuel Tinker back to his seat, the young tenant farmer burying his head in his hands.

"I can imagine what happened in the library," Jane said, realising Lady Westworth wasn't about to tell them in detail what had occurred. "You slipped in whilst Miss Roscoe was waiting for me and confirmed what she had seen. I expect you asked her to stay silent, but you saw she was conflicted and you did not hesitate to stab the knife into her heart."

There was a snort from Lord Westworth. "A thrilling story, Miss Austen, but what about the shirt that was found in Lanbridge's wardrobe? Surely it points towards him as being the one to actually stab Miss Roscoe."

"The shirt is interesting," Jane said, turning to Lord Westworth. "And ultimately it was the key piece of evidence that led us to unravelling the whole case. It was a mistake, one made in panic and desperation, to throw suspicion on Mr Lanbridge."

"Why would my wife do that to her alleged lover?" Lord Westworth demanded, and Jane got the impression he was enjoying this. "Why plant the shirt to try and direct suspicion on to Mr Lanbridge?"

"You were the one who told us that Lady Westworth had not been aware of Mr Lanbridge's true identity until a few days ago. She believed the man living in your house was Edward Stanmore, your long-lost brother. She fell in love with that man, dreamed of a future with that man."

"That is ridiculous," Lord Westworth said.

Lady Westworth spun, and Jane saw the emotion in her eyes. "Why is it ridiculous? To enjoy being loved? To enjoy being noticed for once in my life?"

"Be quiet, Henrietta."

"No, I won't. For years I have stood by your side, smiling and making inconsequential small talk. You bring me out for balls and dinner parties and then ignore me the rest of the time. Sometimes I go for days without talking to anyone but the servants."

Lord Westworth's look of disdain was more eloquent than anything he could say and Jane felt sorry for Lady Westworth, despite everything she had done.

"I was a fool to think I could ever have anything more," she said quietly, her eyes flicking to Phillip Lanbridge.

"You thought Mr Lanbridge loved you," Jane said quietly, "And you thought one day he would take you away from your miserable marriage."

Lady Westworth didn't have to say anything for Jane to know she was right.

"Then you found out it was all fake. The man you had fallen in love with wasn't Edward Stanmore. He was a trickster, out to con your husband. You had killed for your relationship, stabbed an innocent young woman to preserve it, and it had all been for nothing."

"I hated you for lying to me," Lady Westworth said, directing her words to Phillip Lanbridge.

"You took one of the shirts from Mr Lanbridge's wardrobe and cut yourself with a knife, spreading the blood over it and allowing it to dry. There was no way we would be able to tell if the blood was Miss Roscoe's or someone else's. Then you hid the shirt where it would be found in a day or two by one of the maids. You knew it would incriminate Mr Lanbridge."

Jane watched Lady Westworth for a moment then turned to Phillip Lanbridge. "When we came to speak to you at Winchester jail, did you know who had planted the evidence that had got you arrested?"

"I suspected. When I met Lady Westworth in the orchard, I wasn't aware she had seen Miss Roscoe, I wasn't aware we had been observed."

"Which meant for a long time you were not aware of Lady Westworth's motive."

"Exactly. You asked me if I had met my brother in the orchard that night and I told you no, but it made me realise that it could have been our liaison Miss Roscoe had seen, mine and Lady Westworth's, and if it was then..."

"Yet you didn't say anything, even when you realised it could have been Lady Westworth who had hidden the bloodied shirt in your room and orchestrated your arrest."

"No." He looked at Lady Westworth. "I lied to you about my identity and you did not deserve that, but not everything between us was a lie."

The viscountess looked at the man she had loved with tears in her eyes. "I thought you were going to save me," she said quietly. "I would have done anything for you."

"Yet Mr Lanbridge sent you the note from jail saying he had something to tell you, Lord Hinchbrooke," Lord Westworth said, turning to the magistrate, and Jane could see he was enjoying observing his wife's distress. She wondered if he had always been this cold, this unemotional, or if his wife's betrayal had sparked it in him. From the desperate way Lady Westworth had clutched at any opportunity to escape her husband, Jane suspected it had been an unhappy marriage from the start.

"No," Jane said quietly. "That was me. I wanted to provoke a reaction."

"You managed that, Miss Austen," Phillip Lanbridge said, grimacing as he gestured to his injured arm.

"You weren't going to tell them about us?" Lady Westworth said.

"No."

"I thought..."

"You thought I was about to betray you."

"You had already lied to me, I thought it was only a matter of time until you betrayed me as well."

"I did lie to you, Hen, but I would never betray you."

Lord Westworth snorted and shook his head derisively. "The great love story," he muttered.

"What happens now?" Oliver Lanbridge asked, shifting uncomfortably in his seat and looking like he wanted to be far away from here.

Lord Hinchbrooke stood. "Lady Westworth will await trial for Miss Roscoe's murder. Given the unique circumstances and the fact Lady Westworth is a member of the aristocracy, I will send a message to the courts in London and to parliament to see how they wish to proceed with this. Until then I will provide you with a room here, Lady Westworth."

Jane looked at the viscountess. She had murdered Emma Roscoe, stabbed her in an attempt to protect the relationship she cherished. If she had been a servant or a farmer's wife, she would have been taken to jail and thrown into one of the stinking, filthy cells, but instead she would be kept in relative luxury.

"What about those two?" Lord Westworth said, motioning to the Lanbridge brothers.

"Mr Oliver Lanbridge will be charged with attacking Miss Austen in the grounds of Stanmore Hall," Lord Hinchbrooke said, "but I do not think the deception they have spun will be easy to prove. Mr Phillip Lanbridge hadn't yet asked you for anything."

"Let us go," Phillip Lanbridge said, his eyes locked on Lord Westworth's. "You have my word we will disappear, finally we will be out of your life. If you bring charges against us the whole world will be dragged into this and you do not want to be surrounded by further scandal."

Lord Westworth eyed the Lanbridge brothers with disdain, then gave a curt nod. "More than anything I want this to be over."

Whilst Lord Hinchbrooke was mediating between Lord Westworth and Phillip Lanbridge, Jane quietly walked over to Mr Tinker. He was sitting with his head in his hands looking totally dejected.

"Her death was so pointless," he said.

Jane nodded. "I know."

"How could she be so selfish, to take away Emma's life to try and preserve a little of her own happiness? Emma's life was as valuable as hers, yet she snuffed it out like it was inconsequential."

"Emma's life was anything but inconsequential," Jane said, taking Samuel Tinker's hand. "I am glad she had you. I am glad that she was loved and cherished."

"What do I do now, Miss Austen?" The farmer's eyes were pleading, as if she had all the answers.

"You mourn her. You work your farm; you build that life you and Emma dreamed of. Show her you can do it and make her proud."

"Is any of it worth it without her?"

"Sometimes there is comfort in doing an action over and over again. Right now, it might be hard to see the point of continuing, of striving to become the best you can, but in a year or two you will look at what you have achieved and you will see it was worth it."

Mr Tinker stood and looked around the room, shaking his head as if he couldn't wait to get out of there. "Thank you for your efforts, Miss Austen. Even though it will not bring Emma back, it is a comfort to know there will be some form of justice done." He nodded to her formally and then without a word to anyone else he left the room.

"I have had a room prepared for you, Lady Westworth," Lord Hinchbrooke said, motioning to a maid who was hovering in the doorway. "Ginny will show you up and help you get settled."

Docilely, Lady Westworth followed the maid, disappearing into the hallway, leaving behind the two men who between them had led her to take another woman's life.

CHAPTER TWENTY-THREE

"How did you know all that?" Cassandra said, coming over and linking her arm through Jane's.

"It all came together when I saw Lady Westworth in the cell. She risked everything to go there and try and silence Mr Lanbridge, but she hadn't been able to do more than wound him."

"Surely that was because he had overpowered her?"

"I don't think so. He was weak from barely eating or drinking whilst in jail. I think she just couldn't bring herself to kill the man she loved. When I realised she loved him, it all slotted into place."

"What will happen to Lady Westworth?" Jane asked Lord Hinchbrooke as he approached.

The magistrate grimaced. "In an ideal world she would be brought to justice just like any other person who committed a crime."

"But in the world we live in?"

"I suspect Lord Westworth's powerful friends will see to it the matter is hushed up and Lady Westworth is sent to see out her days in an asylum or hospital somewhere."

Jane shuddered. It may not be as brutal as death by hanging, but the asylums were grim places that she would not wish upon anyone.

"Lord Westworth will survive with his reputation unscathed," Cassandra murmured, "although I suppose it will have to come out that he was duped by the Lanbridge brothers."

"I have no doubt that Lord Westworth is already concocting a story to explain away the sudden absence of Edward Stanmore — almost certainly 'Edward' will have decided to return to India. People may speculate, but I doubt the true story will ever become common knowledge," Lord Hinchbrooke said. He shook his head and then turned his attention fully to Jane. "You were marvellous there, Miss Austen. How does it feel to have finally uncovered the truth of what happened to Miss Roscoe?"

"I feel like a weight has been lifted from my shoulders."

"I know who to call on next time I need a scribe for one of my more complex cases."

Knowing the magistrate was likely joking, Jane tried not to show quite how keen she would be to get involved. "I am always happy to help you, Lord Hinchbrooke, whatever the subject of your investigation."

"Don't encourage her," Cassandra said, panic on her face at the idea of another case.

"Might I go and speak to Lady Westworth before we leave?" Jane wanted to talk to the woman alone, to look her in the eye and ask her if she regretted what she had done. It might be a bad idea, but she knew after today there would be little opportunity to do so.

"Of course. Her room is on the first floor, there is a footman outside her room. I believe Lord Westworth is still with her at the moment. Her husband insisted he talk to his wife before he left."

Pleased that she was trusted to walk through Lord Hinchbrooke's home alone, Jane walked out to the hall and climbed the grand staircase to the first floor. There was a footman standing to attention outside a door halfway down the hallway and Jane headed over to him.

"I am here to see Lady Westworth," she said.

The footman knocked on the door and then opened it and went in. Before he could announce Jane, she heard a snippet of Lord and Lady Westworth's conversation.

"…trust you will do the right thing."

"You will uphold your end of the bargain?"

"Mr Lanbridge will be sent on his way unscathed."

"Then you have nothing to worry about," Lady Westworth said just as she noticed the footman.

"Miss Austen to see you, Lady Westworth."

"I shall leave you now," Lord Westworth said, bowing to his wife and striding from the room, not acknowledging Jane on the way.

"Have you come to gloat, Miss Austen?"

"No."

"I suppose not. You are too righteous, too good."

"I am neither of those things, Lady Westworth. Are you comfortable?"

"Yes."

"Lord Hinchbrooke will ensure all the correct procedures are followed."

Lady Westworth sighed and walked over to the window. "Is there something you wanted, Miss Austen?"

Jane was surprised by the directness of the question, but reasoned it was to her advantage not to have to stand here and talk to the viscountess for longer than was necessary.

"How could you do it?" Jane asked, scrutinising the older woman.

"I didn't wake up that morning and plan to finish the day a murderer, it was a series of events that I got swept up in and suddenly there I was with the knife, standing in front of the woman who could ruin my life."

"You could have asked her not to say anything."

"I could," Lady Westworth said with a shrug, "but how would I know she would honour her promise? I had to get out and I was so close after all those years of misery."

"Lord Westworth was cruel to you?" Jane remembered the pressure of his fingers on Lady Westworth's shoulder in the library below.

"Not physically. His cruelty took a different form." Lady Westworth regarded Jane with a complete lack of emotion on her face. "Controlling," she said eventually. "A need to oversee everything I did and everyone I met until it was too much strain and I just stopped trying." Lady Westworth shook her head. "You couldn't understand."

In normal circumstances Jane might feel sorry for the woman, but Lady Westworth was holding this up as an explanation, an excuse even, of why she had felt it was justified to kill Emma. "Are you sorry?"

"Of course. I'm not a monster."

Despite the words, Jane wasn't sure if Lady Westworth was thinking about the life she had cut short or about the impact of her actions on her own life.

Seeing she was not going to get what she needed from the viscountess, Jane turned to leave. "I hope you never forget Miss Roscoe, wherever it is they end up sending you," she said as she reached the door.

The walk downstairs felt long and arduous and Jane almost collapsed into Cassandra's arms as she reached the library.

"I think I had better get you home," Cassandra said.

The room was quieter now. Mr Tinker had long since fled, gone to mourn in private now he knew what had happened to the woman he loved. Lord Westworth had departed too, no doubt to contact any friends or acquaintances that might prevent his wife appearing in front of a judge charged with murder. Only the Lanbridge brothers were left, sitting and talking quietly in one corner.

"I do not need Mr Oliver Lanbridge to be charged for attacking me," Jane said to Lord Hinchbrooke as he approached, concern etched on his face.

"He could have seriously hurt you, Miss Austen."

"Tell them to leave, to go far away from here and never come back."

"If you are sure, Miss Austen. I have to admit I wouldn't mind seeing the back of those two."

"I am sure."

"Go home and rest, my carriage is ready and waiting for you. Perhaps you will permit me to call on you tomorrow, once we have both had a chance to mull over what has happened."

"I would like that, Lord Hinchbrooke."

Guided by Cassandra as if she were a frail old woman, Jane passed the Lanbridge brothers and went out into the grand hallway, pausing only to retrieve her coat. Once in the plush carriage she leaned back and closed her eyes. So much had happened in the past twenty-four hours it was hard to believe now everything was solved, all deception had been smashed through and they finally had the truth.

She knew she should be feeling relieved, but there was something at the back of her mind, something she couldn't quite put her finger on. Allowing her mind to skim through the events of the day without thinking of the details, Jane suddenly sat up.

Moving quickly, she thumped on the carriage roof and, ignoring Cassandra's shocked expression, stuck her head out of the window and shouted for the driver to turn around.

Thankfully he heard her and they were soon back outside Lord Hinchbrooke's front door.

Jane leapt from the carriage and burst into the house, ignoring the footman, who she almost flattened against the wall.

"Miss Austen?" Jane heard Lord Hinchbrooke call out, but she didn't have time to stop and explain, running to the stairs, picking up her skirts and taking them two at a time. She barrelled past the footman standing outside Lady Westworth's room and threw open the door, pausing on the threshold.

Immediately as she entered the room she knew she was too late.

Trust you will do the right thing. That was what Lord Westworth had said to his wife before promising he would leave Mr Lanbridge alone.

Lady Westworth was lying on the bed, unnaturally still. She had taken off her dress so as not to get blood on the expensive fabric and lay in her petticoats and chemise. A knife was sticking out of her abdomen and the chemise and bedsheets were soaked in blood.

For a long moment Jane could not tear her eyes away from the body on the bed. She took in every detail and knew this scene, along with the image of Emma Roscoe with the knife in her chest, would haunt her forever more.

The footman entered the room behind her, followed by Lord Hinchbrooke, both gasping at the horror of it.

"No," the magistrate said, shaking his head. "How did she get a knife?"

"Her husband," Jane said quietly. "When he came to see her, he told her to do the right thing. He must have given her the knife then."

Lord Hinchbrooke moved stiffly to the bed and felt Lady Westworth's wrist, but Jane knew just from looking there was no hope there might be life in her body. Too much of her blood was on the sheets for her to survive.

Jane took a step back, realising this was one tragedy she did not want to be involved in. She heard Cassandra's familiar footsteps on the stairs and hurried out of the room, eager to save her sister from seeing Lady Westworth's body.

"What has happened, Jane?"

"She's killed herself."

"What? How did you know?"

"Something her husband said to her didn't feel quite right. It was only when we were in the carriage that I realised what he meant for her to do."

"Oh, Jane."

"I was too late, Cassandra."

"This is not your fault, Jane, nor your responsibility."

"If only I had realised sooner."

Cassandra took a deep breath and lowered her voice. "Perhaps it is best this way. For everyone."

"How can you say that?"

"The Roscoes don't have to go through the awful torment of knowing their daughter's killer is out there, even if she is confined to an institution. It was unlikely the matter would ever be heard in front of a judge and jury."

"It feels as though Lord Westworth has won. Throughout all he had been in the background, watching everything with that detached manner of his. And now he doesn't even have to sit through the humiliation of having everyone know his wife is a murderer."

"Don't think like that, Jane. Come, you've had a shock, let's go home."

Jane was about to agree when Lord Hinchbrooke emerged from the room, face pale and expression dazed. "What a mess," he murmured, and Jane saw his hands were shaking almost uncontrollably.

Straightening up, she gave him a nod of acknowledgement. "What can I do to help?"

EPILOGUE

"I am quite sure you have better things to do than visit a rickety old man like me."

"I do not believe for one moment you are rickety, and you most certainly are not old," Jane said, smiling indulgently at Lord Hinchbrooke.

It was three weeks since the death of Lady Westworth in the bedroom upstairs and by all appearances Jane was back to her normal, contented self. She did not talk about the images that haunted her when she closed her eyes at night or the prickle of self-recrimination she still felt over Emma Roscoe's death. Perhaps if Cassandra was there she might have confessed how she was feeling, but Cassandra was visiting friends. Jane didn't begrudge her the trip, knowing the events had taken a toll on her sister nearly as much as they had on her.

At least she had been able to start writing again. Each morning she scribbled away furiously, driven as if she were possessed to get the words down on the paper. *Elinor and Marianne* was taking shape and she had started reading excerpts to her family again in the evening. On the outside things had returned to normality.

"I saw the Roscoes yesterday," Lord Hinchbrooke said as he moved the chess piece he had been eyeing up for some time. His hand shook as he did so, but Jane noted it wasn't as bad as a few weeks earlier.

"How were they?"

"Not coping all that well. They have decided to move away. Mrs Roscoe has a cousin who has offered them a cottage in

Sussex. They think perhaps a period of time away from everything they associate with their daughter might help."

"I hope it does," Jane said, remembering the desperate way Mrs Roscoe had clutched at her hand when she and Cassandra had paid them a visit after Emma's death.

"At least they do not have to sit through the indignity and pain of a trial."

The day after Lady Westworth killed herself, Jane and Lord Hinchbrooke had gone together to tell the Roscoes the news. They had sat in stunned silence as Jane and the magistrate had outlined what had happened and why their daughter had been killed. It brought them no comfort that the murderer was dead by her own hand and Mrs Roscoe had sobbed that nothing would bring her daughter back.

A few days later Jane heard that Lord Westworth had paid a visit to the Roscoes and offered them a sum of money to try and compensate for their loss. Mr Roscoe had thrown him out, refusing to take anything form the husband of their daughter's killer.

"I saw Mr Tinker at church on Sunday," Jane said. "He looks devastated too. So much heartache."

"What did I say at the beginning of this case? The motive, the reason someone would think it justifiable to take another's life, would be petty or selfish."

Jane nodded morosely and moved a pawn. Lord Hinchbrooke was a good player, but she had been practicing over the last few weeks. One day she would beat him.

"Let us talk of happier things. What about your young gentleman? Mr Lefroy, wasn't it?"

Jane hadn't disclosed much about Mr Lefroy to the magistrate, but Lord Hinchbrooke forgot nothing and had enquired about him on a couple of occasions.

"I believe he has returned to London."

"You believe?"

"I believe so."

"You do not know for sure?" Lord Hinchbrooke was tenacious when he wanted to be.

"I do not know for sure." Jane held the magistrate's eye and saw him suppress a little smile. She knew not many people spoke to him so directly and that he enjoyed her treating him as if he were one of her family.

"That's a shame," Lord Hinchbrooke said, moving his knight and taking her bishop.

Jane cursed under her breath, her eyes flitting over the board, looking for a way to salvage the game.

Mr Tom Lefroy had tried to call on her twice after the disastrous meeting where he had told her they couldn't be together. Jane had refused to see him both times. There was no need, even though part of her longed to set eyes on him one final time, to pretend he wasn't leaving, that he hadn't decided to follow his family's wishes and seek out a more suitable wife.

Her letters to Cassandra had been therapeutic. In those she had poured out her regrets, her heartache and her wish that things had occurred differently. It had been such a short acquaintance, but Jane could acknowledge now on her part at least it had been love. For a few short weeks she had loved Mr Lefroy and then he had broken her heart.

Jane knew she was young and there was every chance she would love again, but right now she wanted to put Tom Lefroy and her romantic misery as far from her mind as possible.

With a frown she looked at the board, noticing something she hadn't seen before. For a whole minute she regarded the pieces, trying to work out if it was a trap, then she moved her queen.

"Checkmate," she said, glancing up to see if she had really bested Lord Hinchbrooke.

"I was hoping you wouldn't see that," he murmured.

Jane grinned. They had played numerous times over the last few weeks, but this was the first time she had won.

"First you make me redundant in an investigation into a murder and now you best me at chess."

"Do not fear, there is still plenty you have to teach me."

Lord Hinchbrooke looked up and met Jane's eye. "The life of a magistrate is not one most people envy, Miss Austen. It is often a thankless job, a lonely job, but it is unquestionably interesting." He paused and Jane saw the sincerity in his eyes. "You have a talent not many people possess, great imagination. It is a talent I could use. Any time you wish to assist me, my door is open."

Jane stood up. Outside, the sun was beginning to set and even though she had the use of Lord Hinchbrooke's carriage she knew she would be expected at home before dusk turned into darkness.

"I think you know my answer, my lord. I believe we share a rather unique characteristic, that unrelenting quest for the truth. I shall call on you in a week, unless anything untoward happens in Hampshire before then."

A NOTE TO THE READER

Thank you for reading *Death of a Lady*, the first book in the Jane Austen Investigations series. The series follows a young Jane Austen as she encounters murder and intrigue, with true aspects of her family life and writing woven in.

It is always difficult when writing about a historical figure to balance the known facts with artistic licence or interpretation. We know much about Jane Austen's life as she was a voracious letter writer and many of these letters were preserved by her sister Cassandra. They give us a glimpse into the mind of one of England's most beloved authors. Even so, despite the sheer number of letters there are huge gaps, months where there are no details of what Jane was doing, and of course there is the fact that she did not likely commit her every thought and opinion to paper. Even more intriguing are the letters Cassandra destroyed after her sister's death to preserve her reputation. What is left gives us a half-formed picture that people expand and extrapolate in their own way.

I have tried to weave in the details we do know with my own interpretation of her character, imagining how a young Jane might react if faced with the murder of a friend. Given her perceptiveness and insight into human nature, I think it is not too big a leap to think of her putting her inquisitive mind to use in solving the crime.

Thank you for taking the time to read *Death of a Lady*. If you enjoyed the book I have a small favour to ask — please pop across to **Amazon** and **Goodreads** and post a review. I also love to connect with readers through my **Facebook** page, on **Twitter**, **Instagram** and through my **website**. I would love to hear from you. Laura Martin

Sapere Books is an exciting new publisher of brilliant fiction and popular history.

To find out more about our latest releases and our monthly bargain books visit our website:
saperebooks.com

Printed in Great Britain
by Amazon